PRAISE FOR
LILITH SAINTCROW

"Simply put, Saintcrow doesn't f*** around."

— CHUCK WENDIG, AUTHOR
OF *WANDERERS*, ON *AFTERWAR*

"Incredibly timely, well written and important.... A testament to Saintcrow's skill."

— *LOS ANGELES TIMES* ON *AFTERWAR*

"A true faery story, creepy and heroic by turns. Love and hope and a touch of *Midsummer Night's Dream*. I could not put it down."

— PATRICIA BRIGGS, AUTHOR OF THE MERCY
THOMPSON SERIES ON *TRAILER PARK FAE*

"Painfully honest, beautifully strange, and absolutely worth your time. Lilith Saintcrow is at the top of her game. Don't miss this."

— SEANAN MCGUIRE, AUTHOR OF THE
WAYWARD CHILDREN SERIES ON *TRAILER
PARK FAE*

"Lilith Saintcrow spins an incredibly imaginative and delicious tale with vivid language and a story you will not be able to put down. I loved every minute!"—

"Honestly, I wish I'd written it."

"Unique, twisted, lovely, and raw. Just fabulous."

ELDER'S PRIZE

ELDER'S PRIZE
TALES OF THE SANGUINANT
BOOK II

LILITH SAINTCROW

For M. S., who who persevered.

CHAPTER 1

Lookout duty was of course a necessity in any vampire-hunting team, but Layla Cartland wished it didn't involve pretend kissyface with fellow soldiers.

"There's that grey Acura again," she murmured, shifting against warm, gritty bricks. A hot August night, soaking with humidity, had already plastered the pretty black sundress to her lower back. Even bare arms and legs offered no relief; the air was thick as cottage cheese and her toes were sweat-slippery inside cotton socks and combat boots. "Same license plate—and will you quit that? It tickles."

"I hate having my back to the street." At least Pete stopped rubbing his stubble on her hair. He was the only one short enough for her to see over his shoulder, and nobody would suspect a couple supposedly making out between two separate nightclub entrances of good taste, much less surveillance. It was the second spot on their rotation, the only bare patch of wall in sight, and next they'd move to an alley-mouth half a block down.

She couldn't wait.

Layla could probably count the fact that stocky, snub-nosed Pete inevitably got a chubby as a compliment to her own mild attractiveness, though the cheap cologne he dabbed on for every operation involving decoy or lookout made her sneeze. The wall she was propped against thudded faintly with dueling bass beats, a giant's drowsy pulse. The bouncers were leaving them alone, more concerned with the lines of drunks and name-droppers trying to get in or out of the roughnecks' paradise known as Cactus YaYa or the slightly more expensive Blue Moon Spot; wall-humpers would be told to move along if the crowd got more restless, but until then the lookouts were in a golden zone, politely ignored.

"Pete and Layla sittin' in a tree…" Ackerman's voice came over the earpiece, a clear tenor singsong; he was perched on a rooftop wearing his goddamn cowboy hat, probably getting a breath of night breeze as well.

It was rare for him to unbend enough to tease anyone. Progress was being made, hopefully as a result of her own steady encouragement, balancing out the rough teasing other males mistook for therapeutic. Maybe simple, stupid hazing was how a male animals of any species showed they cared.

However, Pete now became even more tense—if that were possible. He was always amped on operations, even simple recon. "Fuck you," he snarled, the throat mic picking it up double and squealing slightly in her poor ear, and Layla had to repress a sigh.

"Cut the chatter." As usual, Dan's voice made her heart thump an extra beat. Unfortunately, the leaps had been getting smaller lately. Especially when she wondered when this entire operation was *really* going to get off the ground. "Steve-o?"

"I got it, boss." Lanky laconic Steve, always professional, drawled over the invisible line. Group chat with vampire hunters, just the thing for a girl's night on the town. "Got three coming in from the west, big black Marias. Guessing that Acura's the lookout."

Or can't find a place to park. Layla didn't bother stating the obvious, but as usual, Ben just *had* to.

"Could be a civvie, looking for a place to squeeze in. Like Pete." Ben's slight wheeze said he was grinning like a jackal, his bushy eyebrows waggling ferociously. "How's it looking down there, Petey? Nice and juicy?"

"For Chrissake," Pete muttered, thankfully too low for the mic to pick up.

Just ignore him; he does it because you respond. Bullies were the same everywhere. Layla patted her lookout partner's side, just over the hard hidden edge of Kevlar.

At least Ben did his job—sort of. Layla could even suppose his clowning might be a bonus in certain situations, like the hair-trigger violence displayed at the least provocation. On the one hand, he'd been overwhelmingly on-target with the two biters they'd already put down.

On the other, it had taken both Dan and Ack to get Ben bundled out of the bar where they'd gathered intel about the Griskov bounty—plus all her own practice at defusing male tempers afterward to clean up the mess, with Steve glowering theatrically over her shoulder.

Finally, the client had unbent enough to agree they were the team for the job—but no down payment, because Ben had fouled the waters almost past soothing. And Layla could be forgiven for thinking she was tired of dealing with mess, physical or emotional, all day every *damn* day.

Every squad member had their own reasons for this kind of work, and bad coping mechanisms to match. You didn't enter a fabulous career in vampire hunting unless you'd lost someone— or unless you had more psychological problems than a stick could shake at.

At least Dan was adamant about not taking on any more crazies, even if it meant a little less firepower. Small mercies, as her grandmother always said, were the only kind a woman ever got.

Not that it mattered at the moment. "I see them," Layla said softly, because she did. Three big glossy SUVs, each black as midnight itself, trundling west along 21st Street. *Huh.* She inhaled sharply. "Three Marias coming in westbound, and two more just joined from Battery Road, heading east. Looks like all the same makes and models; I think we've got extra players tonight."

"Fuck me." Ack, grimly unsurprised—he never expected anything to go smoothly, even laundry. "I see 'em too. What we got tonight, friends and neighbors?"

"He could be leaving early, maybe upgraded his security detail." A crackle from Dan's mic—this time he'd drawn the squawker from the gear barrel, instead of Layla. Another tiny mercy. "Eyes, hold your positions. Ben, Steve-O, stay loose. Ack, take your lock off."

A rash of *ten-fours*, including Pete's murmur. Layla's pulse began to pound, sweat greasy on her neck and arms. A regular old crowded downtown street on a summer night, car horn blaring at the far end, shriek of drunken laughter from a group of college kids spilling out of a bar a block and a half up, faint thread of cigarette smoke lingering on unmoving air. Every salt-soaked inch of her shrank from the assault of noise, light, people.

It was only the adrenaline kicking her senses into high gear, but she still had to suppress a twitch.

"Pulling up now." She enunciated clearly, quashing the urge to yell. Her other hand rested at Pete's nape; he leaned protectively into her, torrid male sweat-smell now edged with the same metallic stress-based cocktail pouring into her own bloodstream. Funny how you could smell the adrenaline, after a while. "Both directions. They've got traffic corked, gentlemen."

Which meant five SUVs full of something bad against their small team. She waited for Dan to make the call. As usual, Suzy's face floated in front of her—not the awful butcher's ruin on the morgue table, but bubbly blonde Suze on her wedding day, smiling beatifically during the waltz, tiers of white lacy dress swaying around her legs. And Dan, his eyes closed, keeping his chin carefully near his new wife's piled curls. He'd looked so handsomely protective, and her best friend so peaceful, that Layla had gone right to the open bar and started in on the whiskey. Two fingers, neat, hold the ice.

At least she hadn't opened her mouth at the wrong time *that* day. No sir, she'd done the best thing possible, and been quiet ever since.

"Egg's cracked." She gazed steadily over Pete's shoulder as the SUVs popped their doors. "Looks like bodyguard details in standard… oh, *shit*."

"What? What shit?" Dan, as usual, didn't like it when she swore. "Give me something better, Eyes."

I've liked you for a long time, Danny, but sometimes you're a real prick. Layla buried the thought as deep as it could go. No use in getting distracted. "It's a biter," she muttered. "Just not ours. Repeat, *not* our target. It's another one; I think…" *Where have I seen that face before?*

"Fuck." Nobody yelled at Ackerman for uttering a blue word, of course. "Angle's bad until a target gets closer to the door. Do you have an ID, Layla?"

I'm working on it. She mentally shuffled every laydown in the past few weeks—the face was familiar, and she *knew* he had to be a vampire. She just couldn't remember precisely which one; the most unsettling thing was that they all looked so goddamn normal until you got entirely too close.

Then the flawless matte skin, the slightly different texture to the hair, and most of all some indefinable, atavistic feeling of *predator, oh shit, run away* were all dead giveaways. It was terrifying how good the human-camouflage was, until you realized there were human monsters too.

Those were entirely out of Layla's control. At least you could feel a hundred percent good, moral, and American about killing a bloodsucking fiend.

"Man, let's just abort," Ben muttered. Pitched right in the sweet spot for his mic to pick up, but not loudly enough for Dan to call him out for either cowardice or defeatism.

Layla pressed her bare shoulders against the bricks; this dress was pretty, kicky, and would be absolutely zero use when the shooting started. She could remember the biter's face, the exact position of the grainy 8x10 photo, seeing it against a stack of manila files—worth their weight in gold, each the product of her own hard work, endless online argument, and constant re-checking.

Her role was clerical, close logistics, and occasional surveillance, which was a pretty way of saying she was a glorified maid-plus-secretary. Still, that was necessary for the smooth functioning of any endeavor. Without her, they wouldn't even *have* hardcopies of the files from O'Shaughnassey's crew, all verified sightings and intel.

Poor Shawn. God.

"Layla?" Dan, warningly. If the operation was called off now they might never get another chance at the biter who owned the Blue Moon Spot, but this definitely wasn't the big blond sonofabitch Roger Griskov.

No, this guy had a mop of curly dark hair, slightly glistening under the streetlights, and a nose that outweighed the entire rest of his face. He unfolded from the backseat of the middle westbound SUV, glancing to either side as soldiers marking terrain always did, and the shape of his chin was even more familiar. She simply couldn't remember the name, though she could smell the cold leftover Hawaiian pizza she'd downed while doing what Ack called *fuckin' homework.*

She was only certain of one thing. "He's a red-stripe." *Let that be enough.* "Skull and crossbones. Do not engage. Repeat, do not engage."

The biter wore a black sweater with leather elbow patches, far too heavy for a sticky summer night, and loose workman's pants—looked like Carhartts, plus heavy boots like Pete's, like Ack's, like her own, no doubt steel-toed as well. The beefy bodyguards moving with him had to be human employees, in dark suits tailored almost well enough to hide the shoulder holsters.

Naturally the biter wasn't carrying. He didn't need to, even a new vampire was dangerous enough—and if civilians noticed him at all they would assume *bigwig*, maybe *mob boss*, and hurriedly look away.

But she knew what he was. Once you glimpsed what lay under the human-looking shells of a few demimonde inhabitants, nothing was ever the same again. She could swear the strange things all but announced themselves into a microphone; the guys, claiming they didn't see the details, called it 'women's intuition'.

When they weren't mocking her for a vivid, 'overactive' imagination, that was.

Pete shifted, and something about the movement might have caught the vampire's peripheral vision. The curly-headed monster glanced in their direction, and for a moment his gaze met Layla's squarely. She hurriedly glanced away—sometimes the creatures could hypnotize, and skull-and-crossbones on any file meant serious bad news.

Her small movement did the trick. She finally remembered the name typed on the manila tab, written on the back of the 8x10 glossy.

Oh, no. No. Fucking hell. "It's the one they—" she began, but it was too late.

A high hard *ratatat*, Ben moving in from the alley across the street and spraying the two eastbound SUVs with a short burst. Which meant Steve-o had to back him up, because once the tango started a hunter did their job, hell or high water. Ack no doubt took his shot too, but the crack of his sniper rifle was lost under the sudden, closer noise.

Pete flinched, an instinctive movement jamming her hard against the wall. She didn't blame him one bit—very little was worse than hearing gunfire behind you, except maybe knowing a biter was there as well. Their earpieces howled with feedback, Dan shouting something; it had to be ignored.

Now the lookouts had only one job.

Run, and maybe save their own sorry hides.

Their escape route was a good one—an alley's mouth lurked just on the other side of Cactus YaYa's entrance; they'd counted off the steps during daylight and on several other nights during recon. Pete's fingers sank brutally hard into her upper arm; he set his feet and hauled, trying to yank her against a sudden eddy in the crowd.

His grip was torn loose and Layla was swept up in a tide of frightened human animals seeking any cover they could, which meant through an open nightclub door barred only by a single red velvet rope. The heavy, polished brass stand it was attached to fell with a clang lost in gun-chatter, pops, and screaming ricochets; it sounded like the biter's bodyguards were returning fire with a vengeance.

Layla's feet dangled a good six inches off the pavement; if she went down, she'd be trampled to paste. She grabbed blindly, getting a fistful of someone's fishnet shirt plus sweat-slick skin, and was dragged past overturned tables as the human wave crested. The screams almost managed to drown out a high-decibel assault of throbbing line-dancing music. Lights flashed, a migraine attack of whirling red-and-purple sparkles, and the poison of panic flooding through the front door spread through the dance space and packed galleries like ink in trapped water. A burst of stench—restrooms down a long hall to the right—and a puff of skunky weed-smell hit her, receded.

No use looking around for Pete, she was on her own. Fire alarms brayed; someone with incredible presence of mind or simply a modicum of drunken mischief must have pulled a lever, because piercing white strobes were now lighting up over back exits. Two of them, if she remembered the Cactus's layout, and now she blessed Ackerman's dogged insistence that she be the one laboriously going over social-media photos, building a layout of both clubs.

Just to be sure.

Owe you a drink, Ackie. Her bootsoles hit the floor; Layla staggered, yanked free of whoever she'd been clutching. Swept onward again, but she'd managed to aim herself in the right direction; now she just had to pray the fire exits really were in working order—and that she wouldn't be crushed or pummeled within sight of escape.

There was a moment of being squeezed between a woman in a fantastic silver wig and tiny bedazzled cowboy hat matched by a beaded dress clinging to her every Amazonian curve, and a person with a high pink-tipped mohawk, a heavy brown beer bottle clutched in one beringed hand. The goddess's breast smashed against the side of Layla's face and the mohawk's hand blindly crawled across her ass—not to grope, but desperately seeking any purchase—before she was spat through a pair of flung-wide fire doors and into the back alley running parallel to 21st, propelled with such force she almost bounced off a bank of dumpsters across the way. The air was only slightly cooler outside, and screams spilling from the club's depths sounded like lost souls in a particularly cinematic hell.

Layla reeled at the edge of the crowd, realized she was going the wrong way to make any planned post-incident rendezvous, and decided to just keep running.

CHAPTER 2

HE ALMOST OVERLOOKED HER, THOUGH IUPPITER'S THUNDERBOLT does not miss when a soldier has made his sacrifices and endured long enough. Or perhaps the gods were indeed dead, and it was only blind luck.

A flash like lightning—pale eyes peering shyly over a heavily padded shoulder, like a dryad in deep woods, amazed at the woodcutter's intrusion. The soldier's gaze moved on, the rest of him already aware of wrongness in the night—heightened mortal pulses, a faint squeal of static from a certain type of short-range communication device, the subtle sensation at his nape meaning prey had noticed a predator.

Not danger, precisely, merely unfriendly attention.

The soldier almost thought his target had hired mortal catspaws to distract Father's chosen sword; a silly measure, but ossification made older sanguinant stupid just as it rendered the young prone to bloodcraze and glut.

Then a stray thread of scent brushed past, sound hurrying after light, storm-roar capable of paralyzing if the flash did not. Electricity was partly tamed nowadays, trapped in switches and wires; still, even in confusing modern times, mortals feared great weather events.

He might have scented her in any case, especially upon a simmering midnight when every exhalation collected in the bowl of concrete called a city street. Yet it was not certain—her kind was, after all, so very rare.

Priceless, in fact. A single breath halted the soldier midstride, images cascading through his skull as he sought to identify the tantalizing odor. Roses, crushed coffee beans, an exquisite stainless musk, all coalescing into those wide grey eyes and straight dark hair pulled ruthlessly back, a glimpse of high-arched cheekbone. There was a mortal male looming before her, leaning close, his hands no doubt roaming over soft curves.

A sudden vengeful snarl contorted the soldier's face, true teeth sliding free as the ever-chained beast roused within his bones. Blinding, utter rage stripped away centuries' worth of dust accreted upon his perceptions, falling like scales from a certain mad prophet's eyes, plummeting like a boy with melting waxen wings.

The assault of fresh color, sound, and other sensation very nearly undid the soldier, an ancient pulse pausing its steady march inside his bone-armored chest. Then a clatter of gunfire began, bullets humming like bees, and mortals began to scream.

For the first time in his long strange existence, the soldier put aside his orders and lawful prey. A new, overriding imperative sank claws into flesh and brain both; he blurred into a light variety of mistform, streaking after something he had never truly believed existed.

There were rumors, of course—*leman*, those fantastical creatures capable of warding aside the slow Gorgon-gaze of accumulating years, a prize every bearer of the Blood longed for. The soldier had never given such tales much credence, despite honoring their telling. After all, if gods and emperors could die, what else might be possible in a wide world teeming with prey?

The challenge was to face Hades with *dignitas*. He had fallen on his sword once, as a mortal. It wasn't so difficult.

She was borne upon the stampede, a jewel amid flotsam. The

soldier arrowed overhead, buffeted by noise and various smoky substances, pushing against air-currents, ready at any moment to dive and tear through fragile mortal flesh if his new prize foundered. The sudden, overwhelming acuity of every sense was akin to a fledgling's first nights after full transition, drunk with the wonder of the Blood—yet far, far deeper.

He had not realized how close he trod to true-death. Ossification had stalked him with infinite cat-quiet patience. Even the control and discipline of his work was a trap, though he had sought to remain flexible by engaging with mortal catspaws and dogsbodies far more than one of his age normally did. His duties as Father's head general necessarily involved contact with security troops, but few pursued it so actively.

That was also part of the game, each interaction with brief ever-changing mortal creatures an attempt at insurance against the inevitable while longing for the unbelievable. Which had now occurred, albeit not quite in the way he'd ever imagined.

She spilled through a pair of wide-open doors, flung free hard enough to clip a corner of the metal refuse-boxes standing sentinel in a spacious, well-brushed alley. He had to restrain a sudden urge to plunge, slip out of mistform, and shield her from the blow, but it was already too late. She was off and running again, quite fast for a mortal. Modern streets were as a rule much cleaner than those of his long-ago youth, yet for a moment he was at the sack of Karthago again, or Korinth, or any of a thousand other cities he had led warriors through.

Screams and wailing rose to foul a night's uncertain peace, though unaccompanied by smoke or cries of murderous joy. The gunfire was fading—his own squad would be withdrawing in good order, knowing well enough to avoid whatever sudden event had necessitated their commander's vanishment. Anything requiring the behavior he had exhibited was above or beyond their own concerns.

They would return to the outpost near the oilfields bearing news, though. And that was concerning. The soldier did not wish to think beyond the current moment, since there was quite enough to do keeping a fleeing leman in sight *and* dealing with the flood of luxurious, unwonted sensation.

He could lose through sheer inattention or mischance what he had just found, unless great care were exercised.

Entirely sumptuous, the layers of deadened emotional callus peeling away as he floated behind her. He could watch while glorying in the freshness, the sheer *newness* of every detail. A clinging black dress with straps over her tender shoulders, the full skirt fluttering, lovely bare lithe legs and heavy boots, a dark braid swaying as she fled—quite the picture, and he dipped lower as she flagged.

Not even a nymph could run forever.

She swung aside, plunging into a small passageway connecting to yet another alley. Was she familiar with this place? Curiosity was another new hunger, burning all through him. How best to introduce himself? The old rumors were clear upon at least one point—a leman was to be taken at the moment of discovery, or swiftly as possible afterward.

Taken, and bitten. Then claimed.

He dove, slipping out of mistform, booted feet cat-soft meeting cracked pavement. Gliding after her, wholly intent, he wondered if he should pray.

Save that for when she is safe. And have you forgotten him?

The soldier had not begun this night expecting he would find himself at once disloyal *and* possessed of divine good luck, but he was now committed. The thrall had risen, a crimson burst in old, almost-dry veins, and he found not only was he awash in magnificent sensation but also—for the first time in centuries— incredibly physically aroused.

Stiff as a gladius, in fact. The need was pleasant in its sharpness; how long had he been an unthinking automaton?

Now he was awake, aware, *alive*. But just as he decided he had followed long enough, that his new prize must indeed be grasped, she put on another burst of speed.

Her pulse sang—every mortal's heartbeat was unique, certainly, but hers was music engineered specifically for *his* hearing. He quickened as well, a hawk preparing for the dive, a giant swan ready to descend upon a staggering girl.

I long to know your name, pretty one. So glorious to *feel* again after centuries spent watching the waters of Lethe rise inch by inch upon his frame, trapped in slowly calcifying body and mind.

Engine-noise, nearby and slowing. A mortal yell.

"Leila! Leila, come on!"

Like a young doe was she, running flat-out as if sensing the predator in her wake. Fists curled, arms pumping, the braid swinging to tap her back, she bolted from the alley and dove into the rear passenger side of a nondescript sedan, quick as a wink. The vehicle barely slowed enough for her to perform the maneuver, yet she did so with grace. One last skirt-flutter, and she was gone.

The soldier paused, struck by unfamiliar astonishment. He recognized another heartbeat within the car; one he had catalogued from sheer habit—the mortal male who had held her against the wall.

Lover? Husband? What true man would let such a beauty wander alone? But mortals were unaware of the rare flowers in their midst—and a good thing, too, lest they make leman even scarcer. Hunting the strange or different was not solely a sanguinant trait, or even confined to the wider demimonde.

Now that he had found such a rare, impossible miracle, everything he had ever heard concerning leman swirled inside him, a collage of tactical responses jostling for selection. It was traditional to remove all encumbrances from a new *aima-glyza*, in order to discourage panicked attempts at escape—and to make their transition to fledgling easier, for the moment she was bitten and claimed the Gift would begin to rise in her flesh.

At least his new objective was almost painfully clear. Father was a problem best solved in due course; the soldier could even anticipate the event with some pleasure.

His chains were now broken, an event any servant longed for, any master feared.

The soldier took to mistform again, following the fleeing vehicle.

CHAPTER 3

AN UNCOMFORTABLE RIDE BACK TO BASE, NOT LEAST BECAUSE LEAN sandy-haired Dan stared in front of the old Taurus like the road had personally done him wrong, refusing to even glance in the rearview mirror. On the other hand, Pete, in the front passenger seat because *of course* he was, kept twisting to look back at Layla.

As if it were *her* fault someone else had jumped the gun.

"It was a red-stripe, skull and crossbones," she repeated, and felt the same old dull hopelessness. Tonight's clusterfuck would absolutely end up being blamed on her somehow. "I just couldn't drag the name up in time. You have to believe me."

"I do," Pete said. Sweat gleamed on his forehead, and his mild brown eyes were for once hot with accusation as he glanced at Dave. "I *told* you not to put him there."

"You prefer him on lookout, then? Or up-top with sniper duty?" Dan shook his head, an irritable flicker tossing too-long fringe out of his eyes. He'd refused to get a trim despite Shawn's crew mocking him, probably because *they* were a weirdly costumed lot in their own right—the tattoos, or the feathers tied in John Dancer's sideburns, were the least of it. "I'll wait to hear what Ben has to say for himself before I decide what the hell."

Oh, for Chrissake. Layla strangled a flare of uncharacteristically intense anger. Soaked with fresh sweat, her heart refusing to slow down from rabbit-gallop, and beginning to feel all the bruises from being nearly trampled to death in a nightclub because *some dipshit* couldn't get it into his head not to pop off before the order was given—that was bad enough. But to have Dan constantly giving that same dumbass the benefit of the doubt just because…

Why?

Because he's a man. She swallowed the bitterness of adrenaline lingering at the back of her palate. "I swear to God it's him. The one they call Nemesis."

The car wallowed as Dan piloted left onto 45th Street. He was playing it cool, just at the speed limit, striking a balance between cautious old granny-driving and the slight rule-breaking of a businessman one past the limit but determined not to get pulled over. This circuitous route back to base was part of the plan.

At least they'd taken her suggestion in *that* regard; a miniscule, qualified victory, the only kind she ever got. But the sense of an invisible, unfriendly gaze on her simply wouldn't go away. Her nerves were a thousand percent shot.

Pete at least had body armor under his civilian T-shirt, for Chrissake. Layla was supposed to be well out of the way before any shooting went down. She couldn't get rid of the sensation of a big ol' glowing target painted on her back.

"You can't be sure," Dan said, finally.

What the fuck? Her jaw threatened to drop. "There's nothing wrong with my memory, Daniel." Layla throttled the unfriendly reminder that she and Suze been the ones getting him through high school—Suze with her head for numbers and ideas of maybe becoming an accountant, Layla for everything else, including every single essay he'd laboriously hand-copied to turn in.

Thinking about it now, she wondered why he didn't just spend that teeth-clenched effort to write the damn things himself.

Layla's memory was a steel trap not just for names but for faces, a major reason why she did so much of the research and recon. But no, Dan said she couldn't be *sure*, probably thinking estrogen was clouding her synapses. Just what did she like so much about him, anyway? Especially considering what she'd seen just before the wedding—and yet he'd made Suzy so very happy, and the way he'd broken down after… after Suze…

After the attack at Paradise Point, and those terrible, dream-like weeks afterward, when both he and Layla had found out how far down the rabbit hole really went.

Pete twisted again, peering into the backseat. "Well, *I* think you did great." As if conferring a huge favor, but it wasn't his fault. Men were just built to be dickheads; if she wasn't so hung up on one particular specimen, she might even like Pete. Certainly he was far nicer than *some* she could name. "And if you say it was a red-stripe then I believe you. But… Nemesis? You're absolutely sure?"

"Curly-headed sonofabitch with a nose like that? And he was dressed the same way as in the file, same sweater even. Plus, he always goes around with a squad of cookie-cutter human goons, and I'd recognize that stare of his after looking at it even once." Layla shivered, though the breeze coming through the half-open window did nothing to cool her off. It was just too hot tonight. She longed for a nice chilled bottle of chablis, a tepid bath, dreamless sleep on good sheets in an air-conditioned room. "We went over the files like eight separate times because of what happened to O'Shaughnassey's crew."

And wasn't that a bitch and a half? Shawn and his group of quiet, scarred, diffident men who had taken their few weeks of adding professional training to Dan's group so very seriously. She'd thought about signing up with them for good, but they were Catholic and took a dim view of girls getting in the way.

Story of her life. Of course, maybe she could be grateful, since just last winter they'd run across a really powerful biter and got wasted in a parking garage, of all things. The footage from that, as well as the autopsy reports, made for some nightmare viewing.

Everything did, nowadays.

"We did." Pete no longer sounded *entirely* dubious, just *mostly*. It was a nice change.

The car veered again; they were getting close to base. The few active storefronts along this street were closed, locked, and bearing metal grilles across their doors; the abandoned ones were boarded up. Both types ignored anything happening before their shuttered gazes.

"I'm telling you I recognized him. We should've aborted." The undeniable, atavistic sense of being watched was really giving her 'the wiggins'. Now *there* was a Suze-ism.

Poor Suze. Poor Shawn. Poor everyone.

"And wait how long for another chance at that Griskov bastard? Where are we gonna find the funding, huh?" Dan's hands were tight on the steering wheel, knuckles pale, and Layla was suddenly very aware of her bare, bruised shoulders, naked knees, the thin material of the dress. "Fuck. *Fuck*. The asshole we were after was supposed to *be* there. He was supposed to be leaving at two, just like always!"

I'm sure he's checking his day planner right now. She swallowed the observation, just as bitter as stale coffee or leftover adrenaline. "Well, if he got word Nemesis was paying a visit, he's probably long gone. We're lucky to be alive, Danny."

Maybe her tone wasn't exactly as soft or forgiving as it could be, but honestly, did she have to be the voice of reason all the damn time? Managing every single man's emotional state as well as his laundry pile was a thankless goddamn occupation, and she was tired.

So, so goddamn tired.

"For fuck's sake." Now Dan glanced in the rearview, and if looks could kill she'd be bleeding in the backseat. "Can you try not to call me that, *Lay*?"

Why do I like you so much, again? She was asking herself the question more and more these days. Her back was positively crawling with gooseflesh; Layla found she was also hugging herself despite the heat and the sweat, fingers slipping against bruised, aching upper arms.

All of her was throbbing like a bad tooth. "Sure thing," she muttered, and settled to stare out the window. Maybe Pete was now watching her in the side mirror; the sense of being looked at only intensified.

She'd thought the night couldn't get worse, but it just had to go and surprise her.

Base was an abandoned, boarded-up machinist's shop out on LaGranda Boulevard, its interior jammed with detritus and a few 'rooms' excavated for their use. Ack had jury-rigged the electricity and Ben, for all his flaws, was a dab hand at guerrilla plumbing, so at least there was a little bit of wash-up before debriefing. Layla could jam herself into jeans and a pink V-neck T-shirt—neither piece too fresh, since she was the only one who did any cleaning at all plus funds were scarce—and tell herself the persistent feeling of being stared at was just post-operation letdown.

She pressed a folded, dribble-soaked washcloth against her nape, ignoring the sharp smell of mildew. Any temporary illusion of coolness was well worth the hassle. "That's him."

The trestle table in what Steve called 'the ready room' held four piles of intel paper and several neatly arranged weapons; at least Steve and Ack spent time tidying *those* up. The rest of the place looked like a bomb had gone off, but the stacked walls of crap helped shield them from outside scrutiny and would slow down cops if any came calling to check for harmless, houseless folk just trying to find some shelter.

NEMESIS, the manila file proclaimed on its tab, sprawled open under a tensor lamp. The grainy 8x10 photo was just as she remembered, and seeing the biter again, even in 2D, was unpleasant at best. *Alias: Nemesis Name: Unk. Age: Unk. Range: Unk.*

Lots of unknowns, but the listed sightings were thought-provoking. If *oh God that's terrifying* qualified as *provoking*, that was. The biter had been all over the continent in steadily widening loops since at least the late 1800s.

Shawn's intel guy Mike had taught Layla how to use shorthand and cross-reference in the particular way real demimonde investigators found most useful. Even he had looked a little green going over some of the reports from Nemesis sightings, and their group had been about as hardcore as it got—fancy new ceramic armor, chain gorgets to guard against bites, crucifix tattoos, Vatican funding, the whole nine.

Fat lot of good it had done.

"You're absolutely sure?" Pete persisted, rubbing his knuckles like he always did when really bad news hit.

"He looked right at me. Of course I'm fucking sure." She couldn't suppress a shiver, carefully laying the washcloth on the table's edge. "I mean, on the bright side, he's probably done for the Blue Moon biter. Maybe we can turn in the kill and get the bounty?" The idea of going back to that particular mobster watering-hold and asking for money just made her more tired. Christ knew she'd probably be the one doing the actual work of gathering a package of gruesome proof.

"Good luck with that." Tall, blue-eyed Ben rubbed at his cheeks, callused palms scraping stubble, and let out a massive beery belch. He'd apparently stopped for a case of suds on the way back to base, which would've gotten anyone else a chewing out from Dan—both for the expense *and* for showing up on a gas-station camera or two. "If we don't have actual footage of the kill, they won't put out. Fucking bastards."

The kill, as if he did this every day of the week. Sure, he'd been part of that terrible two-fer, the baby biters which so far represented their group's only success—albeit more luck than anything else, but still. Layla restrained the urge to roll her eyes.

Which took serious effort. All she could do was wait to see how Dan was going to deal with this.

Their leader just sat in a camp chair, an open Coors can in his hand, staring bleakly at a nearby wall made entirely of stacked, shadowed garbage.

"I only saw the back of his head." Wiry, buzzcut Ackerman had helped himself to a can as well, but he wasn't drinking, just rolling the damp aluminum across his forehead. There were shadows under his bright hazel eyes, and his baggy fatigues had seen much better days. He'd already cleaned his rifle twice and kept glancing nervously in Dan's direction. Now, however, he tipped his chin in Ben's general direction. "Then genius here started shooting."

"Early bird gets the worm." Ben grinned, lifting his beer can, clearly not chastened in the slightest. "We popped some of the hypnotized fucks, at least."

Lots of people signed up to work for individual biters, most unwittingly. The monsters had their blood-drenched claws everywhere, or so it seemed; bloodsucking came with lots of business success, most on the quasi-legal side but no few were entirely on the up-and-up save for entirely law-abiding tax evasion of the sort rich people throughout history had always excelled at. Some of the bodyguards and close personal servants seemed to be as durable as other demimonde species, and the argument over whether they'd been given a bit of biter blood like the stories claimed or were something else entirely was perennial. Some people swore little green goblins and aliens with black bug-eyes worked for the vampires as well, not to mention certain species of chupacabra.

Good help was hard to find for everyone these days.

Steve-o had shoved his whole head into the utility sink; the dark mop glistened with moisture. Now he scrubbed at his underarms with a dirty T-shirt since all the towels were stiff and smelled bad; he hadn't spoken yet. His expression was sour as the laundry.

"Yeah, that's four henchmen who won't be licking Dracula's ass." Ack didn't seem pleased, though he reserved his coldest, most ardent hatred for those provably signed up to serve biters for their own gain. Apparently he'd run afoul of a willing servant sometime in the past, but he rarely elaborated. "But they almost had you and Steve. I think I clipped a civilian, covering you."

"Collateral damage." Ben took another hit off his can, blinking hard—probably against the tingle of carbonation in his nose—while staring at Layla's chest.

She was used to that, so far as was possible. Wearing a bra under these conditions was more trouble than it was worth. At least his constant gawping could explain the sensation of eyes on her every goddamn move.

Steve finally piped up. "That's bad luck, man." He had a nice baritone; Layla often wondered what he'd sound like singing. "Man, I once thought y'all were professionals."

Shawn had offered to let Steve into his group, while turning down Layla in the nicest possible way. Later, Steve had asked her quietly not to let Dan know, and she'd nodded, well aware of the fireworks that piece of information would cause—not from Dan himself, but from Ben.

Just one more service she provided, really. Now there was yet more smoothing the waters to do, and the task filled her with dread.

"We've collected the bounty on two biters already," she pointed out. The fact that the money had been from low-level mobsters who felt a particular type of weird murder-y shit was cutting into profits was neither here nor there; if regular municipal authorities wouldn't pony up, organized crime would. Shawn's crew had been bankrolled by a hush-hush Vatican program, or so they said, but good luck getting the Church to share the collection-plate take with regular old American heretics. "That's good, right?"

"Yeah, well." Steve-o dragged another camp chair toward the table and lowered himself to sit in stages, like an old man.

Nobody would admit Ack getting headshots on two baby fangers with the new ammo while Steve and Dan pumped the rest of the creatures' bodies full of yet more fancy-dancy exploding bullets was more a fluke than anything else. That was just three months ago in Chicago, another operation gone almost-wrong, and she hated thinking about it.

She'd done a great job as decoy, even Ben had to admit as much. Both biters had locked right on her, and she'd led them into the ambush without any trouble at all. In fact, they'd acted skunk-drunk and were still trying to get at her as the bullets hit. And how they'd screamed before falling apart, violated tissues poofing into fine, gritty dust, a sound fit for nightmares if she didn't already have so many.

Mostly centering on poor Suzy.

Maybe that job was why Ben had opened fire early tonight. He constantly talked about getting a few notches in his belt, a phrase which seemed to apply both to vampire-hunting and to sex, but he never mentioned *why* he had taken up the former.

Of course, neither did Steve, but the look on his face whenever the subject came up spoke volumes.

Dan sighed. Everyone quieted, waiting. When he finally broke the hush, though, it wasn't to start the official debrief. Instead, he lifted his sweating Coors can and looked at it like he didn't quite understand how it had gotten into his hand.

"Fuck it," he said, tonelessly. Dim backwash from the tensor accentuated fine lines around his eyes, at the corners of his mouth. "I quit."

A strange murmuring silence filled their temporary, derelict home. A past-midnight train was barreling nearby, rhythmic wheel-clacks like a heartbeat; the formless mutter of traffic was so familiar it went unnoticed until something awkward happened.

Layla's throat was dry. Even the beer, yeasty and pisswatery, was starting to sound good.

"Three years of bullshit," Dan continued. "Four, if you count… just fuck it. I'm going back home, I'm forgetting all about this creepy shit, and I suggest y'all do the same."

What. The hell. Layla had to un-grit her teeth before she could get a word out. "What do you mean, you quit?" Hunting biters wasn't the sort of thing you walked away from. Especially when they killed your *wife*, for God's sake.

That went double for showing up at Layla's door, blubbering-drunk about how Suzy was gone, it was real and Suze was *gone*. And then asking her to go to the morgue to help identify the body, because he couldn't face it alone.

"Do you need a fucking dictionary, Lay? I. Fucking. *Quit.*" Dan glared at her, coffee-colored eyes gone cold and strange, just like when she'd opened the door to the hotel room before the wedding and found him with Cindy Asterly.

No tears that time, no sir. He hadn't even pleaded with her not to tell, just *looked* at her like that.

Like she was a stranger.

"But…" There wasn't enough air in this stupid falling-apart building packed with junk; she sounded like she'd been punched right in the gut. "But *Suzy.*"

Poor, sweet, friendly Suzy, who never hurt a fly. Who never seemed to care Layla's house was on the wrong side of the tracks, who called her *bestie* and even uninvited Mary LaCosta from her thirteenth birthday party because the little bitch had spread rumors about Layla and Bobby Myers.

"For fuck's sake, I didn't even love her," Dan spat, his mouth contorting for a swift, terrible moment. The dark circles under his eyes had somehow gotten worse in the past half-hour, as if years of sleep deprivation had settled in all at once. "She fucking forced me to marry her, all right? Said she was pregnant."

But you did *marry her. Even after I caught you.* Layla stared at him, dimly aware her mouth was slightly open. A weird slipping sensation vibrated under her still tightly laced boots, as if a minor earthquake had chosen this particular moment to strike.

"Uh-oh," Ben mock-whispered, grinning. "Trouble in paradise, Mommy and Daddy are fighting—"

"Will you just shut the entire fuck up?" Steve-o snarled—another shock, he was always so laid-back. "I've had about enough of your bullshit, man."

Layla knew she should say something, anything to fix things, to smooth this over. The words dammed up in her throat, dry and horrible, and Dan's face—once capable of making her melt like ice cream on a hot sidewalk—had turned into a stranger's.

He lifted his Coors can, still staring at her with that cold, awful expression.

Ben belched again, the sound turning into words. "Brrrrr-uck *you.*" He was probably proud of being able to perform that feat. "Shouldn't have a cunt with us in the first place. Bad luck."

Pete turned, his hip banging the trestle table, which squeaked and wobbled alarmingly. "Shut up," he hissed. "Jesus Christ, you're such a fucking amateur."

"None of us are pros," Ack weighed in, and thank God for that. If someone with a dick was playing peacemaker, it might have a chance of working. "Let's just all calm do—"

Ben was, of course, unwilling to be reasonable. "Oh, *you* think you're gonna get in the cunt's pants? She don't even notice you, man, you—*ulp!*"

At first she thought Steve had stood up, walked around the table, and punched him. But when Layla's head turned, she saw Steve still in the camp chair, gazing at the spot where Ben had been. Steve's jaw was loose, blue eyes cartoonishly round, and the shirt draped over the chair's arm fluttered on a stray draft.

Where Ben had stood there was nothing. He'd vanished into thin air.

What the…

She couldn't even finish the thought. A flicker in her peripheral vision, soft *whuff* of displaced air touching her cheek, and Dan's chair hit the concrete, the Coors can describing a high, perfect arc before impact, splattering yeasty white foam. The trestle table wobbled harder, the tensor's glow casting crazy shadows and stacked guns, knives, and ammo clips clattering uneasily.

"*Run!*" Ackerman yelled.

CHAPTER 4

HE HAD DEALT WITH MORTAL HUNTERS BEFORE—THEY HAD BEEN A touch more effective, as such things went, before steam engines and factories. Perhaps something essential had been lost as those technological marvels rose. Still, the soldier had to admit many wonders were built in exchange, and cities in the old days had certainly smelled far worse.

He drifted in mistform near the ceiling for a short while, watching their interactions. The constant internal clock every child of the Blood bore ticked away, a slowly mounting warning. Dawn was closer than dusk, he could not linger overlong—but he was greedy for knowledge of his nymph's mortal affairs, in order to arrange them most effectively.

What he saw was unpleasant. Play soldiers at best, save for the wary bare-chested brute who held his silence longest. Though this location was acceptable for a hidden camp and there was even a touch of intelligence evident in the arrangement of detritus to provide cover, they did not set a watch. No, the men were too busy arguing—and insulting their sole female companion—to notice danger.

Dismally unsurprising performance. Only the half-clad

mortal would have proceeded past the initial application stages for catspaw duties; none were fit for consideration as dogsbodies. Not even cannon fodder, was his final evaluation.

Only *she* was sensitive enough to discern his attention, often shivering and glancing about. The soldier had always thought he preferred women in gowns, but the denims clung lovingly to her legs and the peach cotton top showed her to advantage—though what would not? She was simply, sheerly incandescent, graceful even while holding herself stiffly, clearly *en garde* among male animals.

Indeed the group was laughable, and on the edge of falling apart under its own inconsistencies. The soldier paid particular attention to the one who had pressed her against the wall—her scent still lingered upon him, though also saturating a few other corners of this ramshackle place. The group had been resident some while, and the only real surprise was the large photograph atop a stack of files, his own face clearly captured by film and telephoto lens.

Newer digital devices were easier to guard against.

Sloppy. Realizing just how rigid he had become, how unaware, was chilling. Fortunately she would cure him of that. Sound, sight, sensation poured through him, a glorious welter, and she was so very *distracting*. Tendrils of dark hair escaping her braid framed a soft sweet face; even pulled tight with pain or fatigue her mouth was eminently soft, and her eyes lingered in a shade between wintersky blue and ice-grey, fine lavender lines in the iris. Her cheeks were drawn, her collarbones stood out starkly, and the cotton top's short sleeves could not disguise new, dark-flowering bruises high upon her arms.

The evidence of damage was enough to make the beast in him turn coldly watchful, straining to leap upon whichever of the dolts below had dared lay a hand upon such fineness.

Leila, they called her. An eastron name, ancient even as sanguinant reckoned, lingering sweetly inside his chest like a struck crystal bell.

Then the mortal who watched her most avidly—each time the pug-nosed blond male addressed as *Ben* spoke, a shadow of distaste crossed her expression—as he swilled the watered yellow water they called beer in this benighted age made the mistake of advancing to open insult.

Therefore, this *Ben* was the one to be taken first, and the soldier's only regret was that it was a swift death instead of the lingering agony such behavior deserved. At least the mortal's blood was hot and fresh, absorbed within moments.

Next he took the most competent male—half-naked as a fighting Gaul, plucked from the flimsy chair and dead almost before the soldier reached the roofbeams with a struggling cargo. Just as he finished the last long, artery-pressurized swallow, the first mortal's corpse hit the floor with a deep, almost amusing thud.

Which was lost in a cry of warning, for the mortals scattered—save for the sandy-blond man who had been merely, cruelly dismissive of little Leila. Her pulse had changed as she gazed at the one addressed as *Dan*; the soldier took some pleasure in simply striking the blond's head off its stem instead of draining him.

One precisely calibrated blow, cervical bone-cable snapping, and the soldier vanished before a single red droplet found itself free and jetted high from the stump of a mortal neck.

They were so very fragile. He would have to take much care with his prize both before and after the Gift wore through; leman did not reach the strength and speed of even an elder sanguinant. Perhaps it was payment for their immunity to ossification, and if so well worth the bargain.

Two mortal males and a frightened dryad, all attempting escape through passageways bored in stacked rubbish. The soldier struck again, plucking the speediest contestant—the mortal who had been on a rooftop with a sniper rifle earlier, easily distinguishable from the sound of his hammering pulse. This specimen's blood was a little sweeter than the others', lingering on the edge of cloying since the pancreas was having difficulty.

Diabetic. At least you are spared a lingering decay. The soldier was long past the age of sympathy for any prey, yet a subtle pang went through him. Did little Leila know of her companion's illness?

Not that it mattered. Now there was only his lovely one left, and the male who had held her against a wall.

The soldier was forced to revise his opinion of their group slightly upward, for they had clearly drilled in escape. The male was in the lead, breathing harshly, his glands emitting bursts of acrid terror familiar from any battlefield. It was the scent of defeat, of rout, of hearing Pan's shriek or the clatter of the goat-god's hooves, and perhaps that was how he gained enough speed to outpace even a divine creature.

"Pete for God's sake," she cried, a lost, lonely sound, as the stocky fellow nipped through a heavy iron side door. It banged to just before a clattering—something outside fallen, perhaps deliberately placed to block the exit. The darkness was near total, though no difficulty for sanguinant eyes, and the soldier realized she was about to cast herself upon the sealed exit in an excess of terror, possibly gaining some injury.

Which could not be allowed.

One last time he plunged, hawklike, his arms closing carefully upon tender rose-musk salvation. She screamed, the sound cut in half as the *quietus* snapped about her—peculiar psychic pressure used to keep a fledgling's prey from wriggling, honed and strengthened for many other uses when dealing with mortal authorities or witnesses, and even though the soldier was well-practiced in the art she still managed a startling amount of resistance.

Then again, she was leman. Exquisitely sensitive, a marvelous combination of strength and delicacy, precisely calibrated to shatter the calcified prison of a sanguinant dying by inches. His true teeth ached, attempting to free themselves; the soldier denied them, rising swiftly, shattering a section of the hovel's rotted roof.

Never, he promised silently. *You will not suffer such filth again. I will not allow it.*

Yet this was the easy victory. Much more difficult to keep what he had taken—and there was the problem of Father, as well. The patriarch would not like this turn of events.

He would like the soldier's next moves even less.

More of the terrible numbing ossification broke away, sheets of dusty apathy shaken loose by deep lungfuls of that wonderful, dizzying fragrance. Successive future challenges were even somewhat pleasant to contemplate, despite the sudden, novel, pulse-clenching feeling of having something to lose.

The soldier bore his prize swiftly through sultry darkness starred with electric light, and found, with a sharp wonderful burst of surprise, that he was smiling.

He would have liked to be in a location where he had personal resources, so to speak, but every mortal city eventually accumulated certain places catering to the demimonde. Finding one was simply a matter of looking for a few nearly invisible signs. Not that much searching was necessary in this case; there was a giant glass-sheathed hotel in a slice of downtown very near where he had first scented his new leman.

Very convenient indeed.

A modicum of mental pressure secured all requirements, and the capacious pockets of his trousers—a modern fashion he had nothing but admiration for—also held a pair of cellphones, a wallet full of plastic cards, plenty of the current imperium's cash, and a few other small items. He could travel very lightly indeed, but his nymph might…

Well, she certainly *required*, as mortals did. But she might also *prefer* something other than a march to the next destination, digging camp, orders given, objectives achieved, breaking camp, another march.

Just what her preferences might consist of, the soldier could not begin to guess. Once the reasonably large pink-and-white suite was secured and invisible seals set, he was forced to admit himself… well, not quite at a loss.

But for the first time in a very long while, actually uncertain.

Solicitously laid upon the wide, flower-patterned bed, his nymph was a vision indeed. One small hand lay loosely, palm-up, gently cupped; the other rested against her breast, fingertips touching her heartbeat. Her braid had unraveled, a skein of blue-black silk tangling deliciously across pillow-hills of patterned fabric. Breathing scarcely audible even to freshly sharpened sanguinant ears, pulse slow and regular, her restlessness was neither physical nor visible. Yet the *quietus* swelled as she sought to wake, perhaps with terror still echoing in her fragile, beautiful bones.

Her throat was enticingly bare, and his mouth was full of sweet numbing anticipation. He could sink his fangs in, loaded with change agents to trigger the initial stages of the Gift. It was best to do so swiftly, yet the soldier hesitated.

He stood at the bedside, head cocked, watching.

Dullard. The sharp slap of corrective harshness, necessary for training. Yet this was not combat—or was it? *Will you let the prize slip through your fingers? Take her now.*

She was utterly defenseless. Even with the Gift she could not hope to hold off one such as himself, old and strong, but he did not move. Something was… not right.

The instinct was one he had felt a handful of times over the centuries, and it halted him surely as a brazen trumpet calling vespers. The texture of his clothing was unbearable, every inch of him newly sensitive and the mating-thrall dark wine in his veins, pushing and prodding. He was desperate for relief, to sink his teeth into that soft, enticing pulse, to rip the irritating fabric from both of them and bury himself in what had to be glorious relief.

And yet.

What is known? Start there. Her group had been hunting his own personal quarry—not entirely surprising since Esgard the Varangian had become extremely sloppy, enough to attract the attention of mortal authorities. Father had decided it was time to expand the borders of his own rule in this direction, and the soldier had been dispatched to once again do his duty.

The stacks of paper upon their flimsy table, and the name attached to the picture—*Nemesis*, a title the entire demimonde knew to fear, bestowed upon the soldier by the patriarch himself. Now mortals had heard whispers of it as well.

Is that who I am? What he had become, with the stone-layers of years rising, thimbleful by thimbleful, to drown him?

It had been so very long since he thought of himself as having a name at all. No need for such things when his existence was so blessedly simple, move and countermove dictated by laws of warfare—endless variations, but only a few simple themes at their core. Strategy and tactic both could be used to stay alert, either in complexity to stave off the temptation of glut and bood-craze—the bane of fledglings—or in direct brutal sensation to batter away the languorous killing-sleep which took so many elders.

He had survived so long, reaching elder status and a certain fame. Yet he remembered little of a few past centuries save the violence, the constant work of ensuring Father's safety, the games a patriarch liked to play.

Lamps burned upon the bedside tables, smokeless captive lightning casting loving gold over the curve of her cheek, the blue tones shimmering in her hair, the soles of her heavy boots— of fine quality, her footwear, though far too heavy for such slim, dancing feet.

Think about it, the new, nearly uncomfortable clarity of thought whispered. *Who are you, really? Do you know anymore?*

A name was superfluous. Yet was not *Nemesis* a title? The soldier's eyes half-closed; he stared at a rosy, slumber-chained nymph and wondered what she would call him.

Even that uncertainty was wonderful, sending faint shivers down his back, tingling in his fingertips, the padded hammer of her pulse strike-spreading through every inch of him in warm, overlapping waves. He had been numb for so long any emotion at all was a dangerous blessing.

Now, he possessed a divine cornucopia.

Dawn was nigh. He did not need a fledgling's daylight rest, especially with a near-glut filling his veins, but the sunlight was an enemy to be dealt most carefully with. Just as her fear and fragility, for a leman could be broken or injured beyond repair if their sanguinant were not cautious—or ruthless—enough.

Even shattered or feral, she was too precious to lose. Still, only a fool wasted a god's gift.

Father could be the most dangerous enemy of all, if he did not assume Nemesis dead of age or failed attack. Worst would be if the patriarch realized what the soldier had found and taken, for Antinous held back his own calcification by simple dint of acquisition—territory, treasure, fledgling toys to break and consume, mortal power and influence, all sought bit by bit to add to his stores, to provide a moment's diversion.

It had never occurred to the soldier that there might be something worth the trouble of disobedience. A murmur, a slight movement as the nymph upon the bed fought to awaken, and trembling, absolute certainty took the place of his former loyalty.

Best spoils belonged to the emperor, of course, and the general took first pick of what remained. But even the lowliest of an army's humming hive knew how to hide his own share, whether scraped from the hovels of a burning city or reflexively hidden by a sanguinant who dimly understood one day he, too, would be expendable to his master.

His fangs were out, upper and lower all painfully sensitive. He had to force them away, invoking a control which grew slimmer with every passing moment.

Committed, now. There was no possibility of retreat. In its own way, the lack of choice was a comfort.

Softly, increment by increment, the soldier released the *quietus*, and waited to see how his prize would wake.

CHAPTER 5

Layla thrashed, body and mind spinning on a dark wine-colored flood of vertigo. For an endless, sickmaking moment she was certain whatever had grabbed Ben and Steve had also killed her, but there was bright yellow light in her eyes and the faint squeak underneath her was a huge, soft…

A bed.

King-sized, in fact, with a cabbage-rose coverlet plus tonally matching pillow shams, the entire shebang set smack-dab in a big, pleasant room which whispered *hotel, but a nice one, so mind your manners.* The air was still and dead, blessedly cool in a way that meant someone had paid their HVAC bills recently, and her head gave an amazing flare of pain before subsiding into a dull pounding ache.

All of which was beside the point. She scrambled, impelled by an overpowering, instinctive desire to get *away,* and ended up half-crouching in a mound of decorative bedding, her back pressed against the headboard. Something rattled overhead—a framed print, its lower edge digging into her shoulders. The back of her head brushed the glass, her hair falling into her eyes.

Pinkish carpet, washed-out candy cane wallpaper, floor-length drapes pulled tight over what had to be a huge window, maybe even a tiny balcony. Two nightstands, both with clunky pink ceramic lamps turned up to full. A flatscreen television bolted to the wall over a dresser trying too hard to impersonate rosewood. A door, slightly ajar, showing the dark cave of a bathroom, reflected light gleaming dimly on a suggestion of white industrial tile.

And a vampire.

"What." The word was a mere husk of itself, falling into humming silence. Her voice shook, her throat so dry it could give the Sahara lessons. "The *fuck*."

The biter stood at the bedside, looking mildly at her. His eyes were very dark, his mouth relaxed, and even though his hair was a tumble of black curls each looked perfectly planned, falling in precisely decreed disarray. Straight-backed, hands loose at his sides, wide shoulders at strict angles, chin absolutely level; he looked like a military statue, in fact, since the posture could only be defined as *at attention*. Same black wool sweater with vertical ribbing and well-worn leather patches at the elbows, same indeterminate-dark Carhartts—they were *definitely* brand-name, broken in by hard use—and she was pretty sure he was probably wearing the same boots as in the file photo.

Next to all that, she was a goddamn mess. Her T-shirt was awry and her hair entirely rumpled; her own steel-toed tacticals crushed the pillows and counterpane, and she felt a brief flash of guilt at wearing shoes on a bed.

Which was entirely nuts since she had only seconds left to live, if that. Because there was the red-stripe-skull-and-crossbones vampire, and he was *looking right at her*.

Fuzzy dark flowers dilated at the edges of her vision. Her heart buzzed, pounding like she'd slammed the world's biggest energy drink; the nice cool air had turned to glass and her lungs couldn't drag any in to fuel her starving brain.

The vampire stirred, the fingers of his right hand twitching.

Layla shrieked and tried to push herself through the wall, her legs stiffening uselessly.

A puff of cool air caressed her cheek. The mattress gave a sharp groan because he'd leapt onto the bed, his boots sinking in hard, and his hands clamped around her bare upper arms. Fever-warm skin, callused but oddly gentle—he didn't squeeze, simply held her motionless.

"Be calm," he said, quiet but with absolute authority. "Or I will use the *quietus* again and make you. *Breathe*, little Leila."

Ohshit he knows my NAME ohgod how… And he was mispronouncing it, too, adding an extra syllable as if he could taste every vowel.

Her lungs decided to work again, since it was either that or pass out, and she sucked gratefully at air that was not full of mildew. Someone vacuumed this room near-daily, wiped the surfaces down, changed the linens—there was a breath of commercial detergent simmering up from the bed, though the comforter no doubt held smeared traces of a thousand travelers.

A faint haze of outdoors night and summer heat surrounded the biter, both soothing and terrifying at once. He smelled like a clean adult male after a heavy workout, and it wasn't right, it just was *not right* for a vampire to smell like a person.

"Good," he continued, encouragingly, and that was awful as well. He had a nice, deep voice, almost restful. "Be tranquil, little Leila. You are safe."

That is a goddamn lie. The dark blots threatened to come back, growing over her field of vision; she forced them desperately away, hoping only for one more breath, then another.

"H-h-how…" To top it all off, she was stuttering. *Fucking useless question, Lay. Come on, do something. Punch him. Use all that self-defense the guys were laughing about teaching you.*

But the fingers caging her upper arms were iron; even if he didn't squeeze, she was miserably aware of the sheer strength humming through his hands. He balanced lightly in front of her, with absolute control, and now she knew how a mouse felt when a tiger placed a paw lightly upon its back, not pressing—but ready to, if she moved.

If she so much as *breathed* wrong.

He lowered his chin slightly, peering at her face. The slight motion was also somehow too controlled to be precisely human, and a fresh wave of terror nailed her in place.

"I can explain." The words were evenly spaced, slightly stilted. "Would you like that?"

She couldn't quite place the accent, or maybe he'd just acquired his English from a textbook. How did vampires learn new languages, anyway? Did they attend night classes?

Oh, God. She was going to die as she'd lived, wondering about random, inconsequential bullshit. Layla held very still, wondering if she should pray.

What a time to wish I were Catholic, like Shawn and Mike and...

That was another horrible thought. "P-please d-d-don't kill me," she stammered. It was embarrassing, but she had just that instant found out that all things considered, she'd rather be deeply mortified than outright dead. "Please."

"You are very safe, little Leila." A flicker of eyelids—he couldn't even *blink* like a normal person, for Godsake. "That is your name, is it not?"

Fucking hell, how do you know *that?* How had he found... had he followed her and Pete? Or Ben and Steve, considering they'd emptied entire clips at him and his henchmen?

Where was all his goon-squad backup now? Her own crew, well, she could guess.

Ben gone between one syllable and the next. Steve-o, just vanishing out of his chair. The tensor lamp rocking crazily, shadows dancing... "Are... m-my friends, they're..."

"The one who ran before you—Pete?" He waited, patiently, until Layla managed a tiny flicker of a nod. "He left you to your fate."

Now she remembered the door on that particular escape route was rigged to block itself with a pile of falling crap, cutting off pursuit. Pete probably hadn't even realized she was behind him, too worried with bugging out.

Oh, God. "The… the others?" *You're being so stupid. What do you think happened?*

"Gone," he said, softly. Almost kindly. "You need not concern yourself with them."

Which brought her brain-train to a crashing halt, because it was a statement full of *implications,* as dear old Suze would say, Suzy who had died one rainy spring evening up at Pleasant Point, her convertible's top ripped open like a soda can and her throat, her poor *neck…*

Layla stared at the vampire, who studied her closely in return. Did he look at smooshed bugs on a windshield the same way? The terror was so huge it wrapped around its own axle and became bleakly, morbidly hilarious. What kind of blood-sucking monster put a girl in a hotel room and… what the hell did he *want*?

"Le-i-la." Drawing out her name as if it had three syllables instead of two, though there was no hint of the usual male mockery. "An old name, beautiful. It means *Night*, always a blessing, and eyes like stars. You are no doubt much beloved; are your parents alive? Your clan, your *familia*? Tell me."

What the hell? God alone knew where Layla's wild-child mother was at the moment, and she'd never known her father. Meemaw Catherine was safely in the ground, sure, but she didn't feel like explaining her fucked-up family history to a biter. There was no point, and besides, that was private information.

"Are you going to k-kill me?" What a ridiculous question. Still, she had to know. The words *will it hurt* trembled at the very tip of her tongue; she snapped her teeth shut, keeping them trapped.

"Have I not said you are safe?" The faintest hint of irritation crossed the biter's beaky face, his eyebrows drawing a few millimeters closer to each other, and now Layla was utterly certain she was going to pass out and wake up dead, no matter how ridiculous the notion sounded. "You will live long, little Leila; I will make certain of it."

That was another statement full of implications, but her head—hell, her entire *body*—was so overloaded she didn't have the capacity to untangle a single one. Instead, since holding still wasn't working, it chose the only other option on the table.

Get away.

Or at least, she tried to, pitching herself aside with every bit of strength she could muster. Her left hand struck his chest, and it was like slapping a concrete wall. The vampire's grip on her shifted a fraction; a strange *blip* like a CD skipping in an old player, and his head blurred forward, snake-quick.

Somehow her back met yielding fabric instead of being propped against the headboard and wall. A brush of hot breath on her sweating neck, then a piercing almost-pain accompanied by spreading numbness.

The vampire's fangs closed on her throat.

CHAPTER 6

H_E _{HAD} _{INTENDED} _{TO} _{EXPLAIN,} _{TO} _{SOOTHE,} _{TO} _{CALMLY} _{LAY} _{OUT} _{THE} dimensions of her new status. A man devoted solely to war had no poet's words with which to seduce, even if he longed to try. Yet her sudden doomed attempt to struggle, legs kicking and tender damp mortal flesh sliding under his fingertips, broke the last thread of stringent control.

The soldier's fangs found the sweetly musical pulse they had somehow always ached for. He drew in a mouthful of singing, absolute sweetness, and it burned every other vein-drink he had taken to clotted, muddy ash.

So many words for what she was—*leman, deva, imprima, sang-dolce;* he quite liked the ring of *aima-glyza,* in Greek more modern than Homer's but still ancient as modern mortals reckoned. Honeyed, ambrosial fire filled his throat, a drug more complete than any glut or mortal opiate hit his own slow, ageless veins. A scrape-stinging edge rippled down his body as sanguinant physiology shifted, discovering an addiction lain sleeping for long centuries until the first drop sank all the way to his marrow, followed by blessed, drowning euphoria.

She tasted like victory, like the memory of dusky grapes from his mortal grandfather's estate, like a soft fresh breeze upon a fevered brow. And yet, more. The sensation enfolding him was alien, even as he had somehow always craved its warmth and knew he would do anything, commit any crime or savagery to keep it close.

What else did every warrior long for? The removal of armor, the sheathing of all weapons.

Peace.

He drew again, top fangs working another fraction deeper, and the second draught was impossibly somehow *better*. Complex overlapping tastes, a red-purple scorch of devouring fear, deep dusky blue grief, her totality enfolding him in wonder. Her laboring heartbeat fast as hummingbird wings, a shallow breath stirring his hair as her head tipped back on its slender neck-stem. A drooping blossom, shuddering as it was crushed to his chest; he wanted more, *more*.

But she was mortal, exhausted by terror, flight, a very long and eventful night. His greed met a contradictory, overpowering imperative to protect what he had taken, and candythick tenderness welled from a depth past the beast-lair at the floor of his soul.

One last slow sip, rolled like the finest unwatered wine before slipping down his throat. Now he understood what the rumors whispered of, *now* he understood why any sanguinant lucky enough to find a leman kept the treasure strictly, deeply hidden.

Withdrawing each fang was a wonderful torment, then he paused to lick the marks with infinite care. Change and healing agents were already spreading in her bloodstream, suppressing pain and encouraging initial chemical shifts; now his saliva carried further healing substances from different glands. Slowly, carefully, he gathered every final, marvelous, narcotic drop.

Her scent now bore a trace of burning metal—the residue of agonizing fear, mixed with a dizzying tang he recognized as his own pheromones and markers. A warning, a mark of possession: *this is mine.*

"Ow." An adorable, dazed almost-whimper. "Hey."

He had not felt fear for centuries; now, even that sensation was a luxury. Had he harmed her? It was difficult to raise his head, brace himself on his elbows, peeling himself a few fractions from the slim soft wonder of her body pressed under his, sinking into the bed's embrace. Her lovely knees were pushed to either side of his hips, and the only bar to his desire was a few layers of fabric.

"*Ow*," she repeated, sounding outright aggrieved. Small hands at his shoulders, slipping ineffectually against his sweater as she pushed with no more strength than a starving kitten. Her eyelids fluttered, and her mouth was too entirely succulent to remain untasted for long. "What the *hell* are you doing?"

Only what I must. He strained to think, to clearly discern the next tactical move. He examined her stunned, exhausted beauty as she struggled to compass the situation, then tilted his head slightly to glimpse the marks over her jugular. Yes, the bite was glaring-fresh—primary and secondary fangs on top, the tertiary on the bottom, all properly sealed. No danger there.

His prize stirred beneath him once more, textures sliding, her softness calling to him. The soldier inhaled sharply. Difficult not to simply rip every scrap of clothing free and claim her, but she…

She *deserved* better.

Once the soldier reached elder status he had reflexively, habitually planned for eventual freedom from his Maker's grasp, though the time was never quite right and rising ossification had robbed him of caring enough to initiate movement. This sudden unlooked-for good fortune was more dangerous than any defeat, for it found him pressed for time—always an invitation to error or disaster.

Not only that, but he was called upon for far, far more than simple rebellion. He must not only free himself, but keep a prize hidden *and* adapt to a modern mortal's comfort.

So far as a creature like himself could, that was.

"I bit you." Slightly difficult to recall the proper words, to use her modern tongue; even more difficult to force his true teeth away, restoring the blunt mortal variety unquestionably better for speech. "I will again, sweet Leila. For now, rest."

Surprisingly, her pale eyes flew open and she found enough strength to attempt more pattering, ineffectual strikes. So easy to catch her wrist, pin her arm to the bed; he wanted so much more, but the *quietus* folded over her and sank in, careful pressure applied slowly so as not to damage.

Again, her resistance was far more pronounced than many other mortals', and he found himself charmed by her determination.

But inevitably, eventually, she returned to the arms of sleep—the only other paramour he would ever allow.

"Rest," the soldier repeated, a tender murmur. He even risked pressing his lips to her cheek, inhaling deeply—dim aroma-traces of her companions remained, as well as the faint fading reek from their dilapidated hideout. Both made the beast in him snarl with possessive rage, and the mating-thrall was becoming unmercifully intense. "I will learn, *puella dulcis*. I promise you that."

Extricating himself took a short while, for every brush against her delicate, languid form threatened to break him afresh. His control held by the thinnest hair-fine chain, though, and he retreated to the draped window. Outside, dawn was well under-way, the sun's advent instinctively felt even in the deepest, safest crypt.

He had already stripped the SIM from the small modern 'phone' Father's troops could use to track him; the other, updated every few years, was as secret as could be managed. The wonder of this particular mortal technology struck him afresh, and he marveled at its implications in a way he had not been able to while age-calcification lay thick upon him. Father's newest fledgling, selected for both aesthetic appeal and modern technical prowess, had patiently explained the principles and applications several times, repeating each point so many times as necessary, and finally the soldier had grasped enough for use, as he could most weapons.

Now, though, he could fully understand what the pretty straw-haired youth had been attempting to impart. A shame he would never see young Otto again—unless, that was, events took a truly distressing turn.

Father ordered the pruning of his household's ranks at regular intervals. Perhaps it was the patriarch's favorite method of warding away the creeping rigidity, though the soldier knew his Maker derived a great deal of sadistic enjoyment from watching Nemesis wreak havoc upon those he had more often than not trained and commanded.

Is that who I am? The soldier stopped, turning over the second cellphone in his hands, and looked to the bed.

Now his nymph was tucked under the covers, her boots neatly arranged at the bedside. He had thought perhaps she would not wish to sleep clothed, but if he touched even the button at her denims' waistband—much less the zipper—he would not be able to refrain from claiming her.

The initial event was of some import to leman, or so rumor and lore insisted. Naturally the prize could be psychologically broken past resistance, or even taken unaware… but that was a terrible beginning. Even the fellow soldiers of his mortal life had opinions upon the proper way to conduct such affairs after the first paroxysm of sack and pillage, or when a veteran returned home after doing his duty.

So far he had avoided the worst mistake, or so he hoped. He pressed the power button on the side of the thin metallic rectangle and waited for the electronic servant to awaken. Really the things were akin to the spirits said to wait upon certain gods;

after a certain point, there was very little difference between technology and divine powers.

"Maximus." He heard his own voice, and almost twitched. Singsong talk to oneself could be a sign of accelerating ossification, an irretrievable descent into madness rendering a sanguinant sloppy enough to be dispatched by mischance, human hunters—or their own kind.

The demimonde teemed with predators, visible and otherwise.

He was now proof against fatal rigidity, paralysis, insanity. Every breath freighted with his leman's perfume was further evidence; the sudden relief of that clinging, ever-present fear was worth any tribute she might exact. "That was my praenomen."

Of course his mortal nomen and cognomen were gone, lost to time just as his gens and every human being who might remember who he had been—except for Father, of course.

He will be furious at the loss. Nemesis was a tool to be used, and a faithful one. Yet for some while the soldier had wondered if perhaps his own Maker had decayed past the Rubicon, so to speak. The soldier's plans to escape also included a few contingencies for taking Father's territory and other possessions— treacherous to even think of, yes, but also necessary.

Unavoidable, since any man who claimed to be rational must plan for the future.

At the moment, his first consideration was not freedom but protecting his frail prize. Who would not be mortal for much longer, true, but would remain achingly vulnerable not only to daylight and mischance but also plain theft. For a moment the soldier let himself imagine what might transpire if the patriarch found out and managed to lay hands upon her.

The growl rose from his chest, a sanguinant's battle-warning vibrating in air gone hot and motionless under invisible seals, and Leila's steady breathing halted. She stirred, making a soft sleepy sound, and turned on her side, settling into more-natural somnolence as fatigue asserted itself through the *quietus.*

She might never understand what she had saved him from. He had forgotten even his own *name*, centuries passing under his keel with their changing mortal fashions only worth a few bemused glances. Even studying the ways and inventions of mortal warfare had not been enough to keep him more than partially awake.

If not for her appearance, how long before he succumbed to true-death, either sinking into dreaded but necessary rest or by some error during combat, dying upon an enemy's claws? Or maddened past bearing by the incomprehensible modern world, perhaps even walking into the crucifying kiss of sunlight to seek the relief of permanent oblivion?

A shudder worked down his body. He almost closed his fist, rendering the phone useless as it splintered, but halted the motion just in time. His head tipped back, fangs bared and still throbbing; his own scent had changed, enfolding her lighter, lovely rose-and-musk. A dainty, priceless prize, falling into bloodstained claws.

Very well. "Maximus," he repeated. "That is my name." When she woke, he would begin afresh—a new man, painstakingly learning her preferences, modern ways, and modern mores, insofar as he could.

The campaign might be long; it was rumored some leman never became resigned to cushioned, protective captivity. Nevertheless, each battle would be satisfying in its own right, and in any case he had no other option.

The phone had fallen asleep as well. He woke it with a poke at the touchscreen, granted it permission to update, and began his preparations.

CHAPTER 7

AT FIRST SHE THOUGHT THE GUYS HAD GONE OUT FOR DONUTS AND left her to sleep in, as they sometimes did; she deeply disliked the feeling of being abandoned, sure, but a few hours of peace and quiet almost made up for it. As a bonus, there were no nightmares, unless she counted a particular vivid dream about being trapped in a deteriorating warehouse while a terrifying invisible force whisked her squad one by one into darkness.

Before she opened her eyes, Layla could even pretend the slight headache was a combination of summer dehydration and missing the morning coffee call. Her throat felt raspy and there was an odd heaviness in her limbs, like the fourth-day echo of a super hard workout with one of Shawn's crew.

Thinking of O'Shaughnassey so early in the morning was a bad sign. Layla groaned, rubbed at her face with nearly numb palms, and draped an arm across her eyes. The outside world could goddamn well wait for a few more minutes.

Doozy of a dream. I almost thought…

It was so quiet. And blessedly, wonderfully cool, though she was under tangled covers and her T-shirt had ridden up but good. She'd slept in her jeans again, ugh. Plus, her surroundings outright smelled wrong—no overlapping mildew, old pizza, and gun oil, but canned air, heavily sprayed Pledge, and industrial-strength fabric detergent.

That wasn't a dream. Sudden, inarguable certainty, rising like a shark in dark water. Then the instinctive certainty she was being watched arrived, unwelcome and familiar; memory flooded in, a bright, nasty collage of terror.

"Good evening," the vampire said, and Layla was out of the bed like a shot. The sheets and coverlet tried to stop her, wrapped like clinging seaweed, but she scrambled free—harsh lick of rugburn against her right palm, her knee hitting the pink-carpeted floor hard enough to click her teeth together—and threw herself for the door she must have somehow, on some level, remembered.

Or she tried to. Less than halfway there a pair of iron-hard arms closed around her and she was lifted off madly flailing sock feet. She writhed, attempting to elbow him, to shake free, to kick, but wild motion made absolutely zero difference. A hot, dry palm closed over her mouth, trapping a despairing scream, and a deep, imperturbable male voice purred near her ear, muffled by tangled hair and the thumping of her panicked heart.

"Hush, shhh, little Leila. Be still, *pax*, I do not wish to harm you. Shush, now. Please."

She clamped her teeth into the hand, *hard*. A low, nearly disbelieving laugh brushed her hair, warm breath touching her cheek. She was sweating again, despite the air conditioning. Her nose was clear, but maybe that wouldn't last and she'd suffocate with a biter holding her face.

OhGod please, please don't let me die. She went limp, lungs heaving, air whistling faintly through her nostrils.

"Very good." A faint tremor passed through the steel bars holding her as the vampire inhaled, deeply; he sounded, of all things, almost businesslike. "I am going to take my hand away. If you scream again I will stopper your mouth, very pleasantly. Nod if you understand."

What the fuck? But she did get, very clearly, that he didn't want her to yell, and maybe she could figure out a way to survive this if she played along for a few minutes. Watching for an opening, waiting for a chance—oh, she knew all about that.

Sometimes opportunity didn't bother to arrive, but Meemaw Cathy always said chance favored the prepared. And that was good enough.

Layla managed a tiny nod, chin dipping, rising again. Then she had to loosen her jaw as he worked his hand free of her teeth. At least she hadn't drawn blood.

Vampire blood. Too late—he bit you, goddammit. You know what that means.

One problem at a time, Layla decided grimly, and was finally able to get enough breath into her aching lungs. Violent trembling poured through arms, legs, all the rest of her; she hoped he didn't think she was still fighting.

"Now," he continued, as if it were the most reasonable thing in the world, "I am going to set you on the bed. Please be cautious, little Leila, and move slowly. I have… certain instincts, and they are a little difficult to control at the moment. Again, nod if you understand."

Oh, God. But she nodded once more, trying to make the movement at once definite and conciliatory. What the fuck did he want with *her*? Most of his file was simply a list of sightings, generally right before another high-powered biter vanished; Shawn's second-in-command Feargus had even made the grim joke that maybe Nemesis was a cannibal, cleaning up his own kind. There was another list in the folder as well—hunter groups which had brushed up against this particular biter and dropped off the map.

Sucked into a black hole, maybe with a little *ulp* sound like Ben made when…

The biter glided backward, carrying her along as if she weighed less than nothing, and finally halted next to the tangled pink bed. The leashed strength was just as terrifying when he set her, lightly and with exquisite control, on numb feet. Her legs threatened to give way, rubbery as overboiled noodles, and he steadied her.

"Careful," he murmured. "There. Down."

Her ass hit the bed. It was hard to stay sitting upright instead of sliding right off the edge and ending to the floor; she managed, ignoring the mattress's faint squeak, and squeezed her eyes shut. Her hands knotted together in her lap, like she was waiting in the principal's office after some playground prank. Then it occurred to her she might as well see her own death coming, so she forced her eyelids open again and snuck a quick glance upward.

Same black sweater, on a disturbingly broad chest she now knew was stone-hard, plus warmer than it should be even through a layer of heavy knitted wool. He went still for a moment, and the blank look on his face was utterly terrifying, as if he'd forgotten how to make the human mask work. How did anyone mistake these creatures for people, especially at short range? Maybe biters only let henchmen and hypnotized employees close enough to see the thousand subtle signals adding up to *this thing just ain't right*?

Looming over her like this, he was even more terrifying than last night. If that were possible.

The vampire dropped fluidly into a crouch, finishing the movement by peering up at her through a shelf of dark curls fallen over his forehead. Except for the eerie gracefulness and the way he went utterly, creepily motionless right afterward, it could almost have been kind of comforting, a guy deliberately making himself smaller as if he understood female caution.

"Hello," the biter known as Nemesis said, gravely. "You are very frightened."

No shit. Layla swallowed hard, dry throat giving a tiny forlorn click. She nodded, and once she started, she couldn't seem to stop for a few seconds. Her head bobbed vigorously, until the entire plush, pinkish—Meemaw would call it *dusty rose* —room seesawed like a ship on high storm-waves.

His mouth curved into, of all things, a smile. It wasn't bad, especially as the corners of his eyes crinkled a bit, but the thought that he might show his teeth was suddenly, overwhelmingly *too much*.

So she froze. At least that stopped the nodding; she felt like a goddamn bobble-head attached to a dashboard.

"And very brave." As if conferring a favor, one of her very least favorite tones for a man to take. But the vampire probably couldn't care less what she thought right now, or ever. "You know what I am."

She was trembling almost too hard to breathe, Layla realized. Her head now felt even funnier, light and stuffed with cotton. He'd bitten her; how much blood had he taken? Was she running a few pints short?

Was she a vampire's juice box now? A self-sustaining snack?

"Say it, little Leila." A soft, coaxing tone, again adding an extra syllable to her name. Worst of all, he was smiling—just a little, as if he meant to be encouraging, lips curving upward but so horribly stiff, as if he didn't really remember how to grin correctly. "Let me hear you, so I know you understand."

Oh, Christ. What answer did he want? "You're a biter," she heard herself whisper. Hard to talk with her teeth wanting to chatter, her tongue tangled-numb with terror. "A v-vampire."

"*Sanguinant* is the term we prefer, but you are not incorrect." A considering look, measuring her for God-alone-knew what. His dark gaze was so flat, so closed-off, he could give anyone the heebie-jeebies with just a glance. "You know of the demimonde, then."

It was one thing to have Shawn or one of his guys lecture on proper terminology. It was *entirely different* to have an honest-to-goshness fanged sonofabitch lecture her—especially so casually, patient and expectant as a teacher with a distracted student.

"A little." She couldn't speak above a pained, strained little-girl mutter. "I won't tell anyone, I promise. I *swear*." She hated begging, was helpless not to. Her palms were both sweaty and cold, her throat ached, and waves of scorching and freezing alternated, roaring up and down her entire body like a pair of small dogs fighting over a plush toy.

This was the nicest hotel room she'd ever been in, and she was going to die here.

"Be calm, sweet Leila. You are in no danger." Calmly, as if he thought she'd believe him. He didn't even twitch every so often to adjust his balance, like a human would. No, he just crouched like a gargoyle statue—or a cat contemplating the next helpless, unwitting bird it was about to snack on. "Now, have you ever heard of leman?"

Wait, what? Is that Spanish? Limonada, or… wait, lemon? What the fuck did furniture polish have to do with all this? Or… did he mean lemonade? Was she supposed to mix beverages; did he want a fucking bartender?

Bet he drinks Bloody Marys. The dark, screaming hilarity was a bad sign, and the shaking intensified. Soon she was going to fly apart, in a million pieces all over industrial mauve nylon carpet. What would he do if she tried to escape now? Catch her again, maybe.

But perhaps, just possibly, she could make it.

Stock-still, patient, the vampire waited for her answer. No doubt he was just playing with his food. Either way, the urge to bolt crested, and Layla gave in, rocketing to her feet. If she could just reach the door—

Unfortunately, he was faster.

The world flipped onto its side—no, she was thrown flat on her back across the already-muddled bed, and her arms flailed uselessly. There was a harsh rip of fabric, cold air hitting now-bare legs, and her despairing scream was trapped as the vampire's mouth closed over hers.

His tongue probed insistently, a strange, sweet taste spreading numbness against her teeth; her knees were shoved far apart as his hips settled against her inner thighs. No leverage, her attempt to scoot away doomed to failure; the bed gave a small forlorn creak as a hot, insistent iron bar probed at her most sensitive juncture. Her T-shirt rasped against tangled sheets below and his sweater above; the contrast between its thin comfort and her utterly bare lower half —save for sock feet, her heels scraping against wadded comforter and more thrash-tangled sheets—adding to the confusion.

Another instinctive attempt to wriggle free, the world painted dark red with panic, a stretching and *invasion*. He surged into her, a single thrust sinking deep, and Layla realized what was happening just as another odd, stroking pressure settled a little higher, massaging where nobody else had ever touched her before—her two high school quasi-boyfriends had been strictly limited to above-the-belt petting, and afterward she'd avoided all intimate contact, vaguely repulsed by the thought of further sweaty, greedy male bumbling.

Fire arced up Layla's spine; her back arched, another long trailing cry boiled in her throat, and the creature above her sank a fraction deeper. He braced on his elbows, muscle-corded fore-arms across her biceps, effectively pinning her flat. A strange rumbling growl spread from his chest, vibrating in her own bones. He thrust again, and again, Layla's body shuddering helplessly under the onslaught. One of his thumbs brushed her cheek, almost a caress; his fingers on the others side threaded into her hair.

Familiar pressure rose—as if she were rocking on her own fingers late at night, safe in a familiar bed instead of pinned under a heavy inescapable weight. Her body didn't care. It had been tormented by endless fear, exhaustion, the interminable awful strain of staying alert to variable male moods, suppressing the cold white glare of grief, and so much else. Slick hot impos-sible pleasure spilled through her, a luxuriating relief from all uncertainty, all the dread and second-guessing of her own thoughts.

Tossed over the tipping point, nerves sparking, muscles locking in waves as excruciating pleasure tore through every inch, her body took what was offered. Slack and unresisting, her mouth was full of a candied-metal taste; a single thread dribbled past the fire in her throat. Again and again the pulses tore through her, all coherent thought lost, only an endless *now*.

For her very first time, it wasn't bad.

No dimly remembered mortal fumblings could approach this glory. The thrall struck hard, snapping every vestige of fading control, and even the few feverish, animalistic couplings with female fledglings when his duties allowed or reward was granted were nothing by comparison.

He had been drowning in shadowy violent mortal life, then in the slowly accreting dust of sanguinant age. His head broke surface for the first time in his long existence; pure air stung his lungs, and the source of that glorious liberation shuddered under him. The soft sweetness of her mouth was a city to be plundered at leisure, the slick wet velvet of her core closing around him strangling-tight as her release struck—at least he could please her, though he knew very well fear was so close to survival she was not strictly responding to his attentions.

At the moment, it didn't matter. *First the bite, then the claiming*; that was the proverb, repeated in every language the sanguinant knew. It was true, every word he had ever heard failed to represent *how* true, and his only regret was that he could not take his own final pleasure at the moment.

There was too much else to accomplish. It was only an hour past dusk; he might be able to spirit her from this city with no living creature the wiser. Esmond the Varangian—Nemesis's original target—would be wary after the battle outside his primary feeding-haunt, and though their master would no doubt retreat to the mansion used for certain business concerns, his underlings would be spreading through the city to look for traces of the attackers. It would take some time before Father could assume Nemesis had for the first time not carried out a given duty; if Maximus were swift and lucky he might be accounted dead of either misjudgment or ossification, rendering him free to build a hidden nest for his prize elsewhere while other plans could be laid.

A wonderful possibility, but only that. She was not yet wholly safe, and until that moment he could not allow a single mistake.

His true teeth fought for release, scraping his own flesh. Another's fangs could not easily pierce that wall; still, a thin thread of his own blood was loosed, and passed to her upon a kiss he hoped might at least grant some additional moiety of pleasure, if not ease her fear.

Delicious little cries, his to catch and feast upon. A nymph struck with Venus's greatest gift shook beneath him, tiny jewels of perspiration dewing her forehead, her hair a fragrant dark cloud. In his youth they averred all roads led to the city of emperors, but that was a lie; any highway, byway, or path began and ended here, at his leman.

The arch of existence now had a capstone. She finally lay quiescent, his cheek pressed to hers, her perfect shell-like ear next to his lips. He hungered to move again, to bring her to another gasp-screaming summit, but she was still mortal. A sanguinant's attentions might well prove overwhelming; had not Iuppiter learned caution with one of his dalliances, a princess blasted by unveiled glory?

The comparison might be arrogant, as the soldier stood far more chance of being laid waste by the lovely divine creature in his arms—but it was also apt.

She lay very still, the flickering pulse in her slim throat calling to him, her breathing deep and ragged. The bond was solidified now; he had claimed the treasure.

He possessed a leman. She was *his*, an eternal addiction capable of staving off ossification and creeping-numb death. Now he was aware of precisely what he'd done, and what the act might mean to her. Still buried deep, still tempted to take his own release and any consequences that might bring, he bared his blunt mortal-seeming teeth and sought control.

Her whisper surprised him, lovely still-mortal lips barely moving. "Are you going to kill me now?"

Is that what you fear? The thought very nearly caused him to recoil, stiffening in shock. "Of course not."

Her throat moved afresh as she swallowed. Her pretty lips were chapped, and even with the first application of change agents swimming through her veins, soothing and providing enhanced repair of tissues, the bruises on her arms still glared. Some were clearly finger-marks, and he wondered what the mortal men in that ramshackle building had done to such entrancing, fragrant fragility.

Had he simply done the same? Self-loathing was not new to one of his kind, but this held a jagged razor edge. In its wake followed a flood of bleak shame.

Even that was marvelous, exquisite luxury after so long of no feeling at all—not even grey apathy, simply *absence*. She could drive the blade into his chest so many times as she wished. In each and every instance, he would be thankful for the sheer rushing glory of sensation.

A tiny gleam between her long dark lashes; was she too afraid to gaze upon her new protector? "Can I… are you done?"

I have not yet begun, little Leila. But it seems I have done poorly indeed. "I will move, very slowly. Are you hurt?"

For some reason, the question seemed to amuse her. At least, his new leman began to laugh, causing a fascinating series of tiny shifts and contractions around his shaft. He had to use several centuries' worth of habitual focus to withdraw, inch by slow resisting inch. When he was finally untangled she immediately turned onto her side, curling into a tight ball, and burst into tears.

Sorrow and the consciousness of his own failure was sweet as well, though it pierced his ribs' bony shield as nothing since his own mortal sword ever had. The sumptuousness of mere *feeling* had claws; those shards sank into him and twisted while she sobbed as if her own priceless, wonderful, mortal heart were broken.

The night was fleeing. He would have preferred a bath, a slow gentle ritual to perhaps soothe his new prize, some conversation to accustom her to his attentions. At least the day's deliveries to the suite's outer room, prompted by the 'clean' cellphone, had been accomplished—a paltry offering, nothing to what he would eventually provide, but he was uneasy at remaining any longer in this locale.

Now she was pale and unresisting, though she took a dampened washcloth and scrubbed at her face as if angry at her own tears. Her lovely blue-grey eyes were rimmed with tender inflamed pink, evidence of weeping blurring her beauty in an altogether enticing manner, and she seemed not to notice her denims were shredded.

His claws had stripped those trousers most efficiently, not to mention broken the button on his own. Her shirt was torn at the hem; she plucked at it vaguely with sweet delicate fingertips, attempting to stretch the fabric into covering dark pubic fleece or the lovely curves of her hindquarters, fit for a goddess's statue.

At least in this age, clothing was easy to obtain. When he led her out of the bedroom she stared dully at the suite's carpet, mismatched socks making quiet brushing sounds as she followed the gentle pressure at her elbow. He had arranged the open suitcase on the pink-and-yellow couch in the outer room, hoping at least something among the offerings would meet with her approval.

"There was little time, so…" Was this feeling *awkwardness*? It was just as delightsome as every other emotion returned to him, burnished by her presence. He knew how to thrust a pile of gear at a dogsbody or fledgling, how to bring a squad to readiness with a single word, how to teach weapons care, trigger discipline, tactical awareness.

But how did one deal with a beautiful, numbly staring leman? Especially as she pulled at her shirt's hem again, barely glancing at a pile of expensive cloth?

In the end he selected a dark-red dress much akin to what she had worn the previous night—had it really been such a short while ago? The world, the entire *universe* had changed in a few brief hours.

Her name belonged to a Persian princess; she deserved diaphanous woven-air robes, rings and necklaces dripping with gems to match her lucent eyes, diadems fit for one of such exalted status, anklets of chiming bells. It hurt to see her so thin, so uncertain, in modern mortal rags.

Though trembling, she still offered no resistance when he extended a claw-tip to cut the shirt free; a tiny, clearly fearful flinch tore at his heart. She raised her arms obediently when told to. At least he knew one did not step into this type of garment, and he had very little trouble with the fastening—the zipper up the back, the single button at the top between her lovely frail shoulderblades. Wide straps over her sweetly rounded shoulders, the waistline settled low, the skirt falling in glimmering folds to her delicious, rounded knees.

"It fits," his leman said, clearly surprised. Silken hair, loose and gloriously rumpled, fell to the middle of her back; she pushed blue-black tendrils from her face with a small, irritable motion, piercing his heart afresh.

"Of course." He was not yet expert in discerning her preferences, but he could easily convert tactical gears' sizing to civilian. "Still, you will have to tell me what you like."

All animation and wonder fled. Her hands dropped loosely to her sides, and she turned her head slightly, staring past him.

At the door to the hotel hallway.

Ah. "Thinking of escape?"

A single, extraordinarily vengeful glance—she could slay a man with that look alone, though he was cheered to see any break in the apathy. "If I try, you'll hurt me."

"No." Though he could not expect her to believe as much, Maximus realized; he quickly closed and fastened the suitcase. The mating-thrall was temporarily sated inside his bones yet stirred sleepily at the bare thought of a chase, protective and predatory instincts working in tandem. "It will simply lead to a pleasant interlude, *puella mea.*"

"How do you know my name?" At least she was speaking. Questions led to answers, so he could hopefully begin explanations.

"I heard your companions address you." He paused, straightened, and offered his hand as he had seen modern mortals do. In his day, one greeted friends or prestigious strangers far more intimately. "I… am Maximus. That was—*is* my name. Though you may choose another, if you like; I will answer."

Her forehead furrowed. "Maximus?" Her accent robbed the syllables of their old meaning, but it was also pleasant to hear the word again. In fact, it stirred old dark mortal memories. "Like the… You've got to be kidding."

Did he remember how to jest? It had been so long since he had been tempted to a short, barking chuckle or even the shadow of a smile. Perhaps she would teach him that, as well.

Anticipating the lesson was another pleasure. So many, a veritable banquet crowding upon him, and no risk of true-death by glut. He lowered his hand, a trifle awkwardly. "No. Do you dislike it? Simply choose another." Names were easy as mortal money, as taking a territory and commandeering its resources for shelter, clothing, amusement, prey.

A thin thread of unease trickled through him, lush as any other newly restored emotion. Yes, names could be changed like modern machine-woven raiment, yet he had forgotten his own.

Not least because his Maker had granted him another. Answering to *Nemesis* for… how long? He found, somewhat to his surprise, that he could not guess with any accuracy. Several centuries, as the mortal world underwent metamorphosis and the dust of ages accreted, shifts in prey languages or periodic bouts of battle and murder providing the only calendar-marks.

"Uh. Okay." A faint shadow of interest wrinkled sweet Leila's brow; she brushed vaguely at her tousled mane and shuddered. "What…"

Her uncertainty was only to be expected, even as he longed to banish its shadowy wing. Perhaps it was best to give her an objective. "We must quit this place. There is some distance to travel before dawn."

"You could just leave me here. I won't tell anyone." Slim fingers curled inward, small hands becoming fists. Now he had his leman's entire attention, a pleasant sensation indeed. "I'll never talk about the demimonde again. Or about you."

"We are well past that point, little Leila." *It was too late the moment I caught your scent.* Still, he decided, more details could wait until they were en route. "Will you cooperate, or shall I use the *quietus*? Choose."

"The… you mean knock me out?" She leaned back slightly, rocking on sock-clad heels. The wine-red skirt swayed softly, and he was very conscious of her bareness under the material. "Don't do that. Please. I'll…" His prize trailed off uncertainly, biting her lower lip in a most fetching manner.

If it were not so imperative to move, he might well carry her to the bedroom again. Each moment was a fresh marvel, a new clarity. Very soon he could apply another bite; exquisitely sensitive, she was ripe for the Gift.

Yet his unease intensified still further, sharpening into outright warning. He did not like the feeling of a watch set upon his movements, even if it sprang from mere paranoia. "Then we will go."

"Can I get my boots?" A flicker of hope on her sweet face, gone in a flash—he had become too calcified to notice the quicksilver shifting of mortal moods, but now saw so much more clearly. Interacting with dogsbodies or catspaws had held progressively less savor even if he forced himself to it for the sake of retaining some faint flexibility; he wondered what else he had missed.

He considered her request. Preferable to keep her but lightly shod, to forestall attempts at flight... and yet. He indicated the door to the bedroom and drifted in her wake. She did glance longingly at the curtained window, but all in all, she was remarkably obedient.

For now.

CHAPTER 9

No way to peek between the curtains in either the pink bedroom or the suite's outer room, since the vampire kept a watchful eye as if afraid she might try to take a header through some hotel glass.

He might not have been wrong, Layla silently conceded. In the end, the idea that they might not be very far up and she'd only be embarrassed—or worse, not quickly put out of what might end up being bone-broken misery—stopped her.

But still, she considered the notion. Her brain was struggling through mud, even if the devouring, terrible fear had left her alone for a few short moments. Maybe she was just too exhausted to feel afraid anymore, or maybe the strange, secret lassitude after getting railed to within an inch of her life was responsible.

Try not to think about that. There was so much else to focus on, she just couldn't figure out what to prioritize.

The hallway was carpeted in pale blue, bright with recessed lighting, far cleaner than most houses, and utterly deserted. She found out they were on the twentieth floor as soon as they arrived at the chilly, polished steel elevator; Layla tried not to gape, but this was the nicest place she'd ever been in. And how on earth had he managed to get a dress that fit her? The label said *Kisbain*; it was a brand she'd never even dare to touch in a department store, and it moved heavy-silken against her shrinking skin.

What else was in that big ol' suitcase he hefted as if it weighed nothing?

She couldn't even pinch herself to provoke a bit of clear thinking. She had to make do with flinching as tenderness in a few internal bodily sections reminded her of… of *that*.

What he'd done. What *she* had done, her own body turned traitor—or had it? The vampire acted like he'd already forgotten holding her down on the bed, and she had to look away from her tangle-haired reflection in the elevator's brushed-steel wall.

It wasn't like in movies, or in books. It wasn't even like the porn Ben was constantly watching, though she was pretty sure a lot of people thought sex should follow those weird scripted patterns, right down to waxing hair away in several places. Nothing in high school abstinence-and-disease classes had ever covered this, either.

Was the bite beforehand part of some vampire kink? Did this guy want to turn her into a bloodsucking monster? Why her instead of, say, Steve-o, who was probably far better material?

Layla winced again as the elevator slowed its soundless plunge, her stomach flipping uneasily. Looked like they were heading to a parking level.

How did the biter pay for all this? Many of the monsters were rich, money accumulating around creatures who lived a long time and were capable of hypnotizing humans into hench-folk *or* turning them into plain old regular-ass employees. Once a biter hit a certain age, they seemed to accumulate those hangers-on, plus they switched identities almost at will, and their victims —food or merely inconvenient bystanders, not to mention anyone so foolish as to ask persistently awkward questions— vanished into crime statistics for the year.

People went missing everywhere, all the time, all over the

world. Most were never found. A certain percentage had to be demimonde casualties, swept under the rug or never found. Some folk might even just walk away from their normal lives, start over somewhere else.

God knew she'd vanished out of her own life. Not that anyone had been left to care or look for her, no sir, not with both Meemaw and Suze gone. Dan, of course, had pulled his own vanishing act right next to her.

Now he's really a statistic. She suppressed another flinch, wondering if anyone would find the… the remains of her crew back at base. *Think about something useful.*

What were her chances of escape? Of even surviving? How the great blue northern *fuck* had he gotten a dress in her precise size? It was a far more expensive version of the black one she'd worn for lookout duty, and she couldn't decide if that was a good or bad sign. Was it red because he was going to make her bleed on the fabric?

Oh, Jesus-please-us, what a gruesome thought.

He carried the suitcase easily, but she thought it pretty likely he'd drop it in a heartbeat if she tried to take off. He was just so goddamn *fast*.

And she didn't even have a clue what time it was, though it had to be after dark if the biter was moving around. Assuming she'd only slept a single day, it had been less than twenty-four hours, her entire squad was dead—except maybe Pete, if the vampire wasn't lying—and she'd been…

Well, she was no longer a virgin, at least. Now she had to worry about vampire STDs. Or did she?

A funny slipsliding sensation filled her skull. *I quit,* Dan said, and then the entire world veered off course, descending into this insanity. And that horrible revelation—*I never wanted to marry her, she said she was pregnant.*

But he'd been so broken up about Suze. Showing up on Layla's doorstep, outright sobbing and clinging to her like a baby, his hands roaming. Adamant about digging into his wife's death even though the cops said it was an accident, called him crazy for asking questions. For her part Layla thought he *was* probably a bit unhinged from the shock , but…

Well, it might be time to admit a home truth or two. Suppressing a long-term crush on your best friend's husband did not make for entirely objective assessments. She'd tried to be careful, to look at the evidence around Suze's death, try to disprove anything outlandish.

There was just so *much* once they started digging. And Dan seemed to need her so badly. He'd even been outright affectionate, at first; she'd kind of suspected he wanted to rebound on her. It had taken all her willpower to act blissfully oblivious to that aspect, because of poor Suze and also because some faint but definite voice—maybe conscience, maybe just a twinge of pride—told Layla she didn't want sloppy seconds.

She preferred something *real*, and if she stuck around through the hard stuff maybe he'd see as much.

At least, that had been her hope. And yet… there was the wedding incident.

She hadn't said a word about seeing him with Cindy, she'd listened when he talked about biters and things going bump in the night, she'd looked at the proof he'd gathered, she'd tried to do what was *right*.

Now here she was, kidnapped by a biter. And Dan was dead.

Was he? Could she trust anything a vampire said? *You need not concern yourself with them.*

She could go with what she saw, couldn't she? Ben, vanishing between syllables. Ack, plucked right out of his chair. And the vampire now standing next to her, silent and patient a cat at a mousehole. She stole glances at his beaky profile, her stomach fluttering harder as the elevator stopped.

Not a soul in sight, from the hotel suite to the hallway. When would she see ordinary people again? What time was it now? And Christ, what did he say his name was?

Max. No, Maximus. That can't be real. It suddenly struck her as funny, and she clapped a hand over her mouth. *None of that, no sir. Don't you dare, Layla.*

If she got the giggles now, who knew what the hell else would happen?

The elevator dinged, the door drew aside—yep, a parking level. Outside a larger glass enclosure, concrete walls surrounded patiently waiting cars. Still no sign of another human being.

Had he killed everyone in the damn hotel? She wouldn't put it past this monster, and thinking about it made her gorge rise hot and acid, dispelling post-sex glow.

Or trying to. Her neck throbbed; seen in the bathroom mirror, the fangmarks were classic, vivid, and horrifying. She'd never dreamed of her own skin bearing the pattern—four upper, two lower, the punctures' outer margins white, the centers bright-scabbed red, slight bruise-discoloration spreading to show the arcs of the bite.

Post those on a forum, you'd get a lot of hits. Where's a camera when you need one? Terrible, breathless, almost screamy hilarity swirled next to the thin scorch of bile in her throat.

"Come." The vampire reached over her to keep the elevator door open despite Layla's instinctive, all-too-visible flinch, then herded her out of the box. He also opened the glass door for her, like a goshdarn gentleman, then brushed past and set off as if expecting her to follow.

She did so as slowly as she dared, outright dilly-dallying and still holding back rancid, acidic giggles, breathing hard through loosely cupped fingers. The movement of air against her skin was comforting, a reminder she was still alive. This under-ground level was much warmer than interior air conditioning, though nowhere near soggy-breathless as it would be outside. She examined the cars—most with out-of-state plates, not a local hooptie in sight—and scanned reflexively for any exits.

No chance to find a single outlet for escape, because a sleek black Volvo roused nearby. The sound made her jump before she realized that somehow, the damn vampire had keyless start. Which was even funnier, in the same bleak way as everything else right now, and she was going to commence howling with heebie-jeebie chuckles any moment now.

Researching vampires and other weird shit gave one unhealthy coping mechanisms and a terribly dark sense of humor, but she'd never gotten the howlers this bad. Ever.

Well, this is an exceptional situation, Lay.

The Volvo's trunk clicked open; Max the Vampire settled the big Samsonite with almost prissy care. Then he indicated the passenger side, clearly expecting her to load up. Maybe he wasn't going to open her door, which might have been smart since it could give her a chance to scramble away once there was a slab of metal and glass between them? He probably considered boxing her in to be the better tactic, and maybe this model had kiddie locks.

It certainly looked fancy enough.

Don't let an attacker take you to a second location, all the self-defense classes said. Was this more like taking her to a third, though? He'd gotten her away from base toot-sweet, as Meemaw Cathy put it.

"Are you ill?" Christ, he actually sounded faintly worried. Vampire Max hunched slightly, examining her—he was so much taller it was almost ridiculous, a bear politely inquiring as to a smaller creature's health. Of course, most everyone was taller than her, she'd inherited her mother's small bones and...

Wild, neurotic banshee laughter crammed itself sideways in her throat. Layla kept her hand clapped tight, and *now* her brain had gotten the memo to start up, racing furiously through an utter lack of alternatives.

Oh, God, please. She managed a single tiny headshake. *Please let him just leave me here. He doesn't want me to throw up in his car, right? Please let him be a neat freak.*

For a moment she was dead certain it was the wrong move,

because the vampire went still again, that terrible inhuman motionlessness.

Then his head jerked up, swiveled; a pair of red pinpricks bloomed in his pupils. Layla's heart leapt into her throat as well, crowding out the screaming-meemies but doing a grand job of keeping up the choking, and once more her knees threatened to give.

At least he wasn't looking at her, which was great because the mask of patient normalcy had fallen completely away. His upper lip twitched, lifting, and there was a faint crackling noise in the parking garage's stillness.

She hadn't seen the fangs when he bit her, thankfully. Now they were out, gleaming bright ivory under the garage's buzzing fluorescent fixtures. Yes, it was just as research said and her own neck agreed—two pairs on the top arch, bigger to the outside and slightly smaller inward, one pair on the lower to provide leverage. A distinctive pattern, though there was a lot of squabbling on dark web forums and demimonde-research message boards about whether they grew in constantly like shark teeth.

Nothing was so outlandish people wouldn't argue about it on the internet, even serious-as-hell vampire hunters.

Layla's hip hit the Volvo's passenger-side taillight, and she was faintly aware the impact hurt. *Another bruise*, she thought, pointlessly, as the vampire stared down the row of cars.

A soft brushing sound slid past, then a figure appeared at the end of the aisle, just under the sign proclaiming *MORE PARKING - TURN RIGHT*. The Volvo, taking no notice, hummed happily to itself.

Layla shuddered. The new arrival was man-shaped, a blue-eyed crewcut redhead wearing what she realized was an athletic-fit black tactical shirt as well as heavy workman's trousers just like Vampire Max's. Its hands hung loosely; its boots were very much like the first vampire's as well, but… spit-shine?

That was weird, but even worse were the fangs. Not to

mention two crimson pinpricks glowed in its pupils as well, clearly visible even at this distance.

"Get in the car." Vampire Max's teeth were back to normal, probably so he could enunciate. He stared at the figure like a gunslinger seeing the villain in a dusty old Western, and the thought that a tumbleweed might bumble across concrete between rows of Audis, Acuras, BMWs, and the odd Toyota or Honda was even *more* darkly hilarious.

I'm going to go completely insane. It was a wonderful thought, very liberating.

"It's unlocked." The vampire's hand blurred out, touched her shoulder, and gave the gentlest of encouraging pushes. "Go, now, and *get in the car.*"

Sure, boss. Whatever you say. Layla staggered to obey just as the redheaded newcomer winked out of sight…

…and reappeared, crashing into Vampire Max with a sound like massive billiard balls colliding on the world's biggest felt-top.

They tumbled down the aisle, blurring-quick, and after the collision a rumble filled the air, echoes overlapping and bouncing off concrete. The vibration was faintly familiar—both vampires were growling, a hideous deep grinding noise, and Layla was reminded of Saturday morning cartoons. Meemaw Cathy had loved the Tasmanian Devil, laughing helplessly at the dumb, whirling animated menace every time.

This, however, was bizarro-bonkers real life, and deadly serious as well. The sound alone convinced Layla to get going even before Vampire Max flung the newcomer across the aisle and through a parked SUV, which rocked violently as it crumpled like tissue paper. The momentum tossed Redhead Vampire into concrete wall beyond, causing a puff of dust to glitter under the fluorescents; Layla swore at her legs, trying to force them into working.

Car's right there. Get moving. MOVE!

More crashing and crunching echoed as she staggered along

the Volvo's flank, and it wasn't until she had blindly pawed the forward-most door open, staring over the roof at the dark tumbling smears of fighting vampires pinballing through parked cars and making an almighty racket, that she realized she was on the passenger side.

Oh, goddammit. Never rained but it poured, as Dan was fond of remarking when shit went sideways.

All-leather interior full of new car smell, the stew of chemicals making her even dizzier; Layla scrambled for the driver's seat, the dress catching under her knees, one of which she nearly impaled on the dial masquerading as a gear shift. Thankfully, the Volvo wasn't a brand-spanking new touchscreen model, it only took a few moments of staring at the console before she figured out what the hell.

It didn't help that her heart was hammering fit to snap her ribs, breath ratcheting in dust-dry throat, every bruise on her was tuned up singing doo-wop, and despite being in a sealed metal box she could still hear the growling *and* the crash-thudding as the two biters went at it.

Lots of cars, so if there's a gas leak this problem might-could solve itself. Come on, Layla. Get this show on the road.

There was a bad second getting into reverse, the car revving but refusing to move when she hit the accelerator pedal, but that was taken care of by getting the parking brake sorted out. The car swung drunkenly from of its spot, nearly corner-clipping the SUV on its passenger side, and the vampire-battle roaring went up a notch. She caught a confused blur of motion in the rearview, decided it was now or never, got the Volvo into drive with more wild-ass jabbing luck than anything else, and outright stamped the pedal to the floor.

Adrenaline filled her mouth with thin, runny copper. Layla wrenched at the steering wheel, tires chirping through the turn, and she had no idea which way she was going.

The mystery was solved when red **WRONG WAY** signs bloomed on either side like mushrooms after a hard rain, and

Christ she hoped nobody was coming head-on. "I'm sorry!" she yelped, as the front fender plowed over a line of floppy plastic posts meant to corral traffic in the right direction; she shot onto another parking level, one up from where the Vampire Heavyweight Match of the Century was for all she knew still going on, and saw an exit.

TO 5TH STREET, the sign above it said. There were two problems—she was in the wrong lane, incoming instead of leaving, and to top everything off there was a striped bar across each opening, so the law-abiding citizens were reminded to stop, take a ticket, or pay their parking fees upon leaving.

Oh, hell. Layla realized she was still chanting horrified, meaningless apologies as the car veered through the plastic poles into the 'leaving' lane, and she had a bare screaming second to hope there were no pedestrians strolling alongside the hotel.

Crunch. The bar went flying, the Volvo's windshield blooming with spiderweb cracks, and Layla yanked at the wheel again, tires smoking as the car responded with all its might. Slewing into a wild left turn, she was—amen and hallelujah—finally in what could be considered the correct lane, but there was no time for congratulations or even to take a breath, because now she was steering a stolen car through a downtown, and not only would any nearby cops be interested in wild joyriders but if she hit a poor civilian she'd never forgive herself.

Gripping the cushioned wheel, still screeching *"I'm sorry I'm sorry, I'm so sorry,"* she saw the turn onto Briscoe Boulevard looming. Sharp red-hot relief burst like a firework inside her ribcage.

Briscoe was on a planned escape route for the Griskov job. And really, there was only one place she could go.

A half-hour later she knew what time it was thanks to the dashboard clock, but her face hurt like hell. So did the rest of her;

adding an unplanned car crash to all the other bullshit she'd been through lately was not even really worth complaining about.

Though hitting the steering wheel nearly hard enough to break her nose qualified for a bit of grumbling, she told herself.

Just a little. As a treat.

At least nobody else had been hit. That was the important thing, even if she had just technically committed not only vehicle theft but also left the scene of an accident.

If they put her in jail, would she be safe from vampires? It was a Consideration, as Suzy might say, wiggling her eyebrows.

The abandoned machinist's shop still reeked of mildew and neglect; Layla wriggled through the loosely boarded south entrance and shivered, freeing her skirt from a grasping nail. Cloth ripped, and she was a little sorry—it was a pretty dress, even if a vampire had bought it.

The inside was dark as sin, but she knew the layout from drills and a few moments' worth of feeling around turned up an emergency flashlight tucked deep within a pile of moldering cardboard. Ackerman's suggestion, and a good one.

Poor Ack. She couldn't quite believe he was gone. Of course she might stumble over proof positive in here any moment.

Money. Weapons. A pair of fucking jeans, I don't care if they're dirty.

The flashlight's wavering beam was so comforting she had to suppress a sob, blinking furiously—felt like she had a pair of black eyes, so she would have to find sunglasses, too.

Layla gripped the flashlight hard, wiped at her wet cheek with her free hand, and began picking her way carefully between mounds of wreckage.

Dan had been a hundred percent right. It was time to fucking well quit.

CHAPTER 10

IT WAS NEVER PLEASANT TO TEAR APART ONE HE HAD TRAINED AS A fledgling. A wrenching, the death-cry, flesh falling in rotting gobbets, finally a burst of dry, nearly crystalline dust racing through the tissues as true-death took hold—even the savage delight of victory was faint comfort.

I told you to guard your left side more. Maximus shook away grit, brushed his hands together sharply, and cast a glance over the wreckage. Fairly contained, even with petrol stink simmering thickly in every corner. A single spark could have injured both himself and poor William—both had an elder's strength, of course, and a daywalker could stand the sun.

Perhaps one night he might know what that accomplishment felt like. For now, he had bested an adversary, and that was enough.

An elder strong or lucky enough to survive burning wreckage would at best be deeply scarred, needing much feeding to painfully recover. More likely was true-death, sanguinant tissues being exquisitely flammable at every stage of existence. Only an Archon could deny the kiss of open flame, and there was some question as to whether those truly existed—

or were indeed sanguinant, instead of some other demimonde species.

He did not mind the prospect of scarring so much, Maximus decided. The risk of injury to his leman was another matter, however.

Far more concerning was one of Father's more competent lieutenants—who had been away from the home nest on another task when Nemesis was given orders—appearing in this territory and acting so very strangely.

The parking spot both sanguinant had carefully steered the fight away from was empty. Little Leila had, with admirable presence of mind, fled the battlefield; the sedan, newly acquired and delivered a few hours ago during daylight, was one of the heavier, more safely engineered chariots available.

More importantly, the vehicle bore a small telltale, which the 'clean' cellphone in his pocket—thankfully undamaged, with its hard shockproof rubber case and glass screen protector, more marvelous little inventions—could easily track. Her blood was in his veins, certainly, and he could find her by scent alone if necessary.

This was far more efficient, even if he had to slip from mist-form occasionally to check the glowing screen.

A warm, smog-drenched summer night wheeled underneath him, a galaxy of streetlights and residence-lamps. Mortals ever and quite wisely sought to banish the darkness.

It contained beings such as himself, after all.

Away from his prize, ossification would begin to accumulate afresh within both perceptions and physiology. The process was swifter after bonding, galloping instead of creeping—another reason leman were guarded so stringently.

Why here, William? So hard upon a ranking officer's heels, as well. Any possible explanation opened up dark vistas indeed, making the soldier glad for an extraordinary chance occurrence.

Even Antinous the patriarch, so old and canny, could not account for a leman appearing. She was a divine gift dropped into an undeserving sanguinant's lap—and now wandering unprotected once more.

A plume of steam rose skyward, growing larger as he followed the phone's helpful guidance. Sanguinant did not suffer nausea even after glut, save by fading psychological reflex during the fledgling stage; yet a certain discomfort began in his midriff as he ascertained that yes, the evidence of burning or disaster seemed to be marking the very location where his leman's chariot had come to rest.

No. The useless reflex to pray—whence had that arisen? He had fallen out of the habit over a long lifetime, and suspected one miracle was all he would ever be allowed. Too much, in fact.

For if those who had granted him a glimpse of Elysium in the shape of a star-eyed nymph noticed the error, they would no doubt snatch her away.

The black car, shining and whole less than an hour ago, now rested its mangled front end against a concrete retaining wall. A looping trail of scorched rubber showed where the charioteer had lost control and skidded; said driver's door hung open, forlorn, and above the tableau several blinking caution-lights warned of a sharp curve ahead, road turning to run parallel to railroad tracks.

His boots touched the top of the wall; he crouched, gazing down at what his leman had wrought.

There. A hint of roses and musk, drifting upon still, humid air. The road was deserted in either direction, lights shining blankly over its concrete flow. It was amazing, how there could be such solitude even in close-packed mortal warrens.

A half-familiar location. He had seen this road wheeling underneath not too long ago as he streaked through the night, carrying a precious burden.

Upon the previous eve, in fact.

Ah. I see. His face felt strange. The smile was a mixture of rueful admiration of and fresh anxiety over sweet Leila, who had taken the wheel, fled, and aimed for a place she would find familiar.

Many survivors of rout or catastrophe did the same.

Her scent flared and faded, a coppery edge sharpening its deliciousness. His true teeth, so recently unsheathed for battle, throbbed afresh; his hands itched, longing for her flawless satin skin. She was moving, perhaps impelled by sheer stubborn terror, risking ever more damage with eacch act of fruitless struggle.

Cursing was a waste of energy, yet he did so inwardly as he streaked along her wavering trail.

The same tired, abandoned building slumped near iron rails, a fresh hole in its roof grinning at the sky. Maximus slipped through that ingress, the need to find her threatening to force his old, strong heart into quickening; he throttled the urge, and did not have to strain to catch voices echoing in a dark refuse-choked well.

"You brought it here!" A male mortal, working himself to a pitch of violence.

And the only voice Maximus wished to hear, a soft sweet soprano, crying aloud in terror. "Pete, don't, I'm still me—"

There. He *moved*, blurring through space in mistform, swift as an arrow.

A sharp, terrible bark of gunfire.

CHAPTER 11

SHE DIDN'T STUMBLE ACROSS ANY BODIES, SO *THAT* WAS LUCKY. OR so Layla told herself.

The jury-rigged power was out, the entire base dark as sin. Her flashlight's anemic beam traced the overturned table, the scattered camp chairs… and found no sign of paper or the stacked weapons save a single gleaming clip, discarded on the floor at the very edge of the ready room.

Layla's breathing refused to settle, harsh and hard like the heavy panting of a horror movie victim just before the slasher showed up for his final flurry. There wasn't much creepier than an abandoned building at night, especially when she wasn't sure if she'd turn a corner and find a corpse.

Still, someone had clearly picked up the files, not to mention guns, ammo, knives, and other gear. Had it been the vampire? Or Pete, or someone else?

Her eyes were swelling badly from stopping an airbag with her face, or maybe she was developing fear-based claustrophobia. Thin, tenuous flashlight glow seemed to be getting weaker all the time.

Are the batteries going dead? Christ, that's just typical.

She felt her way along mostly by memory, heading for the

supply room. Her personal sleeping cubby was the only one behind a locking door—Steve-o had insisted on that during move-in, glancing significantly at Ben, who had been telling Dan a steady stream of dirty jokes while they racked gear.

Oh, God. She would *not* cry. There wasn't any time for that bullshit, she had to think about what she'd do if whoever had cleaned up also grabbed the cashbox and the keys to their only remaining transport—a wretched, ancient Jeep Wrangler barely capable of freeway speed, but good enough for getting out of this city and a full gas-tank's worth of miles in any direction.

She wasn't picky. She never had been, really, and current events just continued the trend.

The flashlight swung, tracking a small skittering sound, and if it was rats she was going to scream because Christ-Lord-Jesus she *hated* having big ol' naked-tail rodents running around looking for food a man couldn't bother to put away.

"*Fuck!*" A yell, a popping click, and Layla screamed, throwing herself behind a mound of used laundry.

Knees and one elbow hit hard, flaring with fresh bright-red pain; she almost lost the flashlight but rolled just as Ack had taught her, the back half of her cry fading into an inglorious wheeze. Ended up against a pile of old, splintering wooden crates, which quivered on the verge of toppling, and if she died in a junk landslide it would be funny, it would be absolutely *hysterical—*

Silence. She lay, trembling, clutching the light to her chest. The red skirt, pulled so high her bare unmentionables were probably showing, was wadded under her hip.

"Jesus Christ," Pete whispered. "Layla? Is that you?"

"I got everything packed." Shadows from the glare of a much bigger, fully charged emergency light played over Pete's sweat-gleaming, dirty face as he led her along familiar corridors; he was bloodshot and haggard in dirty jeans and a torn camo T-shirt. By the looks of it, he'd been jumping out of his skin since last night.

Layla could absolutely relate. "But... You're *sure*? All of them?" Stunned, stupid disbelief was all she could scrape up. Somehow, hearing him say it aloud made everything horrifyingly real.

"Yeah. Dry as doornails, damn near mummified. I put 'em near the east entrance with their IDs, so at least next of kin can..." Pete shook his head, the boxy yellow plastic light jittering in big capable hands. Towers of junk around them seemed to shift, re-settling only when he halted, peering at her. "I'm sorry. I know you and Dan were tight."

"I can't believe he was about to quit." Why couldn't she say something useful? Layla found herself smoothing the dress's soft, heavy skirt over her aching hip with her free hand, rubbing over and over as if soothing a small animal. "I'm glad you're okay, though."

"Yeah, well." Pete glanced over his shoulder, nearly running into another stack of wooden crates, their sides plastered with ancient, faded fruit labels. "You're all banged up. What happened?"

You would not believe me if I tried to tell. Or maybe he would. Layla opened her mouth, closed it again. Where the fuck could she even begin? "I... it's a long story. I'm just glad someone else made it."

"Me too. I'm glad it's you." Pete's mouth pulled down on both sides, a quasi-grimace making him look at least ten years older. "Fucking Ben's probably the reason it found us."

"I can't even guess." Still, the idea opened up a horrible can of doubting worms. Why on earth had the vampire grabbed her? Just because she was the only girl? Maybe he'd been feeling lonely, wanting a little of what Ben would call *R&R*. "I want to get changed. Are my clothes still here?"

Where else would they be, Layla? You think Pete was going to take your panties? A stupid question, but at least it got the conversation off her own whereabouts during the last twenty hours or so.

"Yeah, 'course, but hurry up. I want to get us on the road." He stepped into what had been the supply room, playing the light over an unholy mess. He'd packed in a hurry, looked like.

"You want me to go with you?" Layla sounded surprised even to herself. Her flashlight blinked; the batteries were indeed dying, so she clicked it off to conserve what little juice was left.

"Shit, girl, there ain't nobody else left." Pete gave a grim chuckle; her own threadbare, hitching laugh rose alongside. "Just wish I could figure out how the fucking thing *found* us."

"Smell? I mean, nobody does any laundry." All in all, Layla found she was feeling a bit better. "Just give me five seconds to get into some jeans."

'Here we are." Pete halted, since the flashlight had found her cubby door. He swung around, and the beam glared directly into her eyes. "Shit, sorry. You're gonna have a pair of real shiners soon, I put the first aid in the…"

Ouch. Layla nearly hit herself in the forehead with her own dead flashlight, her hand jumping up to block the sudden brightness. "Hey, watch—"

"Sonofa*bitch*." Pete blundered back, shadows dancing, a sword of light bouncing crazily as the yellow plastic case hit the floor. "What the *fuck*, man?"

"What?" Layla yelped, backing up as well, almost going ass-over-teakettle into yet another pile of mildewed cloth—tarps, maybe left from previous inhabitants, slowly congealing into a lump. "*What?*"

"You're *bit!*" he yelled, and his hands were suddenly full of a pistol. A very big one, in fact, Ack's Desert Eagle, loaded with the special biter-shredding ammo. Its mouth looked huge and very black, shaking but definitely pointed in her direction. "You're fucking *bit*, you bitch!"

Oh no. Her heart was in her throat again, choking her. "Pete—"

"God*damm*it! You're bit!" The pistol's mouth wavered, as if he couldn't quite believe what he was aiming at. If it went off now, he might miss.

But at that minimal distance, he also might *not* miss.

"I'm sorry!" Her hands were now up, one freighted with a partly dead tube of metal and batteries. "The vampire, he grabbed me, I'm sorry! Pete, come on, I'm still me, I'm—"

"You brought it here!"

That wasn't a bad guess, really. But the very idea hurt, slicing cleanly through any relief at finding someone she knew still alive. The mad thought that she could throw the dead flashlight at him rose, whirled away; Layla's boot sank into the piled tarps and she almost went sprawling once more. "I'm still me!" she shouted, knowing she should be quiet, be calm, talk him down, but for *God's* sake he was going to shoot her. "Pete, *don't, I'm still me!*"

BOOM.

CHAPTER 12

He would grant their mortal toys a scant measure of efficacy, especially when wielded by the untrained or incapable. The strike hit his right shoulder, a hammerblow refusing to pierce the modified scapula, and flowered into sharp bits of metal perhaps capable of bleeding an unwary fledgling. It took a moment of concentration to seal his own flesh, denying exit to any drop of vital fluid, and he knew the wet red killglow was in his eyes as he gazed down at his leman.

His left hand curled about sweet Leila's upper arm, careful not to squeeze; he steadied her gently. Bruises puffed over her pale eyes, her pretty nose swollen, a cut at the corner of her soft mouth; she was much the worse for wear. What part of the damage had been inflicted during wild flight or accident, he wondered, and what was the product of this coward's fury?

Roses, copper, exhaustion, the light delicious musk, and that hint of fresh coffee. Mortal food could be a pleasure, though much lost its savor as age mounted. Still, she smelled downright edible, though terribly weary and no doubt in some pain.

"Leila." Softly, tasting her name, attempting to ease her fear. "You are… alive. Good."

She stared up at him, as if she could not quite credit her own senses. A tear collected on thick charcoal lower lashes, wrung free by shock or injury, and traced down her bruised cheek. Her lips, split and terribly chapped, trembled. A sorry state for a nymph; he must take far more care with her fragility.

Gods did not like their gifts misused.

A squeaky whisper from behind him. "Oh, *fuck.*"

Maximus blurred into motion, the whispering speed shading into mistform. His hand closed about the mortal male's, and almost before he finished fully resolving into denser corporeality he *squeezed*, hearing the crackle of breaking bone. Smoke rose from the gun's barrel, pointed safely away into the mountains of detritus.

The male howled. Stocky and dark, curl-haired, he was the one who had held Leila against a brick wall, his hands roaming her slenderness; not only that, but he had fled with no attempt to protect her—although, Maximus admitted, the *ignavus* would have died with the others, had he tried.

Now this absolute poltroon had committed an even graver sin. Tearing prey in half was too quick, crushing every remaining bone in a frail mortal body would be satisfying but might disturb sweet Leila, evisceration was messy and might also unnerve her. What was left?

"*No!*" A hoarse shout, a metallic clang, a light pattering of footsteps. She did not flee—no, now his nymph crossed the space between them and flung herself at his back, her scraped and swollen hands grasping his left forearm. "No, please, no, don't hurt him, please don't—"

The male screamed, an agonizing wail. Maximus's true teeth sprang free; the *quietus* descended, squeezing no less sharply than his fingers. The cry died on a gurgle, and the mortal stilled.

Now decisions could be made.

Leila continued to tug at her sanguinant's arm, achieving nothing—she could not hope to move him with physical force. Still, the soldier hesitated and turned his head slightly, chin tucked almost to his shoulder. To catch her in corner-vision was also piercingly sweet, a glimpse of lingering beauty.

She froze, slim fingers tangled in his torn sweater-sleeve. "Please," she whispered. "It's not his fault, it's best practice, okay? Please don't hurt him."

There was a suspicious weight in Maximus's throat; his back twitched, flesh expelling the last few bits of shattered bullet. Ejected with some small force, they pattered into darkness; he had to force his true teeth away. He could easily drain this prey, take her to rest, and consider at leisure what had transpired in the last few hours. The night was old, she required rest, he had much to think upon.

Once more his plans were disarranged. But that was the nature of battle. *Fog of war*, the mortal theorists called it, and they were far more correct than they knew.

Another flurry of tugging. "Please." Frantic pleading, wholly unaware of her own power, blind to the inevitable result of misplaced mercy. "Please, Max. It's Max, right? Maximus. I'll do anything you want, I promise I'll cooperate, just please, *please* don't hurt him."

How very strange. Yet she was a woman, and a modern mortal at that. He had already let this male vanish once, despite her companions' attack upon Father's dogsbodies and more importantly, the rule that it was always best to rid a leman of any lingering emotional ties. Initial severity aided in adjustment to their new status.

No sanguinant survived long without understanding cruel necessity, whether momentary—or permanent.

He eyed the male, who quivered under the *quietus*. She offered far more resistance to that invisible pressure, but then again, she was leman.

His leman.

The soldier leaned down slightly, took a good whiff of the mortal male. Naturally the scent was already fixed in memory; a predator did not forget such things. But he wished to drive the point home, not least for the nymph who hung upon his arm, trembling with pain and fatigue.

"You may go," he said, though it irked. "I suggest you return to whatever home you have and forget the demimonde. If I catch sight or scent of you again, nothing will save you." What else could he add? "Remember always that you live only because *she* wishes it."

One final squeeze, small bones grinding, flesh turning to paste, the metal of the gun making a low, unhappy sound as it bent. Great clear drops stood out on the mortal's brow; his pupils were huge, and *quietus* denied him the questionable relief of howling in agony.

I can always hunt him down later. A comforting thought, but should he do so without his leman's knowledge?

Maximus decided that was a decision for another night. He dropped the hapless coward, took up his wandering prize, and left the *quietus* to drain away its own accord.

Upon the outskirts of the city, a cracked, fraying paved driveway barred only by a cattle gate rose up a slight dusty incline to a compact two-story farmhouse, the slight prominence surrounded by nodding metal pumps drawing crude petroleum upward. He circled the structure thrice before deciding it was clear, and there was a certain grim satisfaction in circumventing the security system—held in passive mode since the mortal troops who had accompanied him to this outpost would be well upon their way, returning to Father's abode for new missions.

Or they had been cleared from the board by ruddy-haired William.

The latter was far more likely, as the mortal soldiers' loyalties might be rendered suspect or superfluous to William's require-ments. Besides, active measures were expensive, and despite his vast wealth the patriarch Antinous was something of a skinflint.

None would expect a traitorous soldier to take refuge here; if luck was kind, news of the ruddy youth's demise would tarry upon its way to the patriarch's ears.

Despite its seeming remoteness and dedication to the machinery of extraction, this place was surprisingly adjacent to more densely settled slices of the city. Its only drawback was a lack of access to highways leading outward, but since those could be under watch by now—and other means of egress surveilled as well, the soldier suspected—it was a fine place for a wary wolf to hide, gather his thoughts, and tend his prize.

Carrying a wounded, semiconscious leman was a thorny pleasure. He pressed his lips to her temple, attempting to express some measure of comfort; she fit in his arms as if specifically sculpted for the perch.

The true value of this lair was not the outer shell, though during daylight the dogsbodies and mortal troops he had selected for the original task—removing Esgard the Varangian so Father could take this territory—had been comfortable enough. No, the stairs leading to a concrete-sheathed basement were far more useful, and the saferoom at their foot reasonably well equipped.

Securing the single entrance to that haven was a distinct relief, as was the glow from incandescent fixtures. The furniture was old and heavy—bedstead, large fully stocked wardrobe made of fragrant wood, a plain wooden chair the soldier had hardly glanced at during his first visit, judging it fit only to hang a holster on. Of more immediate concern was the bathing-room. The plumbing was antique and robust, heavy porcelain slightly discolored with age, but the tub was cast-iron and quite capacious.

Invisible seals shimmered into being, and he surprised himself with a sigh. Safe enough until next sunset, and now he had time to consider what he might be required to do in order to not merely take his treasure from this city but also permanently safeguard her.

He finally realized his clothing consisted mostly of fluttering rags. Her dress was better, though still torn and stained; they would have to make do with what remained in the wardrobe.

First, though, his sweet star-eyed Leila required proper care. And feeding.

CHAPTER 13

SHE KNEW BITERS WERE STRONG AS WELL AS FAST, BUT BEING princess-carried by one moving at freeway speed was something else entirely. Layla huddled against the shreds of a vampire's sweater, her eyes squeezed firmly shut, and tried like hell not to think about what she'd just done.

You saved Pete. That's worth something.

Was it? The cracking, bone-snapping sounds as the biter squeezed, faint traces of steam rising from the back of his right shoulder as if—had he been shot? Pete going cheesy-pale, metal squeak-screaming as Ack's pistol deformed under the pressure, a spatter of blood hitting the filthy floor…

He's still alive. I saved him.

Was it selfish to wonder who the fuck was going to save her? *You oughta look out for yourself once in a while, pumpkin,* Meemaw Cathy always said, but Layla didn't want to be like her mother.

Anything but that. Samantha Cartland's number one was always her own sweet self, and she had unloaded toddler-Layla at high speed during what was supposed to be just a short family visit. Meemaw hadn't ever complained—her grand-daughter wasn't a burden, naturally—but Layla was always conscious of her born status as baggage.

She'd spent her entire young life trying to be useful, to make up for it.

Vampire hunting seemed like a good way to change all that, though she and Dan couldn't hope to catch the one who got Suzy up at Paradise Point. Even well-funded hunters with access to painstakingly gathered research operated at significant disadvantage, and law enforcement liked sweeping weird things under the rug. Their group's small successes had been incredibly hard-won, though garnering them the attention of O'Shaughnassey's crew. Scheduling the meetup between groups had been a nightmare of cautious security measures, but worth it in order to get some expert opinion on Suze's case.

Probably a baby biter, Shawn had said, shuffling through the familiar, dog-eared crime scene photos. *Since the kill's too messy, but normally solo prey isn't savaged like this... Jaysus, the claws went right through the cloth top, look at that.*

And the funny look on Dan's face during that entire discussion. What had he been thinking? Had he already wanted to quit, but couldn't because... why?

Four years is a long time. But still, we were just getting started. They'd even had two whole bounties, which was more than a lot of so-called professional groups bragging on the forums ever managed.

Not that it mattered. Even well-armed, professional crews could be erased by a single old, powerful biter in a matter of moments. Layla herself was only helpful as research, logistics, surveillance.

Or bait. And now she was beginning to have dark suspicions about the two young monsters their crew had bagged, both going straight for her while making those horrible sounds.

The wind-roar cut off, the sense of motion slowed. Weird— had she fallen asleep, carted around by Vampire Max? That was funny too, in a dreamy, disconnected way. Of course, she'd promised to cooperate, let him do what he wanted.

She could just check out, really. Unhook herself from her

body, let the world roll right over her. *Que sera, sera*, like Meemaw's favourite song. Whatever would happen could continue without her; the entire goddamn world could simply arrange itself as it pleased.

"Leila." He was saying her name, still with that funny accent. "Open your eyes, little leman."

What is with this guy and the citrus? It didn't matter, nothing did. She didn't have to do a goddamn thing; she'd promised to cooperate and by golly she was a limp noodle, offering no resistance at all. If he didn't like her style, he could just…

What would he do?

It didn't smell like a hotel, though they were definitely inside. Dusty, with the indefinable sense of a previous hurried cleaning, something she was more than familiar with from taking care of every dilapidated hideout Dan's crew had ever landed in. Even Shawn's group seemed to take it for granted that she'd pick up after them as well, heedlessly strewing clothes and packaging everywhere.

Shawn and Feargus bullied her boys into racking their own damn weapons, though. She had to admit that had cut her workload by a significant amount.

It was blessedly cool, and was that running water? Which reminded her, she hadn't needed the bathroom since getting back to base last night, which was weird but could be dehydration. And she was hungry, but that was the norm more often than not these days, with vampire hunting budgets tight as hell. Tight as the bodice of Suze's wedding dress, needing to be sewn on.

I should have told her the truth. But Suzy sometimes seemed to suspect Layla's lingering high school crush, and it was better to just be quiet.

Safer. If she just watched Dan from a distance, letting the feeling be a soft secret sting in her chest, there was no risk of fucking everything up.

Except somehow, despite all her strenuous efforts, she had.

The vampire held her easily, shifting Layla around like a giant doll. Her boots were tugged off one at a time, socks loosened and peeled free. The relief of getting footwear off after a long day was so intense, she didn't even mind what her toes must look like. A slight soft sound, like scissors through heavy cloth. Sweat—and probably blood, or other substances—had glued the pretty red Kisbain dress to her skin; she tried not to flinch as strips were peeled away.

Oh, God. What is he doing now?

The vampire hissed a long soft indrawn breath, as if pained. It was ridiculous—what could hurt a superpowered monster? But there was the whole fight in the parking garage; getting thrown through a few cars might put a dent in anyone's day. Then he'd hunted her down and stopped Pete from shooting her.

Not Pete's fault, really. Best practice meant just that; if a fellow hunter got bit, they were unreliable. You just couldn't take the chance they'd turn into a vampire's faithful employee. Contamination by *anything* demimonde was an automatic ticket out; that was why O'Shaughnassey's crew had those fancy chainmail gorgets.

Except the collars hadn't done any good. The grainy footage of their last job was absolutely pitiless in that respect.

Layla forced her eyes open, or at least so far as she could. The swelling on her face was now having a heyday, and every other bump, bruise, and scrape took the slight movement as permission to make themselves known.

Loudly. In fact, the sudden symphonic crash of physical misery was so intense she inhaled sharply too, as if copying him.

The vampire paused, holding her braced on one raised knee. His curls still looked designer-tousled despite being wildly windblown, and the only evidence of the night's events was his sweater and Carhartts both torn all to flinders. Same dark eyes, only this time with no glaring red dots in the pupils, and there was no sign of the fangs. He had one booted foot on the edge of a giant cast-iron bathtub, and had finished peeling the dress off her.

Oh, for Chrissake. Now she was completely defenseless; not that it mattered. Just business as usual.

"Warm water," he said. "It may sting. Test it."

This was no weirder than anything else that had happened to her lately, and her face was so messed-up the fiery blush rising up her neck might not be evident. The bathroom fixings were the half-antique sturdy type any Pottery Barn catalog would be interested in copying, from the pedestal sink to the ancient commode with its water tank attached to the wall, a chain dangling gently for flushing.

Was he going to drown her in the tub? The vampire shifted, and her toes tapped the rising water. Blessedly hot, very nearly perfect.

It was indeed going to sting. Layla nodded and braced herself, stretching her leg so she could slither out of his grip. If she got in the tub herself, maybe he wouldn't hold her head under.

That makes no sense.

Her attempt didn't work. He kept a good grip and lowered her gently, making a small clicking noise with his tongue as if to a frightened animal.

Layla blinked back tears. "It's fine." Her voice cracked. *It's all fine, I can take it. Just let me sit down for a minute.*

"Very well." Max gave her a considering look, as if suspecting a fib or outright whopper, and pushed gently at her shoulders until she huddled in the very center of the nearly full tub.

Nasty scrapes and ripening bruises paraded up and down her legs, but if she hugged her knees the ache didn't seem so bad. Her back was a solid metal bar of pain, her neck throbbed, her fingers were swollen. Even her hair hurt. The vampire moved away, but only a few steps. Layla gingerly settled her wounded face against her knees.

Okay, take a breath. Think about what to do next if he's not going to drown—

A splash, a wave of warmth, and the water level rose dangerously close to the rim as a much larger body settled behind her. Not only that, but heavy muscular legs were suddenly to either side, pressed against the tub's borders. His toes looked human enough, and so did his knees; that was weird. Stranger still was his arms curling around her, and Layla swallowed a yelp as she was drawn back.

There was no way to avoid being draped over his chest, and zero chance of ignoring the evidence of arousal pressed against the small of her back. Well, he'd had a fight; according to the hunters, what came afterward was a fuck. Even Shawn's guys went to the bars looking for companionship after an operation or practice—and to confession as well, if they could find a cathedral of the proper type.

Oh, jeez. She just hoped whatever he'd do, it would be quick. And that she could catch a nap afterward.

Sleep sounded *great*. Even, perhaps *especially* if she never woke up again.

The vampire brushed at her tangled, sweat- and steam-damp hair. "Tilt your head back." His voice rumbled against her back, and she suppressed a shiver.

I don't want to. But she'd said she would cooperate; if she didn't, would he find Pete again and do something horrible? It didn't seem outside his abilities at all.

Her chin tipped up. The back of her head fit almost exactly in the hollow between his shoulder and collarbone. It was even… restful, she supposed, and her tired muscles all let go at once. "Are you going to hurt me?" She sounded very small and very frightened, even to herself.

"No." His hand paused. He shifted slightly; it was almost, *almost* soothing to be held, buoyed by warm water and enclosed by someone so much taller, broader, stronger. "I remember this was pleasant enough, in its own way."

Something pushed against her lips. Startled, Layla tensed, but the edge of his wrist was under her top teeth, and a warm numbness filled her mouth. His other arm had snaked across her bare chest, pinning her shoulders, and even as she tried to pull away she realized what the fluid had to be, what he was doing.

She had no choice but to swallow.

A hot smooth hit like good tequila though lacking any alcohol sting, and the liquid seemed vanish halfway down her throat. Another gulp followed; Layla was caught between struggling and the promise to cooperate, between utter exhaustion and the consciousness of *fucking vampire blood* trickling down her chin, burrowing into her esophagus.

Then the heat dilated, a soft irresistible scorch eating all physical pain. A smooth burn like expensive whiskey on an empty stomach, hazy cotton filling her skull, and she was floating.

Wow. A slow, dazed thought. Like the headrush after taking four shots and sliding off a barstool to hit the dance floor, like the first draw of really good weed through a freshly cleaned bong. She'd never done anything harder; this left both spendy booze and Humboldt Gold in the dust.

Now it tasted like the tangerines Meemaw Cathy brought home sometimes after her monthly check, bought from the roadside stand at the southern edge of town. Always child-Layla's favorite things; she could just about eat herself sick on small sweet-tangy fruit. Then it changed, between one mouthful and the next, into a bang-on taste of her grandmother's famous chow-chow with the spicy, peppery edge nobody else on earth could make, filling her eyes with tears and making her poor scratched-up broken heart leap as if so many years could be erased and she could hug Meemaw again.

That's my girl, her grandmother would say, and for a moment all would be right in the world.

The persistent scratching in her throat was soothed, the deep unpleasant rumble-pain of bruising retreated. For the first time in what felt like years a sense of complete physical wellbeing poured through Layla, all discomfort vanishing along with the constant torment of anxious uncertainty. It kept changing, from just-baked dinner rolls to dark clover honey, from tea sandwiches to sweet tea itself—good things, *wonderful* tastes meaning comfort, safety, a refuge from all fear.

The vampire eased his wrist free of her lips. She couldn't even wonder how he'd cut himself, she was too busy struggling with the urge to grab his arm, clamp her mouth to the wound, and get another dose of memory-laden painkiller—even if she was always scared of eating too much, and sometimes had lain in her childhood bed at night wishing she wouldn't grow out of her shoes or clothes, since they were so expensive and Meemaw only had the monthly check plus a few pennies from taking in sewing work.

If she got greedy now, what might happen?

The thought drifted away. Blessedly, the warmth didn't quit, settling behind her breastbone and expanding like a balloon, pushing down her legs, along her arms. Finger- and toe-tips tingled; she blinked hazily, managing to lift her right hand.

The bruises on her forearm were shrinking in fast-forward, their edges turning yellowy green instead of deep fresh red-purple. Scrapes on her knuckles now seemed days old instead of livid and fresh. Golden light from incandescent bulbs, hazy and wonderful, stroked her wet skin; when her fingers twitched slight rainbow dazzles followed the motion.

Christ have mercy, I'm stoned on biter blood.

The urge to laugh returned, nearly overwhelming. It wasn't the screaming-meemies but genuine amusement, however drugged or disconnected. A giggle bubbled in her throat; she forced it down, licking her lips for any remaining trace. *Holy cow.*

"See?" His voice was deep and soft, a tiger's purr vibrating along her bones. "No pain, little Leila. Let it work."

I ought to be scared. But the floating, numbing relief was too intense, wiping away fear-twinges almost before they could begin. There was still something she wanted to know.

"Why are you doing this?" She had to concentrate to form the words; at least she didn't sound drunk, just sleepy.

"You need healing." Water lapped as he shifted, smoothing her hair once more, finger-combing as if he had some experience with the operation. "And this will render you stronger, more durable. I feared the worst, finding the car."

Oh, crap. She'd almost forgotten crashing the Volvo. "I'm so sorry about—" she began, a sudden sharp spike of unease very nearly managing to break the flood of warm forgiveness, of pure relaxation.

"No, you did as you should." As if he forgave her. Which was great even if conditional, as all male forgiveness tended to be. "It served its purpose. Better the chariot than my leman."

Was he calling *her* a broken-down car? This was fucking confusing. "What's with you and the lemons, huh?"

"Leman." More careful enunciation—much less stilted now, the ghost of a strange accent merely hiding behind the words, not poking through every syllable. "It means *beloved*, and *companion*. You are a gift of the gods."

Man, are you in for a surprise. "That's not me." Maybe she should have kept her mouth shut, but all this was just too confusingly hilarious. Beloved? Who the hell even used that word anymore?

Another rumble in his chest, turning into words. "You do not compass your own value."

I'm a fuckup, sir. My own mother didn't even want me. This was why she avoided weed and too much booze; not only did it let bad thoughts out of the barn but it was a good way to get hurt by any male in the vicinity.

Every woman knew that danger on some deep level. Just part of living in a world made for men, that was all.

Still, the cascade of sparkles around every movement was fun to watch. She lost the thread of hurtful memory and when he moved again, she barely noticed. Quiet encouragement in a deep, soft voice—*lift your arm... tip your head back, good... close your eyes*—as soap slid against her skin, as water spoke in its own liquid language, as for once simply existing wasn't painful but almost kind.

Helluva drug, she thought, hazily, and gave up wondering when the agony of living would start again.

She was too tired to care.

Lᴏᴠᴇʟʏ ᴛᴏ ꜱᴇᴇ ᴛʜᴇ ᴇᴠɪᴅᴇɴᴄᴇ ᴏꜰ ᴅᴀᴍᴀɢᴇ ꜰᴀᴅᴇ, ᴛᴏ ʙᴀᴛʜᴇ ᴀ ʜᴇᴀᴠʏ-lidded leman and gently chafe languid, beautiful limbs to dryness. To carry her to the bed, arrange her in its precise center, to sample a velvet mouth freighted with the taste of his own blood. The Gift was rising swiftly in her now, urged along by a Maker's initial feeding; the memory of her drawing against his veins was pleasurable torment, the rising thrall a prickling goad only salved by pushing her legs apart and driving himself into her hot, slick center once more.

Her back arched, starry eyes half-opening. Maximus froze, an unwelcome awareness of how a mortal female might interpret this act sending cold trickles down his back. Glacial ice meeting the volcanic heat of her core, his own existence steel caught between the two; he was helpless to withdraw, yet could not advance.

"Christ," she whispered. "You could just find a regular girl-friend, you know."

"No." His teeth—both true and camouflage—ached desper-ately. So did the rest of him, held in precisely painful equipoise. He needed to move, *had* to, but what would that cost? She had already been battered and terrorized well past mortal bearing, and now he was doing… this. He could barely find words in her modern language, struggling against a sea of contradictory imperatives. "Sanguinant, we need… *I* need this. You."

"Nobody needs me." Achingly quiet, resigned to the idea, as her heavy charcoal lashes drifted down.

The statement was so utterly, incredibly bizarre. Had her mortal companions been blind to the miracle living among them, unaware of a divine gift burning golden amid the piled trash of their warren?

"Then I am nobody," he murmured, and was tempted to laugh. A good soldier must be wily as Odysseus if he expected to become a general, and now he must not only keep what he had found but become a patricide as well.

Nemesis's orders had been to murder the sanguinant elder who held this territory. There was no reason for one of his fellow senior legionnaires to be sent so closely afterward… unless Father intended to discard an elder son.

Eldest son, as a matter of fact. *Primus inter pares*, once, but none of Maximus's coevals had survived so long, nor been sent upon so many sensitive, complex missions. William had been a good pupil, the finest among his crop, being groomed for a command of his own.

No more. And he had to wonder why William had acted so oddly, appearing in the parking structure. Certain aspects of that fight were worrisome.

His leman's hips shifted, a wall of pleasure swamping her enthralled sanguinant, returning him to the immediate, vivid, overwhelming present moment.

"Oh," she breathed. "Okay."

For a long, breathless moment he thought she accepted necessity, accepted *him*, and his chest expanded with intense, murderous relief before he realized it was merely mortal fatigue and the narcotic effect of feeding from a Maker. Were that lacking, she would no doubt struggle as she had before.

He had his praenomen again. Unfortunately it was the title of a traitor, a patricide in the making, a beast assaulting a defense-less nymph.

Worst of all, he had no intention of stopping.

His body tensed, shaft driven to the hilt. He battered the gates of Elysium itself, as her soft hands rose to grip his shoulders, as she moved with dreamy slowness. Cast into phrenzy, he nevertheless grimly held his own release at bay until her pleasure was unmistakable, tiny gasping cries lost in his mouth battening upon hers, the hot satin of her innermost sanctum clamping rhythmically.

Then he was lost as well, spinning, drowning, his only anchor shuddering below and around him. Damned and driven, chained and liberated at once, he pressed a kiss to her humming pulse before driving his teeth in, and the taste of his salvation bore the smoke-laced edge of his very own, his *only* fledgling.

The world halted. He collapsed onto her, merciful blackness covering every sense for a brief eternity, and even in that abyss a single word beat in time to his old, ruthless heart.

Leila. Leila. Leila.

A tiny, experimental wriggle, setting off another cascade of pleasure. He raised his head, and she went still. Was it fear, or discomfort?

"Shh." Maximus stiffened, propping himself on elbows. Had he crushed her; could she breathe? "Don't."

"Huh?" Another tentative shift, her hips twitching. "There's… it's… Is that normal?"

Of course there were distinct differences in physical structure, though all sanguinant had been mortal once. "The shape changes." Groping for words to explain was a constant difficulty, but one he could be grateful for. If she were disposed to listen, it meant at least a measure of resignation to her new status.

"Barbed, as an arrowhead. I am fastened for some short while. Try to relax."

"Sure, *relax*. Uh-huh." Finally, her legs wrapped about his waist, slim pretty ankles hooking together. She let out a long, drowsy sigh sounding suspiciously like relief. "Oh, thank God. That's better."

His heart, pierced and soothed at once, gave an incredible leap. "I will remember as much."

She paid no attention, lost in the blur of feeding. "Monster blood." A singsong whisper. "High on monster blood. Wow, what a trip."

Very little matched the opiate pleasure of your Maker's ichor, given initially to strengthen the Gift and afterward as a reward for good behavior or marked success in carrying out orders. A leman's presence overpowered even that rapture; could she understand her own importance, that a few meager drops of her breathing presence outweighed centuries spent fighting the slow rise of ossification?

"Hey. Max." She bumped his shoulder with her palm, perhaps used to requesting attention from her former companions in blunt manner. "You're making me a biter, right? Is that what this is?"

Biter. It wasn't the worst word, he decided. "Sanguinant." A pedantic correction, and he risked brushing her cheek with his own. She did not retreat from the caress, nor did she attempt escaping his weight. All in all, he could be cringingly grateful for such grace. "Yes. You are given the Dark Gift, little Leila."

"So I'm... ugh." Even her soft disgust was attractive. "I'm gonna have to suck blood?"

"Only mine." If he must pay with his own veins for her grudging compliance, it was only right. He would give much more for far less—and if she ever gifted another creature the touch of her fangs, he would wait for her to finish draining the prey before tearing it to shreds. The certainty was immediate, instinctive, and overwhelming. "I will hunt for us both. You will learn what it means to be leman."

He waited for some response, but there was none. She had sunk into unconsciousness; he realized dawn was well past. Soon she would suffer Sol's advent as a fledgling always did, rendered helplessly somnolent until dusk loosened daylight's bonds. Full transition would be swift for one so sensitive, especially with frequent feeding.

The thought was extremely pleasing.

Maximus lay still, breathing her in, and even while cursing himself for what he had just done, he knew he would never take another road.

CHAPTER 15

One moment she was high as balls, lying naked underneath a vampire. The next, Layla was conscious of a pillow against her cheek, a large quiet space around her that didn't smell of mildew or rot, and a deep inarguable sense of physical health she hadn't felt in forever.

It was a cliche to open her eyes and think *where the hell am I*, but the situation sort of demanded as much. This might take the prize for 'weirdest thing to happen since your best friend got eaten by a biter', though there were other serious contenders.

She'd been living in the Twilight Zone for four fucking years, after all.

It wasn't just vampires. There was so much other crazy shit in the world's floor-cracks, from the little green henchmen some swore served old biters to the staircases in the woods, from the Bermuda Triangle to the Dyatlov Pass Incident, from wendigos to yetis. Mothman, the Jersey Devil, the hunters who specialized in werewolves, chupacabras, or Sasquatches instead of vampires, an entire enchilada of bizarre mythological bullshit come to screaming, carnivorous life. The only thing more unsettling than the weirdness was the determination over ninety-nine-point-nine percent of humanity displayed in ignoring its reality while consuming reams of fiction on the subject.

Ackerman had once remarked it was even kind of a backhanded comfort, since actual monsters were a lot less terrifying than things some human beings did to each other. *Almost makes you believe in God*, he'd said, and Layla couldn't help but agree, having been more than half awake in high school history classes.

Now she had to face the fact that she might be irrevocably part of the bizarro zone, just not on the side of humanity. Was he really going to turn her into a biter?

I'd say that ship has sailed, Lay. You'll be a henchwoman at best, a baby biter at worst. How are you going to deal with that?

She lay very still for what felt like a long time, testing her fingers and toes, taking internal inventory. A few twinges in her lady-parts reminded her of being held down and railed *again*, and she had to admit he wasn't bad at it. If she was turning into a complete slut—but that was stupid misogyny talking, right?

Christ, that was almost the most confusing thing about the whole deal, her body deciding it liked… well, sex *was* a biological imperative. The whole bride-of-Dracula thing in the movies always looked like it felt good, so maybe it was a case of fiction following reality for once.

She didn't appear to be sleeping in a wet spot, at least. It was so nice to feel clean again, come to think of it. Cold-water showers and washcloth scrubdowns were fine, but hardly satisfying.

Layla stirred, cautiously peeking in every direction. She raised her head, taking in the terrain.

A relatively large windowless room, walls painted pale eggshell. The bed was huge, soft, and the sheets reasonably fresh, a thick scratchy grey wool blanket providing just enough weight and warmth. A huge chifforobe of dark wood loomed across from the bed's foot, and a plain wooden chair was placed precisely between the bed and the right-hand wall, where a door stood ajar, showing tile—bathroom, and she was blushing again, since there wasn't enough monster blood in the world to make her forget *that* part of the festivities. Another door to the left, shut tight, most probably the exit.

Good to know.

Max sat wedged in the room's empty corner, head down, arms loose over his knees, hands dangling. Another black sweater with leather elbow-patches, slightly different work trousers, boots laced tightly. He was completely motionless. Was he asleep? How many of those same outfits did he have, and where the *hell* had he gotten clothes from?

It was odd. He looked almost lonely, sitting like that.

You are out of your fucking mind, Layla. That thing went through your crew like a hot knife through butter, and he's fucked you twice now. Or is there another word for the event? You did get kind of enthusiastic about parts of the whole thing, remember?

She felt like she was thinking clearly for the first time in ages. A dark film had been peeled away from her vision, and her ears nearly twitched like a rabbit's. She could see little chips and gouges in the paint, every ding on the varnished wooden bedstead, count the threads of the cotton sheets. There was a regular, slow *ka-thump*, pause, *ka-thump* in the stillness, though the air was still and close, as if the place was soundproofed.

Reason it out. You can do this—you're not the brightest, but at least you can chew what you bite. Meemaw always said that was more important, anyway. Layla scooted back to lean against the headboard, arranged her knees crisscross-applesauce, and tried to think systematically.

Nemesis killed other vampires, the red-stripe file was very clear on that—and usually ones who were being real bastards, though according to most hunters the only good biter was a dead one. What if, just *what if* he'd interpreted Ben opening fire as another bloodsucker's human employees getting the drop on him?

Which brought up the question of precisely why he hadn't

killed her back at the base. Maybe sheer sexism, because she was a girl? Some of Nemesis's listed targets had been female biters; Shawn and his crew were very definite that girl bloodsuckers were fast, tough, and incredibly hard to put down in their own right.

Then there was that lemon-leman stuff. Did Max actually want a girlfriend, or did he want little vampire babies? There wasn't any research swilling around on that particular subject; most who studied the demimonde agreed it couldn't be done.

Still, the biter who had taken out O'Shaughnassey's crew was reportedly capable of walking around in sunlight, as some of the really old ones were said to. That particular monster had also survived a car bomb, standing in leaping gasoline flames while being peppered by the new fragmenting ammo. Knocking up a human probably wasn't outside an old vampire's capabilities; she had to at least consider the notion.

Then I am nobody.

Another flush, rising from her neck to fill her cheeks with fire. You couldn't take what a man said during sex literally; she was inexperienced, sure, but she knew *that* much. Now he'd gotten what he wanted and infected her with vampirism, he was probably going to say *so long, thanks for the fun* and disappear, leaving her with a habit for red stuff and the prospect of being hunted by people she might once have corresponded with for research.

Layla didn't think she could bite another person, or do some of the horrible things vampires seemed to enjoy. The very idea filled her with unsteady revulsion. All the research said biters were downright addicted to blood and acted correspondingly; still, plain old humans didn't need a habit to be assholes.

The solid, blocky bedstead creaked, a brush of warm air stirred Layla's hair, and the biter appeared right in front of her without the benefit of stretching, yawning, or even standing up and walking across the room.

He shook his head as he settled into a crouch, tossing those gleaming curls back, mattress giving a sharp squeak as his boots sank deep. At least his eyes were dark, without those wet crimson sparks spreading in the pupils. He went completely still again, peering at her like he was surprised to find a girl still in his bed after a night spent doing… what he'd done.

What *both* of them had done, since she hadn't exactly hated the whole experience. Did she have to take responsibility? The spinning inside her head wouldn't calm down so she could decide.

"Leila." Gravely, as if reminding himself of her name. Or at least, his version of it; she couldn't place the accent at all. "How do you feel?"

Completely fucking confused, even if all my bruises are gone. A ghost of the deepest aches remained, but only that. She hadn't felt this good since well before graduation, really. "F-fine."

A pause. He clearly weighed her response and found it insufficient. "You must tell me if there is any pain. Any discomfort at all."

Oh, shit, do you really want to knock me up? "Uh…" She might as well ask. "Are you trying to have vampire babies?"

His mouth opened slightly; fortunately, his teeth looked dentist-perfect human at the moment. There was no sign of fangs, and she had to wonder if she'd develop big sharklike chompers.

The very thought filled her with even more of that wobbling, stomach-flipping disgust.

Max the Vampire stared at her. He seemed, of all things, thunderstruck by the question. Was she not supposed to guess his grand plan? Or was she way off-base?

"Ah. No." It was weird to see such a powerful monster look, of all things, slightly embarrassed. "Sanguinant are sterile; our only progeny is in the Blood. Why? Did you long for children, in your mortal life?"

Christ, no. The thought that she might end up a mother like

Samantha was a good argument for hundred-percent abstinence. So was freedom from STDs.

Which brought up another question. "What about vampire diseases? Do I have to get checked out?" Where did you find a clinic for that, anyway? And that term, *your mortal life*. Did that mean she wasn't human anymore?

She didn't feel any different, except for being relatively well-rested. And unbruised, and clear-eyed.

Oh, crap. Was this what vampires always felt like? No wonder they were so strong, so unholy fast. There were definite advantages to that, she decided, but weighed against the liquid diet and all the murder, well…

"Diseases?" He repeated the word as if it were foreign.

Help me out here, big guy. You ought to know about protection if you're going to be sticking that thing anywhere. She was treating him like a human guy, she realized, and maybe that was a bad call. "I'm sorry, I just don't know. We haven't been hunting for very long."

It was kind of a lie, though old bloodsuckers would probably consider four years less than a lunch break. Then she could have kicked herself—sure, remind the big scary bloodsucker that her group had shot at him and his human friends.

Where were *they*? Was she going to be introduced to his employees? The thought of getting to know a whole new group of men was tiring, even if she felt physically great. Layla found herself pressing back against the slatted headboard, aware she didn't even have a sheet to cover herself with. Just her bare arms, hugging hard and attempting to shield her chest, fingers pressing in hard like Pete's as he dragged her away from an operation gone wrong.

The room blurred, wavered. Was she going to fucking *cry* now, too?

"Leila." His hands clasped her shoulders, feverish-hot against her cooler skin. "Shh, hush, sweet Leila. There is no need to weep. I can explain."

I wish someone would. Anyone, even you. She forced the tears down, had to swallow several times before she could speak.

"Great," she said, in a thick, blurred voice hardly recognizable as her own. "Okay. Do I get some clothes?"

The chifforobe turned out to contain two neatly racked rifles, a Bowie knife hanging in a holster, and two pistols carefully settled on a lined pull-out shelf. No ammo, though. Which was probably for the best, since he watched her examine the weapons. She kept her hands clasped behind her back, but no doubt he was wary of anyone who looked at guns that longingly.

Hell, she wouldn't have minded the knife, just for something to hold.

The big freestanding closet *also* held several iterations of what he was already wearing—sweater with leather elbow patches, Carhartts, and now she knew he liked black cotton tube socks and boxer briefs. Fortunately, it also held a few pairs of charcoal sweatpants and dark T-shirts; she could tighten the drawstring on the former and was almost lost in the latter, but she'd worn guys' underwear before.

Even tighty-whities were far more comfortable than thongs, in fact. She would've liked to fit into the current offerings, but they were too big. So, commando and braless it was.

Not her first time, and she was sure it wouldn't be the last. Almost freeing, in a way.

Vampire Max obligingly extended a single pointed, razor-tipped claw—the human-seeming fingernail growing and sharpening like a very good special effect, which made her feel a little faint—to trim the hem on the sweatpants. Knotting the shirt at her midriff got most of the extra material out of the way.

She probably looked ridiculous, but that never hurt anyone. At least the clothes were clean, plus they smelled faintly of detergent instead of mildew. "I just never thought of a vampire in sweats, that's all."

She was also doing great at making conversation, or so she thought. Probably inaccurately, but if she kept talking, it might distract the biter from doing anything… else.

"Ease of movement during combat training. Dogsbodies and fledglings both require instruction." He stood at what might be considered a respectful distance, though he'd tried to help her get dressed.

When she said *I can do it myself* he'd backed off, a flicker of something unnamable crossing his face.

"Yeah, so, I'm sorry one of our guys opened up on your… dogsbodies." It was a new word, and one she didn't particularly care for. Plus, Layla was apologizing about Ben's behavior for the millionth time, and the irritation at having to do so pinched her conscience hard. "We didn't know you were fellow hunters."

"Fellow hunters." Another unreadable flicker. He repeated her words carefully and seemed to be trying to mimic her accent as well, as if he didn't have much experience speaking good ol' American.

"You're Nemesis, right?" If she could display some bona fides, maybe she wouldn't start out at the bottom of whatever weird ladder *this* hunting group had. "You hunt other biters. Vampires. San-whatevers."

"Sometimes." His knifelike nose wrinkled briefly, mouth turning down, and he closed the chifforobe with a distinct, gentle click. "When Father commanded it."

Okay. Now there was a piece of news; she was finally getting somewhere. "Father?"

"My Maker." Gravely, like saying *the sky is blue* or *water's wet.* "Antinous, the one who granted me the Dark Gift."

I'm learning a lot of fresh terminology. "Dark Gift." Layla cast around for a good place to have more discussion, but there was only the one chair. The bed didn't seem quite safe, but she marched to its foot, dropped to the floor crisscross-applesauce again, and politely indicated a nearby patch of carpet for if he wanted to join her. "Like, I'm going to turn into a biter, too?" Would that make this 'Father' her grandfather?

Another extremely uncomfortable thought. Especially since she was still a little tender downstairs, so to speak.

"You are different." Max glided to the spot she pointed at and sank down into another easy, fluid crouch, graceful and controlled through the entire motion. If he was nervous at having his back to the door, he didn't show it. "Leman do not acquire even an elder's strength and speed, though a fledgling's is more than sufficient. You will never suffer the bloodcraze or have to fear the killing sleep. And as you age, you will not ossify."

"Hold on." She raised a hand, briefly, as if in the classroom, and put it down as soon as she realized the complete ridiculousness of the gesture. "You've gotta explain this lemon thing. Please?" A belated tack-on addition, she didn't want to sound pushy.

Go figure, she was sitting in a vampire's sweatpants and treating him like one of Shawn's hunters, asking for clarification on demimonde technical slang. On the one hand, it was clearly working to keep him occupied, and adding to her store of knowledge as a bonus.

On the other, it probably wouldn't do to get overly comfortable with this... with him. His gaze, dark and still, hadn't left her once since he hopped up on the bed.

Being watched this closely was unsettling as fuck.

"Leman are very rare." Carefully, visibly choosing each word as he sank further, finally coming to rest sitting, mirroring her own position. "Most sanguinant spend centuries without ever confirming your kind exists, though we are on the whole instructed very carefully by our Makers or elders. It is part of the Ecologue—ah, what every member of the Blood should know." His hands settled loosely on his knees. Straight-backed as a dancer, he didn't seem uncomfortable in the least wearing boots while sitting tailor-fashion.

Rare. Okay. Layla wasn't sure that was a compliment. She braced herself against the bed; it was getting to be a habit.

"For a normal sanguinant, the moment one receives the Gift, there is danger." Recited softly, like he'd given this speech before. "A fledgling may glut and suffer bloodcraze, and that often brings true-death. When dawn loses its grip, then one is an Elder and the risk of glut is much reduced, though still present. Of more concern is the killing sleep, when a sanguinant goes dormant, sinking into lethargy. Starvation occurs then, and can bring true-death. Age adds strength and experience but also ossification—a rigidity, physical and otherwise. We become inflexible, apathetic, numb. And that—"

"Brings true death," Layla supplied, eager to be a good student. Research was her primary role, after all. "Right?"

"Indeed. Very good." A nod, and a slight smile. He was so straight-faced, the tiny movement had an outsized effect. "The only cure is a leman. *You* will not suffer glut, nor killing sleep, nor ossification. And the sanguinant who claims you, bonds with you, is freed of those dangers."

Wow. That's… that's something. "Wait a second. Are you sure? You've never seen a leman—" Pronouncing it very carefully earned her another nod. She was making progress, good for her. Even if her head felt a little light, squeezing all this new stuff inside. "A leman before, right? So how do you know?"

"It is," he said, quietly but with finality, "unmistakable. I knew the moment I scented you."

Maybe that was why he'd stopped in the street and looked at her? "Was that when Ben shot at your crew?" *So did Steve and Ack, though. Can't blame just one person.*

Here she was, sitting across from a monster, trying to be fair and precise like in post-op debrief. At least he wasn't chugging beer and blaming her for everything under the sun.

"Very nearly, though it did not matter." Vampire Max was

back to straight-faced, nearly robotic information-giving, though his accent was getting a lot better. All in all he seemed a little looser now, though she couldn't decide if that was a bonus or a new danger. "In that moment, everything changed."

Is that good? Tell me it's good. She had a sinking feeling it was exactly, precisely the opposite. "Changed how?"

"To find a leman is a miracle, sweet Leila. Immediately upon doing so, a sanguinant will take the prize. All other considerations are secondary at best. *First the bite, then the claiming.*" The final sentence had a strange rhythm even for his accented delivery, a proverb or something translated from another language.

This is a lot to take in. "Let's leave that for a second." Her voice shook. "How old are you, anyway?"

His curly head cocked; he considered the question. Was it rude to ask? His right forefinger twitched, and she realized he appeared to be silently counting.

Go figure, biters looked incredibly human while doing mental math.

"Two millennia?" he finally said, not quite sure. "A little more. Time blurs, after a certain point, and one ceases to care."

Wait a minute. "You're... two *thousand*..." It wasn't possible. He had to be joking; did he only mean two hundred? That was incredible too, but somehow a little less outlandish.

Her head hurt. The sensation wasn't physical; the mind lodging in her brain-meat attempted to wrap itself around what he was saying, failed, tried again. Why *this* was the biggest hurdle after everything else she couldn't tell, or maybe she'd just lost the ability to absorb strangeness all at once.

"Give or take. Age often brings strength, but is not the only consideration." His eyelids dropped slightly, and his gaze turned distant instead of scorchingly attentive. "I have known for some while that I surpass my Maker, but it was... again, difficult to care. There was no reason to do anything other than follow orders. I am a soldier, sweet Leila."

Good Lord. She wished he'd stop calling her *sweet*; it wasn't as dismissive as some nicknames, but still. "I've hung out with Army guys," Layla managed, an utterly inadequate response. How the hell was she supposed to deal with this?

"Hm." Momentary brooding fled, and the biter's dark eyes were now hot and direct. "I was sent to kill the holder of this territory. The elder we met last night was one of my fellows—a serjeant, perhaps, you would call it? I believe Father has found me superfluous to requirements, and may very well suspect I would not succumb to a single junior. In any event, I have a leman now. I will not let you be taken."

Holder of this territory—he's got to mean Griskov. A sergeant, huh. But that wasn't the most concerning concept here. "Taken?"

"Oh, yes. Leman are priceless, my Leila." He lingered over her name, tasting it with that strange extra syllable. "If another sanguinant discovers your existence, they will seek to acquire you. If by some chance I am killed, the one proved stronger in combat will immediately bite and claim you for bonding."

"Wait. Just hold on one cotton-pickin' minute." *I sound like Meemaw.* "Kill you? And…" *Claim* her? Like she was a piece of lost luggage? Layla sagged against the bed, glad of something solid to lean on.

The idea of screaming and running away was incredibly attractive, if she could just figure out which direction to go.

"You need not be troubled," Max-the-vampire said patiently. Another twitch went through his strong, tanned fingers, slight tapping motions—apparently even two thousand plus years of being allergic to sunshine didn't bleach a biter, which was a completely useless detail to fasten on but Layla couldn't help herself. "I am possessed of more than enough savagery to protect what is mine. You may in time come to…resign yourself to your new status. Once I have dealt with matters in this territory we may go wherever you like, and I will endeavor to make your captivity tolerable."

Territory. Captivity. New status. "Do I get any say in this whatsoever?" Go figure, even with the flood of purely physical wellness plus strangely sharpened senses—if they really were, if she wasn't just imagining it—she still felt distinctly wobbly. The urge to leap up and just start running was overwhelming.

Nowhere to go, but she had to get out of this room. Just *had* to.

"We will travel wherever you like, live as you please. I will feed you, I will tend to your needs, and I will not demand affection. Only a certain resignation, which I am prepared to enforce. But we may speak upon that later." Broad shoulders rolled, settling—a preparatory movement, one she'd seen other guys perform. On him it was the elegant shrug of a cat waking up, deciding to take a stroll through the garden and see what birds were available for snacking. "It is past dusk and I must find the battlefield. You will stay here, where it is safe."

"Wait." Layla stared as he rose, unfolding just as gracefully as he'd settled. The conversation had taken a *distinct* turn, and the sense of the world slipping into madness was more pronounced than ever. "Hold up, you're just going to..." Her face felt stiff, her lips numb, and the rest of her lingered in the 'woozy' category.

Was he serious about leaving her here?

There were no windows; maybe she could pick a door-lock or two. If she was really infected with vampirism, though, busting through walls like the Kool-Aid Man might be an option.

Figuring out what to do afterward was the real problem. She didn't even know where she was, except maybe still in the city.

The vampire bent, offered his hand. When she didn't move, he simply leaned a little further, clasped her arms, and drew her upward. Once more, the truly horrible thing wasn't how strong he was—more than likely she'd develop superstrength too, that was a heckuva thought—but how *controlled*.

How careful.

Vampire Max held her upright, still wearing that faint smile. "This is a saferoom; while I live it will remain sealed, and bar the entry of any sanguinant or mortal. Even should the structure above be breached and collapse, you will be unharmed. I will return before dawn to feed you."

"You're just... leaving me here?" *There's not even a television, for Chrissake.* Layla couldn't help it; she shot a glance at the chifforobe.

"Only for a short while." He set her carefully on the bed before he left, sure.

He also took the weapons with him, slinging both rifles with quick habitual movements, checking the pistols before sliding them into shoulder-harness holsters he also shrugged over one arm, and making the knife disappear under his sweater. It was like seeing Shawn's guys suit up, complete with the tiny clicks and metallic sounds.

Worst of all, he didn't use the door, just walked up to it and blinked out of sight. A soft sound, a puff of warm breeze, and her vampire kidnapper vanished.

CHAPTER 16

Naturally his prize was stunned; how much she truly understood of their parley was an open question. Yet how painfully delightful were her determined attempts; she had a most fetching habit of frowning slightly while absorbing a piece of new information, pursing her lips so temptingly it took concerted effort *not* to take a kiss.

Or the rest of her, in entirety. Though she had stared at the mortal weaponry with something approaching longing, and he was forcefully reminded of another danger to leman—the despair of delicate, intuitive creatures held in captivity, no matter how cushioned.

Self-harm was a distinct risk, to be treated with all seriousness. He had carefully inventoried the saferoom before taking his own variety of rest, attempting to make certain nothing within it could be improperly used by his new prize.

The deeper changes of the Gift were proceeding apace; she was already somewhat more durable than a mortal. Still, he had combed the entire space thrice as she slept, then upon his exit simply removed the mortal weapons to a space outside the seals

—having no need of them, for his own claws more than sufficed —and was reasonably satisfied.

To lapse into healing near-somnolence without the risk of killing sleep, to surface from soft restorative haze and find sweet fragrant Leila awake, regarding him shyly from the tumbled bed… those were wonders enough. Her inquisitiveness, the sight of her in clothing meant for his own use, her apparent distress at being parted from her new protector, were far deeper pleasures.

Of course the last could be simple fear of the cage. He did not like leaving her in such a state, even temporarily.

His instincts, however, proved correct the moment he slipped from the sealed saferoom into darkened hallways, and sharpened further as he plunged into a humid, scent-crowded mortal night. The old habit of leaving any lair near-undetectably—a skill learned almost before his first fledgling glut—once again stood a soldier in good stead.

This outpost was being watched. The sense of unfriendly attention was immediate, prickling the fine hairs if he had been in anything other than mistform; Maximus drifted in darkness as the surrounding rows of oil pumps bobbed their ungainly heads.

Hunters sent by Father, or suitors come to call? Both?

Troubling indeed. William's behavior had been somewhat strange, pausing to show himself in challenge instead of simply, efficiently striking from thin air. Not at all how the young fellow had been taught to handle efficient removal of a target, and furthermore, the other sanguinant had been most obliging in Maximus's efforts to keep the battle from drawing too near the newly acquired mortal chariot—no, *car*, he must use the modern tongue whenever possible now—and its precious cargo.

Almost too cooperative, well-trained red-haired William, despite the resulting awkwardness of prime tactical terrain removed from both combatants' use.

Maximus's new capacity for emotion was both an advantage and its opposite. Possessive instincts rose in a blinding crimson wave, threatening to throw him from mistform, send him plunging into open violence, tearing through any who would *dare* approach his prize. Set against the urge was cold experience born of battles uselessly won; it was one thing to conquer, quite another matter to hold what was gained.

She was safe enough, though thoroughly sieged. If others knew of or suspected a leman's existence—the hotel had been a calculated, unavoidable risk—the worst thing he could do was verify her current location.

He had intended to visit his original target this evening, ascertaining whether William had managed to erase Esmond the Varangian. Now paying that particular social call was the only proper move, for either way it would draw attention away from this seemingly abandoned villa.

So long as he remained undetected while leaving and returning, that was. There was no way to smile in mistform, but the sensation of baring his true teeth was still marked.

Maximus drifted free of encirclement; orange citylight bounced from thickening clouds moving from the east and a seashore within a few hours' steady movement; both sky and ground were seething with unease. Sanguinant eyes could easily pierce a veiled sky to find the river of stars and a waxing, almost-full moon smiling beneficently behind the mask; he wondered what Leila would think of the view.

So much to show her, to anticipate her wonder. A piercing pleasure, even as he realized the sharp edge of his perceptions were already slightly dulled. Calcification would return swiftly; he could not be away for long.

Best to get started, then.

A wholly natural prickling discomfort intensified as Maximus slipped through outlying urban areas, working towards the city's core and avoiding steadily thickening bands of unfriendly attention, occasionally hearing a rumble of thunder many miles distant.

No rain tonight, he decided. *But soon.* And finally, he reached what he suspected was the first battlefield of the evening.

The street where he had first sighted his ambrosial nymph was alive with mortal merrymakers, even more crowded than it had been that memorable eve. Steady heart-thumps of music throbbed through the clubs, taverns with live shows adding layers to cacophony, a bolus of vehicle traffic partially blocked yet forcing its way through orange cones and fluttering yellow tape, a great beast's digestion sluggishly performing its duty. Perhaps the mortal authorities were still attempting to discern what precisely had happened, though no few were the modern cities where nocturnal—or even daylight—gunfire was hardly a matter for notice or comment.

More tellingly, the entirety of downtown was under heavy sanguinant watch. Shadows flickered upon rooftops, in alleys, and the sounds of mortal celebration or intoxication held a hard, almost-bitter edge.

Maximus ignored the ring of fidgeting fledglings—so much heedless, intoxicated prey milling about was an invitation to glut, no matter how well-fed the predator. He paused only to mark the locations of scattered elders placed to keep rein upon the appetites of youth, and the dogsbodies standing guard at the Blue Moon Spot's open doors felt only a brief piercing chill as he slipped past.

The dogs reeked of newness, a scant mouthful of their Master's ichor still working outward through mortal tissues to grant strength, speed, a modicum of greater awareness. Nothing compared to a leman's natural sensitivity, of course; the memory of her scent, held close to his skin in order to not alert demimonde passers-by, was at once a balm and deadly distraction.

He had not expected ossification to return quite so quickly once he stepped from her charmed circle. An elegant, object lesson; the thrall was already waking inside his bones as well, the beast in him dissatisfied with her absence, craving another blinding, wonderful possession.

Soon, he promised. *When these enemies are dead.*

Two floors brimful of carousing children, the music an assault no less than the flashing lights, constant pressure of warm damp mortal flesh, the reek of alcohol, stimulants, adrenaline, sex.

Above all, blood. Their pulses rising and falling in surf-roar waves, their breath full of information on health and lifestyle choices, their bright gazes roving, their chatter yelled over pounding electronic bass. It would have been agonizing temptation save for his leman's taste upon his tongue, the burning addiction proofing him against any other vintage.

He could easily drink without the kill now, another hard-won skill rendered effortless as breathing by the simple fact of her existence. All other blood, even that of fellow predators, had become mere water. Nutritious, certainly, and of value both for his own needs as well as carrying nourishment back to his prize.

But there was no mounting, tempting urge to gorge, to bathe in hot red saltflood. Only the icy knowledge that every sanguinant in this building—and there were quite a few upon the third floor—must be erased before dawn, along with several combat groups in other key areas of the greater urbs.

His battle tonight was both feint and winnowing.

Any survivors of Esmond's line or allegiance must think Antinous had struck in order to widen his territory; if Father sent others in William's wake, they must assume Nemesis or one of his lieutenants simply carrying out the work. Neither could suspect a leman, and if they already had intimations of her existence tonight must introduce uncertainty of the prospect.

The more they doubted her existence, the better.

A first breath of doom was visited upon two elders standing guard in opposite, darkened corners of the ground floor. The male was a stocky fellow with dark hair cut in a thick leonine ruff, the female slight, thin-lipped, and dun-haired, bearing the marks of malnutrition in a mortal childhood about her eyes and mouth despite the burnish of the Gift. Praetorians both, since this was a post of high dignified responsibility, requiring of great control; he paid them the honor of swift painless passage. First the woman, whose dark gaze stuttered upward in disbelief the moment he appeared; she managed a claw-swipe which almost touched his sweater before his right hand pierced her abdomen, thrust upward, grasped the cardiac muscle, and gave a swift squeeze. His left, claw-freighted, sheared through her neck, snapping reinforced bone, and her tissues were dry enough the fatal burst of glimmering dust went unremarked in the dimness.

At least, unnoticed by the mortals. But Nemesis was already away, using every erg of whispering speed to blink across the dancefloor in a single leap, treating the male to a swift, stunning head-blow, skull rebounding against a heavily painted brick wall glistening with the condensation of mortal breath and outside humidity.

That was merely a love-tap. Maximus's claws pierced a sanguinant throat on both sides, every substance save bone collapsing. When his palm met reinforced cervical spine it was a simple matter to close his hand and yank. Usually the move was simply one more moment in combat, though tricky and techni-cally difficult.

However, a burst of muffled satisfaction at victory slid through him. Emotion was a luxurious gift, even with its distrac-tion-drawback riding tandem.

The male had fed more recently; wet rot sloughed through his tissues before being eaten by glisterdust. None of the mortals noticed, only a few rubbing at their eyes as the building's HVAC systems blew grit across the floor, struggling to push fresh oxygen over packed, gasping dancers. Nemesis passed between mortals crowding the stairways to the second level, and the dance-space here was packed with stomping, stamping, thrashing celebrants, nearly all dressed in black, a different music vying with the din from below.

More sanguinant upon this level as well, and the light was dimmer though steady strobe-flashes gave the appearance of stuttering movement, some bulbs emitting the spectrum which granted certain substances—cloth or paint—a certain glow to mortal eyes. Another half-dozen of his own kind died nearly unaware, showers of grit timed to burst between stammering fluorescence.

A clot of dogsbodies and elders lingered at the foot of a second stairwell, its open maw crossed by a line of a red velvet rope. Nemesis realized he was grinning, true teeth bared and the battle-roar beginning in his chest, for he recognized both of Esmond's senior advisors in conference among the clearly worried soldiers. Jumal the Red, with his bare-shaved head glinting under stinging light, and Raleigh the Golden in what was her accustomed garment of leather strips clinging to pore-less, stone-hard skin still bearing the color of a mortal life spent under the kiss of desert sun.

The Red saw him first, but it was too late. And their presence, both Red and Gold, meant Esmond was certainly present in this haunt.

Nemesis's strategy was working so far, its beginning stages a success. Now all that remained was to eradicate every scion of the Blood in this building and burn it to the ground. The mortals could make shift for themselves.

I am glad she does not see this, the soldier thought, before the chill clarity of battle took him again. The blunting of his reflexes was worrisome, and he hoped to return to his leman's arms quickly.

Unfortunately, that fond desire was in vain. For Esmond the Varangian knew Nemesis approached, and had a few plans of his own.

CHAPTER 17

"For fuck's sake," Layla hissed, glaring at the door. "You've *got* to be kidding me."

Well, she wasn't so much looking at the heavy wooden slab which probably weighed more than she did, with its brass hardware and a shiny, relatively new deadbolt keyhole sitting smug and prissy, well aware of its own importance. She was occupied with something else entirely.

Something invisible. Or rather just *barely* visible, rippling in her peripheral vision like heat rising off faraway highway on a deadly dry summer afternoon. A sheet of near-shimmering force lingered along the wall, and now she knew what Max meant by 'seals'.

How in the hell was such a thing even possible? The demi-monde was full of weird shit, sure, but this was certifiably *insane*.

No fan-vent in the bathroom, though air had to be exchanging somehow because humidity wasn't accumulating on the walls. The light fixtures were recessed, giving off a serene golden glow, and impossible to reach even if she clambered onto the pedestal sink. Attempting to climb on the toilet-tank attached to the wall was a no-go, there just wasn't enough space to wedge herself atop it.

She landed on her feet after two attempts, clicking her teeth together painfully though catching her balance each time, and decided that experiment had used up most of her daily luck ration. She'd probably break her damn leg if she tried again.

Even the single chair didn't help. There was simply nothing to grab, no way to get close to the fixtures, and bouncing said chair off the invisible curtain only got her a clatter and nearly falling on her ass when she dodged the backfire of *that* stupid plan.

The chifforobe was unscalable even if she pulled out the rolling shelves. Every attempt to monkey up its internal architecture and get near the ceiling was a dismal failure. The thing was either fastened to the wall or so heavy she couldn't tip it despite the newfound sense of vital strength coursing through her entire body, and trying to climb on the bed's headboard got her nowhere as well.

She could rip up the sheets and blankets, sure, but what the hell would that get her? Punishment? A funny shaky sensation went through her at the prospect.

He hadn't precisely hurt her yet. Unless you counted... the bed. Which she avoided after her initial attempt to climb on the headboard, or settle the chair at the head of the mattress and get near the ceiling that way. Even looking at the rumpled woolen blanket and plain cotton sheets was uncomfortable, not least for the strange half-submerged thrill shooting through her entire nervous system.

Hormones, or fear? Both?

Layla stroked the invisible curtain, wincing slightly at the prickles racing up her arm. Poking tentatively with fingertips gave a slight uncomfortable zap like biting on tinfoil, and slapping the solidified air outright stung as if she'd hit a brick wall.

Well, she had in more ways than one, really. What did *a short while* mean to someone who had lived two-thousand-plus years? All this nonsense about lemans and true death and captivity, and worst of all, Layla was thirsty.

That was an understatement. Her throat was impersonating all the world's greatest deserts at once, parched as Death Valley, dry as the Gobi.

Cool water from the sink only made the burning worse. It didn't feel like strep, but she couldn't really check her tonsils because the bathroom had no real mirror. There was an oblong of burnished metal—looked like brass—fastened to the inner panel of the chifforobe's left door, but its surface was too cloudy for details and anyway, she had to hop to get a glimpse of her face, because it was set for someone much taller than her.

Which essentially meant *anyone*, but still.

No windows, she couldn't get at the door... some indefinable sense told her she was underground, though she couldn't be entirely sure. There was a faint hum which might be HVAC, the light fixtures, or something else entirely. The strange slow *ka-thump*, pause, *ka-thump* had vanished when Max left, and her own pulse was uncomfortably loud in her ears along with the ragged working of her lungs.

Every once in a while she ran a fingertip over her teeth. No chance to brush them, but they didn't seem any sharper. The taste lingering in her mouth was strange, almost spicy, and only made her fractionally more thirsty each time she swallowed. The lights seemed to be getting brighter, and all told she was as uncomfortable as it was possible to be.

Nah, if the power goes out you'll find out it can get worse.

Wasn't that a merry thought. She made a complete circuit of the two rooms, feeling along the invisible curtain as high—and as low—as she could reach.

And she ended up right back where she started. Staring at the door, again, her hands curling into fists and releasing.

Trapped. Helpless.

Of course, she wouldn't have minded this invisible-seal trick while traveling with Dan and the guys. Sleeping with one eye open around a bunch of men was a recipe for perpetual exhaustion, and now Layla could admit she'd never quite trusted any of them.

Even Dan.

"But I *liked* him," she blurted, the words bouncing off bare walls. The weird shimmercurtain didn't muffle her voice, though the air was so goddamn dead in here. She was going to end up a claustrophobic mess.

Did you really? Her stupid, hyperactive brain, unable to figure out any way to escape current circumstances, decided on the time-honored amusement of Picking Apart All Layla's Past Mistakes. *Sure, you had a thing for him in high school, and he knew it. All the times he grinned at you while Suze was looking t'other way, all the homework you did for him.*

"We were just kids," she muttered, and stamped back to the bathroom. The towels, hung up neatly on door, sink, and wall-tank, were almost dry. Max had clearly arranged things for maximum airflow; she'd done her best to replace them in the same configuration.

Christ, the vampire picked up after himself better than any adult male she'd hung out with.

Yeah, you were kids. But did you ever think finding him with Cindy just before the wedding was a little too neat and convenient? He didn't even lock that door, and he must've known you'd be along to bring his cufflinks and boutonnière. That was your job, since Suze was finishing up getting her hair done.

"None of my business," Layla countered, setting off for the bed. The need to be doing something, *anything*, buzzed inside her bones, filled her muscles with shaky heat. "She wouldn't have believed me anyway."

Had Suzy really been pregnant before the wedding, or thought she was? She hadn't said anything to Layla, but some things were private even between besties.

There were always secrets, from anyone.

Okay, different question. What was she doing alone up at Paradise Point? They never found another body, but…

Maybe Suze had gone up to the local makeout spot to think things through. She'd claimed to be happy, sure, but sometimes Layla wondered during their monthly Olive Garden dinners. Fancy pasta and cheap wine, habitual giggles as they endlessly recycled high school jokes, Layla talking about her job running a cash register at the box store, Suze about her only part-time gig at the Craft Depot, since Dan had a good position at the factory and wanted the trailer kept up.

He'd fallen behind on the payments after Suze's death; consequently, only the sale of Meemaw's doublewide and the land it was on had funded their first two years of vampire hunting. Picking up Ben and Ack off the demimonde message boards, then Steve-o last year as the best of a bad batch of tryouts…

"Christ." Layla stood next to the bed, temporarily overcoming the weird shaky feeling enough to snatch up and hug a plump pillow, its case plain white cotton like the sheets. "Everyone I ever really talked to is dead."

Suze, the bright bubbly cheerleader, had always looked set to achieve escape velocity from their hometown. Layla would never have believed *she* was the one to travel, even if only in junked-down jalopies looking for free wi-fi to download more forum posts, collating sightings, research, bona fides. Or to sit with rapidly warming Cokes in crappy rundown honky-tonks while the men talked in low voices over cheap beers about patterns, firepower, endlessly shooting the shit.

The shit was now done shot, Meemaw would say.

Layla had been content being Suze's longest-term bestie, content to tag along with Dan's great revenge quest, mostly content to do research, lookout, decoy, laundry. At least she was *needed*.

What was she now? Alone, infected with vampirism, and literally fucked several ways from Sunday.

She didn't even know what day of the goddamn *week* it was. Layla swayed back and forth, clutching the pillow, staring at the half-made bed, and wondered if the vampire was ever coming back.

And what she'd do if he didn't.

The lights didn't flicker, nor was there really any warning sound. But the strangling leap her heart gave a bare moment before Max winked into existence right inside the door—and the invisible curtain—nearly knocked her down, and the brush of warm air across the room was such a relief she also let out a strangled yelp.

He swayed, and she dropped the chair—she'd been poking in desultory fashion at the force-field, more out of boredom than expecting real effects. The chair's back hit plain beige carpet very near her bare feet, and the next thing she knew she was next to the vampire, grabbing at the waistband of his Carhartts.

Or what was left of them, because it looked like he'd been run through a meat grinder, passed over a hot barbecue, and dipped in seventeen flavors of holy old hell besides. The guck was layer-crusted in some places, steaming in others, and a great deal of it looked like blood.

Dried, and fresh. Along with multiple strata of other crap she couldn't hope to identify.

He let out a weary sigh, one muscled arm curling over her shoulders, and she had to hope he wouldn't fall straight down because he was a lot heavier than he had any right to be— certainly he outweighed *her*, by a long shot—and ending up under a heap of dead vampire was a terrible, terrible prospect.

They're supposed to go poof and go grainy, though, aren't they? The others did. He didn't look dusty, though, which was a relief.

Sort of.

Max took two drunk-staggering steps away from the invisible curtain. Then he half-turned, threw his other arm around her, and went utterly still. Which ended up smooshing Layla's cheek against his broad, filthy chest, his chin resting atop her head, his entire body curving protectively around hers.

He was breathing, at least. The *ka-thump*, pause, *ka-thump* was back, and she knew what it was now, beyond a doubt.

Layla was vaguely aware of babbling. "Oh no, no no no. You're gonna be okay. You're gonna be all right, Max."

What the fuck? Have you forgotten what he did to you? But still, she couldn't stop stupidly chanting comfort, her natural reflex to care for a stranger in need drowning nearly every other consideration.

At least until the invisible curtain got taken down. Would she ever see outside this stupid two-room prison again?

He repeated the sigh, and she realized he was sniffing her hair. Inhaling in great gasps, in fact, as a wave of shudders passed through his very large, very hard frame.

"What *happened*?" Muffled and frantic, she couldn't move. His arms had tightened just short of crushing; plus, even beaten to hell with his clothes reduced to dirt-crusted shreds, something hadn't changed. He still had a respectable hard-on, and it was shoved right up against her. "Max? Max, *talk to me.*"

"One moment, *puella mea.*" The last bit was a little slurred. "None of the blood is mine."

Are you sure? She'd seen a lot of bravado while hanging out with vampire hunters, but this was in a whole different league. "You look awful. What the hell hap—"

"*Pax*, sweet Leila." At least the near-drunken slurring eased up, though he didn't let go of her. He'd turned into a statue. "Let me be reassured of my leman."

Reassured? You absolute asshole. "I'm the one locked up down here if something happens to you." She couldn't even wriggle away; the goop on him smelled awful, but the worst was the nasty edge to the thin, curling steam rising from several gaps in his clothing. Had he gotten hit by a car-bomb, like the biter who took out Shawn's crew? "But I'll bet you never even thought about that, did—"

"You have a lovely voice. Keep scolding me." Did he sound *amused*?

For fuck's sake. Now she was sorry she'd been worried, even in the slightest and for only a few heartbeats. The fact that she was about to read a goddamn *vampire* the riot act was somewhere between disturbing and justifiable. "You are a jackass."

"And you are the gift of a goddess, turning me into a man." He exhaled sharply; his grasp loosened—but only a fraction. "How do you feel?"

How do I feel? "Like I was left in a prison cell while you went off and did something stupid. I could starve to death down here; do you even care?"

And now she was certifiably nuts. She'd gone from being terrified he'd kill her to being worried about vampire impregnation, to absolutely wanting to *shake* a big dumb lug who—all things considered—reminded her a bit of Ackerman.

"I told you the seals would release upon my death. Not that you need worry on that count." He drew himself up and very gently unwound his arms only to take her shoulders, pushing her back a step, two. Then he examined her, his eyes glittering in a mask of crud, his curls full of sticky-looking grit. "How do you feel? Do you thirst? I will feed you, and then—"

"Oh no you don't." Layla tried to pull away, achieved nothing, and settled for glaring up at him through strands of her own hopelessly tangled hair. "You're not getting me tripped out on monster blood while you're all covered in guck. Come on, right to cleanup with you. Do you have a first-aid kit?" If he did, it was hidden so well she couldn't find it; she'd been over every inch of the place.

"Unnecessary." A short, sharp shake of his head, tiny glittery flakes dropping free of gleaming dark curls, and he let go of her —slowly, one finger at a time. "But very well."

I am bossing around a two-thousand-year-old biter. How long had he left her down here? "Are you going to tell me what happened?"

"I found the battlefield, and somewhat more. You may be pleased to know there are many less sanguinant in this city now. Though that is a mercy of short duration, I am afraid." His boots were scarred but whole, making soft whispering sounds as he turned away, gliding for the bathroom; there was a small cascade of ripping and the ruins of his sweater were torn free. Muscle flickered in his back, deeply defined straps and shapes.

She also spotted glaring, livid stripes under the dirt. Layla's jaw nearly dropped, and she hurried in the vampire's wake.

CHAPTER 18

sacrificed a damp towel to scrubbing and almost wished his
leman were a bath attendant with a scraper and a pot of oil.
Despite that, modern plumbing was more than worth the lack of
such civilized pleasures; the tub was full before he finished the
brute work of cleansing.

He would have very much liked to see her in a chiton, bare-
limbed and intent upon the work of tending her soldier's skin. A
useless, impossible phantasy, but pleasant nonetheless.

She leaned in the bathroom doorway, watched him scrub
caked grit and blood from his hair, and when he tossed the
blackened towel upon the pile of spent clothing Leila finally
spoke.

"What are those?" One graceful, finely boned hand, pointing.
Even the frailty of her wrists was so achingly beautiful; he would
have liked to simply stand and gaze in wonder, though she
might find such scrutiny unnerving.

"Hm?" He lifted his arm, gazed down at his ribs. Was she
concerned for his wellbeing? Unlikely, so she must be merely
curious. Still, it was a sign of interest, and deserved a proper

answer. "Claws. That one was a fledgling; he forgot to strike a little lower. Silly."

"You…" She swallowed, hard, pale eyes round. The Gift was burning bright in her, stripping away mortality, burnishing her skin, her hair alive with blue highlights under electric glow. "On your back, too?"

There was no shortage of injuries upon his corpus, most closed solely by force of will at the moment. A hard-won skill, semi-consciously encouraging a sanguinant's natural healing capability, and one which separated elders who would survive a little longer from those who might more easily fall to glut or killing-sleep.

The stripes would fade over the course of a few feedings, though the marks could be disconcerting at first. "Scratches. I am not of an age to bleed easily."

"But don't they hurt?" A child's question, or simple empathy. She was so very tender, a statue of Hebe the Merciful brought to bright rosy life.

Sometimes pain is best. Judiciously applied, agony could be used to hold off the creeping stony numbness for a short while. Yet too much and the edge was lost, apathy rising despite ever more severe injury. "At first. Not now."

He was clean enough, the soldier decided. Lowering himself into hot water almost wrung a groan from his throat, perilously close to an old mortal's noise. A short soak, then he would feed her; he could admit she was correct, it was entirely unfit for a leman to be sullied with the corpse-remnants of several sanguinant and dogsbodies, even if much of the former had burned away into steam and the latter had also served to fuel his combat.

He had drunk deep, conscious of the need to carry sustenance to his prize. And now he also possessed an edge no other living creature knew.

For once, it was enough.

"I'm sorry." A flush mounted to her soft, sculpted cheeks. "I'll leave you alone so you can—"

"No." *Please.* He could beg, if necessary. It would not take much effort at all; this was far more pleasant than one of Father's punishments. "Speak to me, if you will. It was a… an eventful night."

Sweet Leila lingered, visibly weighing the invitation. "Are you sure?"

"Very." *You cannot know how much.*

Perhaps his visible weariness overcame her trepidation; she tiptoed into the bathroom and sank to kneel upon tiled floor, gazing over the tub's rim. "What happened?"

Maximus tried to imagine her concern was affectionate, but phantasy only stretched so far. There were far more insistent, not to mention practical, problems to hand. "I was sent to this territory to kill a certain sanguinant."

"Roger Griskov, right?" Was she anxious to please, or to show some knowledge of the demimonde? Her arm twitched, perhaps wishing to settle against the rim; she leaned back slightly at the same moment, denying the urge. "The guy who owns the Blue Moon Spot."

"Is that the name he was using?" The need for mortal identities would become far more marked now that he had a leman to care for. A welcome challenge, far gentler than his usual duties. "He was known in the Blood as Esmond the Varangian."

"That's a mouthful." Layla hesitated, then crossed her arms after all, resting her elbows on the tub-rim and regarding him solemnly. Her eyes gleamed, the sweet curve of her mouth no longer tight with pain. "He generally left the club at around 2am, heading back uptown to that big old mansion. We were going to get him in transit that night, if he showed."

Brave for mortals, especially considering their few numbers and the pathetically small amount of weaponry in their derelict camp. Either courageous, or exceedingly stupid—but the attempt had brought a leman across his path.

A god's gift, indeed; he could grant them that much. Maximus studied her expression, the exact curve of her forearm pressed against the tub's lip, the soft flush to her cheeks, still so painfully thin. She required much more feeding—another pleasant duty. The mating-thrall was entirely, agonizingly alert now, focused unblinking upon her every breath, each slight shift, the pulse fluttering in her throat.

"I was lookout," she continued. "Me and Pete. I recognized you from the files." Was that a flash of hope, transparent in those blue-grey eyes? Or was she simply exhausted from a night spent safely trapped, anxiously feeling the weight of approaching dawn upon an almost-fledgling body?

In any case, she had no one else to speak to.

"I see." Maximus held to stillness, letting the water settle. It was possible to wait until the fluid was smooth as glass, a some-times-interesting test of patience, but the sight might disturb her. To keep her visible, and calm, for as long as possible was another battle, far more intense and satisfying than simply clearing terri-tory. "You may consider Esmond no further danger to anyone, sanguinant or mortal."

Would the news please her?

"That's good, I guess." Her brow was wrinkled, however, that positively adorable frown of concentration. "He does some horrible... I had to go over the files pretty extensively, and they were awful. Was it the blood-crazy? Is that what you call it?"

"Some, perhaps." How could he explain to this earnest, deli-cate miracle that cruelty was often an end in and of itself, espe-cially to one judged worthy of the Dark Gift? Every child of the Blood was once a mortal, their natural capacity for violence given refinement and intensity by virtue of longer lifespan and greater strength.

"Well, there was a bounty on him and we needed the fund-ing." Yes, she was clearly anxious to please. Currying favor with her captor was a brave, intelligent move, especially as the sharp tang of fear colored her mouthwatering scent. "But you probably know all about that."

He was aware of mortal hunters financing their vendettas in various fashion. Most often their efforts were an irritant; to hold a nest or a territory long-term, judicious cleansing of those sanguinant liable to attract mortal notice was advisable. "Somewhat." *Let her stay. Let her be soothed.* "I learned a great deal tonight."

Now, safely behind seals and breathing her in great starving lungfuls, he could think upon the entire lesson-list.

Primus: Father had sent William to eliminate a powerful eldest son grown too ossified for proper duty.

Secundus: Maximus could safely assume it was not—or not solely—because the patriarch suspected a descendant's strength surpassed the Maker's. Had that been the case, a single soldier would not be nearly sufficient. No, it had to be that Nemesis was seen as no longer useful enough, being caught in age-rigidity— which the chance appearance of a leman had now freed him of, but that was a different matter.

Tertius: The plan had clearly been for Maximus to be murdered while exhausted from achieving Esmond's murder, or the Varangian would at least be weakened by an unsuccessful attempt and finally dispatched by the second attacker.

Either way, Antinous won the territory and Maximus had not been expected to survive. Yet all plans had foundered upon a single nail—sweet star-eyed Leila, now watching him so very closely.

Which led Maximus to another list of logical certainties. *Primus*: William had discovered the fact of a leman and sought to challenge for the prize. *Secundus*: Esmond, questioned before his violent death, had also been aware, most likely from the same source—the hotel staff, though mortal, had been possessed of enough puzzle-pieces for a wary opponent to suspect the event. Not only that, but any surveillance footage would grant more than one clue.

More logic, unreeling in a chain. Had the woman Maximus was sighted with been a mere fledgling, he would not have acted thus. His behavior had not been the irrationality of ossification but instead must be something else.

For another thing was known of Nemesis: He had never made a child of the Blood before.

Ergo, for his opponents, there was only one possible explanation.

He was adrift in the sheer luxury of thinking clearly, of *knowing* he possessed clarity because his leman's fragrance enfolded him, because she rested so near. He would gladly fight a thousand such bloody campaigns—or more—to win even a fraction of that gift.

"Yeah?" Leila's gaze avoided his, skated across his chest, touched on the small hollow before his shoulder, skipped away. She rested her pointed chin upon her wrists, though his lovely prize was not nearly so relaxed as the posture might suggest. "What did you learn?"

"I was sent here to die." A simple truth, perhaps all she needed at the moment. "Indeed, I was very close to true-death; I was calcified, growing sloppy and apathetic."

"I can't imagine *that,*" his leman muttered.

"Thank you," he replied, gravely.

Leila stared at him for a moment, the very picture of startlement. Then, amazingly, she began to laugh—warm, merry chuckles, casting slight ripples across hot water.

Suddenly, none of the night's wounds ached even slightly. Maximus stared at her, mouth slightly open; his leman wrapped her arms about her middle, rocking back and forth, her shining dark hair swaying, every trace of watchfulness or fear fled for an endless, marvelous few moments.

It was enough to make him forget what lay ahead. This outpost was still under watch, the city's exits—roads and other-wise—still barred by sanguinant who had no loyalty to Esmond. Which could only mean Father was coming, perhaps only to view his new territory, perhaps to do what William had been unable to.

Follow the logic, soldier. There was another possibility, one he must account for.

Maybe, just maybe, Antinous also now knew of her existence, and meant to take what his eldest son had found.

CHAPTER 19

delivered so deadpan she just couldn't help it. Once started, she also couldn't seem to stop, and was a little afraid she'd hurt herself by the time the laughter bubbled down to stray rivulets.

It was hard to be afraid of a naked vampire in a bathtub. Of course, trying not to look at anything impolite was an exercise in futility; she couldn't help but stare at bit at his proudly erect cock; did he just wander around all day with a hard-on? That seemed uncomfortable as all hell, according to everything Layla had heard. More to the point, his undercarriage seemed regular human-shaped despite the hazy memory of a different feeling buried in her own body. *Barbed,* he'd said—or had she just imagined it?

Thank goodness she was sober at the moment, not high on monster blood. The memory of inebriation was equal parts disturbing and strangely attractive. Was she going to be a biter-blood junkie? That was a question for another time, simply because she didn't want to think about something so terrifying at the moment. She had all she could handle quite literally right in front of her, lounging in a brimming bath.

In any case he seemed utterly unself-conscious of nudity, whether his own or someone else's. Maybe it was being old, maybe it was being a biter, or maybe he'd just had enough time to get over little things like Puritanism.

He *predated* Protestant prudery, in fact, and the thought provoked another wild cascade of chuckles; when Layla finally managed to get herself back under some kind of control she found Max watching her quizzically, wearing a slightly abashed grin as if he didn't really get the joke but was happy to be included.

It was a very *human* expression. Had he loosened up, or was she actually getting used to a bloodsucking monster? She wiped her cheeks, rubbed at her mouth with the back of one hand. Her knees ached a bit, braced against cold tile.

Good Lord, stop cackling. "You're actually pretty funny," she said through a few leftover, hiccupping giggles, and immediately realized it sounded dismissive, or worse. Guys didn't like being laughed at, especially by a woman.

"Good." Thankfully his expression didn't alter, except for the smile widening. He was looking more human by the second. "I… it's been a very long time, since I found any humor in my existence."

That's probably the understatement of the year. Layla sobered, chewing gently at her lower lip. *Oh, my God. Am I getting Stockholm syndrome'd?*

Because at the moment, he really didn't seem that bad. And that was deeply chilling.

Any amusement was well and truly doused. Silence filled the bathroom, slopping against the walls, broken only by the small plink as a drop of water fell from the high-arched faucet over the tub.

She had to say something, break that dangerous quiet. "I was afraid you weren't coming back."

"I told you I would." All hint of levity vanished. Vampire

Max was back to poker-faced intensity, watching her almost hungrily. "I cannot stay away."

Oh, hell. "Please don't leave me locked up again." It didn't matter, since she was in absolutely no position to exert any control here. He was a *biter*, for Chrissake. He'd torn through her entire squad in a matter of heartbeats; only Pete was left, and hopefully her fellow hunter had hightailed it back to his hometown in Montana. "I promised I'd cooperate. And it's not like I have anywhere else to go."

The vampire said nothing. Layla studied his face, carefully; an idea had been in the back of her mind ever since he disappeared, tiptoeing in the darkness like a biter itself.

Steve-o had talked about Army training in case a soldier was captured. From where Layla was sitting, pretty much anything was permissible if it would get her out from behind the invisible force-field, and she could figure out everything else—including what to do about possibly someday craving human blood—later.

It took more courage than she thought she possessed to straighten, balancing on her knees, and extend an arm. Her fingertips hovered a half-inch from Max's shoulder, his deltoid making an almost perfect triangle. Every scrap of him was well-defined muscle and sinew, nothing extraneous; she felt pretty out of shape by comparison.

She took a deep breath, and gently traced the short, brutal scar running down into the hollow between his shoulder and pectoral muscle. Whatever had hit there had cut deep, and she repressed a wince at the thought. The bath had to be hot, but his skin no longer felt feverish despite the steam. Droplets glowed on his coppery tan; the texture was different than human, pore-less and matte, incredibly smooth. Dirt, blood, and other guck wiped off with a towel he'd folded and swiped very efficiently, as if he'd done it so often thought wasn't required.

How many times had he gotten home from a fight covered in God-knew-what, to be that practiced? Just like tying his shoes.

Sure, he'd erased other biters, but he also *had* to have snacked on humans. Which should she concentrate on, what half of the equation carried more weight?

The scars weren't ridged or puckered, just discolored. Had the terrible glaring one trailing across his stomach shrunk a bit, or were her eyes fooling her? She touched the edge of another, a jagged slash across the right side of his chest, and irrationally, now she wondered if Pete's shot at base really had hit him.

Stay on target, Lay. You're about to do something really smart or incredibly stupid.

The vampire didn't even appear to be breathing. Eyelids lowered to half-mast, lashes damp, he stared at her like a starving cat presented with a bowl of kibble.

"Don't lock me up," she whispered. *Let's see how well I can bargain.* "Please?" Her legs were a bit woozy, but she managed to unfold a bit, her palm skating up to touch his neck. The *ka-thump* of his heartbeat continued, nice and steady; she didn't dare peek at the other half of the tub to see if he was still standing to attention, so to speak. Her fingers found his nape, sliding on damp skin, and if she hitched herself up and braced her ribs on the rim, she might be able to get close enough.

Amazingly, the vampire obeyed that gentle pressure, leaning toward her, lowering his head. Water rippled.

Her lips touched his. It was goddamn awkward, balancing precariously on a flared cast-iron edge, her toes slipping against damp tile, and she hoped her breath wasn't horrible. The vague spice in her mouth reminded her of being high on monster blood, and *that* wasn't a thought she needed.

I am no good at this sort of thing. Please let it work, though. I'm trying awful hard.

A splash, a tumbling confusion as she overbalanced, and Layla bit back a surprised yell. Water geysered up—she was lifted, a tug at her waistband, and fabric ripped. Falling, a jolt of impact, another massive splash, and good God the entire bathroom was going to be swamped.

That was beside the point, however. Because Max had, with terrifying, casual strength, simply stood up, carrying her along, and stripped away her sweatpants, not to mention clawed the T-shirt to scraps. Then he simply dropped, controlling the descent with negligent grace, and she was on his lap in a half-full bathtub, clutching those very broad muscled shoulders. A familiar, very insistent pressure poked between her legs, eager to burrow further.

Layla froze, and so did he.

Her ribs, still feeling the rim's imprint, heaved as she tried to sort out what the hell. Her knees were pressed hard against the sides, and if he let go of her waist gravity would help the hard, hot nudge at her opening push deeper. Layla couldn't decide if this was a bad or good sign, especially since he didn't move.

Shit. Oh, goddammit. Did not *expect that.* There was such a thing as a half-baked plan working entirely too well.

Max was still staring at her, heavy-lidded though thankfully without any wet red pinpricks in his pupils. A humming went through stone-hard muscles, leashed strength just on the edge of exploding.

"I will not leave you here alone again." A soft, rumbling whisper.

For a moment the words didn't make sense. Her breath caught, and a strange uncoiling sensation deep in her belly was half terror, half a dark excitement she didn't care to examine more closely.

Oh, my God, do I actually like this? Layla fought to keep her own eyes wide open, to think clearly. "Good." A high-pitched, breathy little word. "Everyone leaves me behind. I'm tired of it."

Was she actually using her body to negotiate with a vampire? She hoped Meemaw wasn't watching from heaven, but then again, Lay had known she'd never reach the pearly gates. There wasn't any point in trying; she'd settle for saving her own miserable life and maybe getting out of here.

The spellbound quality was draining from Max's expression; his gaze sharpened. "I told you I would—"

Don't let him think. Layla wriggled, hips rocking, and plastered her mouth to his, her tongue sliding between thankfully human-seeming teeth. An excruciating moment of worrying whether she was just going to embarrass herself—he could shove her away, decide he didn't like her initiating action, maybe he only got off when she struggled? She knew that was what a lot of guys preferred, thinking a girl was a slut if she acted like she wanted anything at all.

But no, he seemed interested. At least, one part of him was; she slid, aided by silken hot water and gravity, halfway onto his cock.

Not only that, but he returned the kiss with surprising force, inhaling the short sharp hiss she made at sudden penetration. So far, so good—she let herself respond, flutter-probing, hoping she was teasing and tempting instead of licking like a Pomeranian. Kissing was supposed to be a matter of practice, though Suze had averred you either had the knack or you didn't—

She didn't want to think about Suzy. And then, maddeningly, his fingers tensed, biting into her middle. All movement halted, both of them locked in stasis once more.

Goddammit. Really going to make me work for it. Okay. She moved, finding a better angle. Her legs were wrapped around his waist, two people crammed into the tub which all of a sudden seemed to have shrunk, and she hoped she wouldn't get a faucet in the back if things got more active.

Or went badly.

The kiss deepened, a half-familiar numbness filling her mouth. Layla rocked a little, finding he'd cooperate after all, and so far, her halfass, entirely insane plan was going great. Especially since her entire body had lit up, nerves crackling with electricity, fresh jolts rising with every movement, and a wicked, delicious pressure found her clit as well.

How the hell is he doing *that?* But she had to think, she was in a good position—a *great* one—for negotiation, and there wouldn't be a better time.

His mouth pursued when she tried to pull away. It took two tries and tipping her chin up before he got the idea, but that could have been a mistake because he turned his attention to nuzzling down her throat. If he was going to bite, she was absolutely defenseless.

Not that it was a big change. "Max," she whispered. "*Max.* Please. Listen."

"Hm?" A sleepy, inquisitive noise. His hands loosened another fraction; she sank further, an exquisite stretching. "Leila." Drawing out her name, tasting it.

More than once, Layla had been forgotten in a corner while men discussed how bitches used sex to get what they wanted, a certain kind of male laughter *hur-hurr*ing around the room.

She was going to find out if it actually worked. "I'm cooperating," she gasped. "See?"

"Leila…" An honest-to-gosh groan. His movements were a lot less graceful now; he was clearly trying to find her rhythm though she could keep *just* ahead of his attempts, and a heady sense of power rose with the pleasure, filling her skull.

She could keep him off-balance, if only for a little while. It was a wonderful development, a great change, and an absolutely terrifying risk. "Promise me," she cooed. *Am I really doing this? Jesus.* "Promise you won't leave me behind."

The growl started, vibrating in his chest. Strangely, the sound wasn't entirely frightening, if only because she had so much else to worry about before her body took over and everything else was pushed to the sidelines. Oh yes, now she understood how this was power, and could be exercised.

It might be the only currency, the only *control* she had. Fine, she'd use it, for as long as possible.

He made some sort of answer, but the words were strange and harsh, a foreign language. Clearly nothing her few years of high-school Spanish could untangle; Layla pushed at his shoulders, her back arching, still keeping just barely ahead of his attempts to work deeper, to overwhelm.

Then his fangs drove into her throat.

CHAPTER 20

A SINGLE MOUTHFUL OF HONEYSALT AMBROSIA WAS ALL HE COULD safely take from her fragility, but it satisfied as no amount of gorging upon mere mortal or fellow sanguinant could. His leman cried out, a sweet husky sound bouncing from tiled walls and floor; her limbs loosened just a fraction, just enough for her to settle entirely upon his phallus. Driven deep, a blade sunk to the hilt in its dark, willing sheath, every weary year of his existence narrowing to a single point.

All the battle, the striving, the agony was dissolved, shredded to nothingness by the taste of his leman, the feel of her closed about him. Every bloodstained moment, every wound, every cry of murder or victory, every bitter defeat or frenzied plundering was nothing compared to this glory.

She was lost in her own pleasure now, water rippling as she undulated in his arms. Forcing his fangs to slide free and sealing the punctures was a duty he could not avoid, performed swift and thoroughly before freeing a hand to cup the back of her head, guiding her to his mouth once more so she could share the taste of sheer wondrous beauty.

He had the march-pattern now, working with her slight body as velvet heat strangled his shaft. Words vibrated in his throat, riding the battle-roar filling his chest, both beast and mating-thrall howling for possession. Promises, blandishments, endearments he had never thought would escape his lips were lost in the kiss; how could she think he would not return to this?

To *her*?

A great rushing stillness filled the room. Outside, his enemies lurked; those who would steal her slunk to hide in daylight holes. He barely cared at the moment—she was safe, she was his, and she lingered upon the cusp of release, holding off the crisis with maddening intensity, just beyond his reach.

No. I will please you, at least. It is all I am allowed.

That was the punishment of finding something so beautiful, so unstained, and grasping it with bloody hands. He could long for her affection but would only receive a measure of tolerance—if he were lucky, if he were blessed by whatever god had decided, in a momentary fit of graciousness, to drop her in a soldier's path.

More than enough.

So, ruthless as ever in combat, he pursued that stillness. Found it, pressed hard upon the shy swelling nubbin of her *landica*, and tipped his beautiful storm-eyed nymph over the edge.

More cries, her shaking and shuddering, his own body slipping control for a brief eternity, cradling her as the cataclysm raged inside his ageless flesh and her no-longer-wholly mortal form.

It was well past dawn, the Gift already reaching toward the high flame of transition inside his leman; she was clearly weary from a night spent in anxiety. It was easy to slip a bit of the *quietus* over her, the lightest of psychic pressure. He drew a claw along his chest, blood welling to the surface yet held from spilling free, and guided her head downward. Her mouth fastened sleepily on the slash, drawing with exquisite care. Each swallow caused his entire being to thrum, a string played by delicate fingertips, and he let her take full measure before closing the slash.

The floor was no doubt awash. Tub-trapped water cooled to tepid, though a sanguinant's bodyfire could more than heat such a small amount. Maximus was content to simply keep his drowsing prize warm enough. She resisted full sleep for some short while, though he thought she would not be able to do so again. For a slight crackle of bones shifting passed through her slenderness, and as her downy cheek rested against him the tiny movements of jaw and maxilla told him her true teeth were forming.

No pain for his nymph, both the change agents and his ichor providing narcotic ease. Her final metamorphosis into the Blood would be lost in deep restorative slumber; he stroked her dark, silk-clinging hair and enjoyed the last brief peace he might ever know.

When he could slip free of her flesh, he carried her to the bed, arranging her slack dreaming limbs, and tucked her in securely. Clothing himself, rearranging a few items—what had she been doing with the chair, he wondered, before deciding it did not matter—and strengthening the invisible seals occupied him well into daytime. The sun was high overhead; he had until dusk.

Covered with the scent of a divine gift, ringed with the feel of her, his very blood sighing her name, Maximus longed to recline at her side. It was impossible; he was not fit to rest upon a nymph's bed.

Besides, he had to plan.

How many times had he put his back to a wall, sitting with knees drawn up and arms draped loosely, his chin down as he stared at a patch of ground between his heels? Often, during his mortal life, he had done so with gladius lying nearby, his shield propped next to the opposite shoulder, both silent, trusted companions.

After his own violent, agonizing conversion, he had used

almost every weapon mortals could dream of. Eventually his own claws more than sufficed, though there was an elegance to some invented implements. Even an old, strong sanguinant might well require something ingenious to carry out orders.

Or to protect a prize.

What will he do? You know your enemy well, predict him.

Maximus drifted between trance-rest and the peculiar focused concentration of strategic anticipation. Attempting to simply flee this city was certainly preferable, but unlikely to succeed. If even one other sanguinant knew of lovely Leila, he would merely be shifting the battle to another locale. His opponents would not cease the hunt until dead or in possession of a leman; wherever he stopped to rest his prize, the terrain might not be so well suited to his purposes, nor scouted thoroughly enough to be properly utilized.

The ground here was prepared; besides, he now possessed an edge no other creature knew of, not even his sleeping guerdon. There was a time for flight or for withstanding siege, then there came the moment for turning upon pursuit with the fury of a cornered beast.

A better opportunity was exceedingly unlikely to occur, especially since the bond with his leman would only deepen. At this point even a single night spent away was too much; his effectiveness had waned with alarming speed during the final few engagements before dawn.

Besides, if his now-chief opponent's opening move was as Maximus suspected, Leila might well be broken by complete terror, though physically unharmed inside the seal. Even a leman driven to feral insanity was too precious to lay aside, and he could keep her contained for centuries while patiently waiting for recovery.

Yet he did not wish to, especially if by some mischance he did not kill his enemy and the hunt commenced. No matter which way he turned the situation inside his skull-case, a logical conclusion was unavoidable. He *must* win here, now, and entirely. There was one slim chance to surpass all previous battles, a single gamble he would never have a better chance at winning.

Fellow sanguinant called him Nemesis, and apparently even mortals heard those whispers; if he accomplished this, he could consider himself worthy of the name. Never mind it had been first granted by Father—no.

By *Antinous*. He could no longer call his Maker anything but a danger to be eradicated.

Sweet Leila would more than likely grow to despise him, as he could now admit he hated the one who had seen a dying soldier upon a Hispania battlefield and granted the Gift almost as an afterthought. Maximus had survived the change, and for millennia he had fought when commanded, killed when required, drank oceans of blood, trampled those Antinous wished erased.

No more. This would see an end to it, one way or another. His only regret was for what his nymph would have to suffer upon the next dusk.

CHAPTER 21

Her evil plan had worked; he apparently wasn't going to leave her imprisoned much longer. Which was such great news Layla almost didn't mind flicking into consciousness like a light switch and nearly levitating off the bed in a single twitch.

If she could just stop losing her clothes, she'd call it a definite win. The torn sweats were part of a sodden heap in the corner of the bathroom, along with the ruins of Max's yesterday outfit plus a towel full of congealed grit and dried blood, topped with the shirt he'd sliced off her last night when the bathtub interaction really got going.

Thank God he didn't seem ready for a rematch. Instead, he watched while she used the sole clean washcloth to scrub up in approved vampire-hunter fashion, and he even laid out the chifforobe's very last supplies on the bed, which was now neatly made with hospital corners.

Apparently vampires, unlike human males, could do basic housekeeping.

He was just the same—sweater, trousers, boots. But he'd cut down a T-shirt and the last pair of Carhartts for her, and torn the last T-shirt into strips to act as a belt. The work pants were still ridiculously balloon-y, but her legs weren't bare and he might not rip the tough fabric quite so easily.

It was a cheerful thought.

"So we're going to make a break for it?" She was almost lost inside his last clean sweater, attempting to find the neck, floundering in what felt like acres of black wool. "Because this Father-guy—"

"Antinous." His accent was a lot less janky now, but the name sounded super ancient anyway. Max tugged at the sweater hem, held the shoulders so she could get her arms through, and perhaps there was a ghost of a smile lingering in his set, remote expression as she rolled the sleeves up and irritably shoved her hair back.

The deep, inalienable sense of physical health had intensified, if that were possible. The only trouble was the lights glaring— had he turned them up while she slept? And even if she wasn't craving monster blood her mouth still felt weird, as if she'd just had a thorough cleaning by a not particularly gentle dentist. Still, she felt as if she had a reasonable handle on the last few days; so long as she kept thinking about the most immediate problem, she wouldn't have to dwell on, for example, her prospective status as a biter.

Did other vampires adjust the same way? Could she somehow reverse the process? If, for example, Max met with an accident before she got a mouthful of human blood… the stories were conflicting, movies and folklore swilling around and the dark web forums full of argument on that score.

One problem at a time, Layla.

Her hair wasn't hopelessly knotted, either, any tangles parting under mere finger-pressure. Layla tipped her head back and decided on the tightest French braid she could manage, since they were going to be moving fast. No elastics, but she could make do with a strip of T-shirt or trouser hem. "Antinous, yeah. Okay. What do you need me to do?"

It actually felt fucking wonderful to be planning an operation. Maybe Max, all two-thousand years of expertise, wanted a vampire-hunting partner?

A tiny worm of pride poked its head up in Layla's chest, though there was plenty not-so-good to be had in recent events. Such as, oh, ninety-nine percent of her crew being eradicated and this guy being directly responsible, as well as his habit of tearing her clothes off *and* the fact that she'd basically seduced him last night.

Maybe she was turning into a monster, a real Dracula hoochie. If that got her out of hock and with a clear shot at escape, though, it could be worth the price. Teaming up with hunters you didn't personally like was part of the game.

The truly inescapable question returned, like a dedicated bill collector. *What if you end up snacking on humans, though?*

"I would ask…" Max trailed off.

When she turned, he was studying her, dark eyes narrowed and his mouth a thin line.

Ohfuck. Had she made a mistake right out of the gate? She stared back, fingers frozen, her throat suddenly dry with fear instead of yesterday's terrible, consuming thirst, and even the sense of buzzing, energetic well-being couldn't cover a jolt of dark red fear.

The steady *ka-thump* of his heartbeat didn't alter. He could almost certainly hear her nervous, jumping pulse.

He took a step closer, then another. Layla stood, arms raised, stupidly holding a half-finished braid, and could not even begin to tell what he was going to do.

But he halted just at the edge of her personal space, gazing down at her. What was it like to be so tall, so powerful? She'd extracted a promise to not leave her locked up again, but really there was no recourse if he decided on take-backsies—or even just 'forgot', the way men always did when they didn't care for an agreement.

"You are in full transition," Max said, finally. "Much stronger and swifter than a mortal, though those may still inadvertently damage you with fragmenting ammunition. I will clear any dogsbodies present as a matter of course, but accidents happen. Listen to your body, it will protect you so far as it can. As for the sanguinant..." His lip lifted; she watched, fascinated, as the full set of fangs appeared with a slight creak-crackle noise, then retreated before he continued as if he hadn't just snarled like a wolf. "As for them, once you are scented no bearer of the Blood will risk damaging you. Fledglings will be dizzied by your proximity and strike at those nearby in an attempt to weed out other claimants. The elders will drive the battle away from your vicinity if possible, always seeking to catch you. And there is a very high chance you will be caught."

That's a lot to take in. "Once I'm scented?"

"You are leman." Flatly, maybe daring her to disagree. "The least hint of you will alter the battlefield completely; other fledglings will be made outright drunk by your presence."

Which brought up the question of the two young biters her crew had dispatched. Even Ben had commented on how they'd both gone straight for Layla; for a single mad instant she considered telling Max about that, seeing what he'd say.

Thankfully, sanity hurried to reassert itself. If this guy found out she'd been party to vampire murder, it might convince him to change his mind, leave her imprisoned for another night.

Or for good. And that, as Suze would say, was *no bueno at all.*

"So..." Layla worked all the information around in her head, arriving at what she hoped were reasonable conclusions. There were concerning bits, like *once you are scented* and *you will be caught.* Still, she could figure out the details later. Right now, she had to appear at least mildly useful, and thankfully she had a bit of experience in that department. "So you need me to decoy? That's great."

Max settled on his heels briefly, as if physically pushed back by the notion. "Great?"

"Yeah. I mean, my main duties are research and logistics, but I've been the lookout before. Decoy duty is like that—it's how we got… never mind." A strange, almost crazed relief filled her chest; he must have been worried she wouldn't understand the concept. As heady as seducing a vampire was, the proof that he considered her capable of actual work was an additional shot in the arm of her self-esteem. At the moment, she'd take anything. "So which direction do you want me to go?" *I don't even know where the hell we are.* She resumed braiding, her fingers suddenly working again.

"It does not matter." Max's expression had changed again, gazing down at her like she'd done something incredibly unexpected—or made an embarrassing bodily noise, it was a fifty-fifty bet. "The important thing is to submit if you are caught. Do not struggle. You may be jolted during transit, but you will not be injured; do as you are told. Survive, and I will arrive to collect you apace. Do you understand?"

Do as you're told was pretty clear. Still, Layla didn't like the sound. "Collect me?"

"Of course." The snarl returned, though his teeth thankfully didn't change this time. Red pinpricks glittered in the center of his pupils for a brief, heartstopping moment. "It is a terrible thing I ask of you, Leila. You will see a great deal of savagery this night, but understand this: *I will find you.* All you must do is survive until dawn."

"Dawn." Her internal clock was all fuckered up; she swallowed hard. Seeing his eyes light up like that was pretty horrible. Would her own do the same, on some distant day? "Sure. What time is it now?"

"It is just past dusk. Now, listen. You are for all intents and purposes a fledgling. When the sun rises, you will sleep—if we are separated and you are by some chance not held by an enemy, you must find a place well away from daylight to do so. Anaphylactic shock and combustion are unpleasant, and I will not have you thus harmed. Understood?"

His tone was oddly familiar, like Shawn giving orders to his crew or Dan laying out an operation. "Ten-four." Her braid was finished; she had to move in order to get a strip of material from the pile on the unmade bed. "I need something to tie this with."

Max was silent as she tied her hair, maybe doubting her comprehension. She was used to that from male creatures, even if he clearly expected her to hold her own on decoy duty. Now she wondered if he'd been watching their team, judging performance, and selected her?

Nah, couldn't be. She could brood over the hows and whys to her heart's content once she was out of this goddamn prison. Right now the important thing was getting free—the calm, flat *you are a fledgling* statement took second place to the prospect of fresh air, even if it arrived with another vampire or two and one of those snarling, car-destroying fights.

While the biters were all occupied with each other, she might be able to slip away. Her chances were better if she had some kind of superspeed now. The problem of blood-drinking, though...

Oh, God. Focus on what's in front of you.

She shook her braid and bounced on her toes lightly, glad he hadn't destroyed her boots. She looked ridiculous and the sweater was too heavy for a summer night, but that didn't matter. *Run away and find a place to hunker down, let the vampires sort it out* wasn't exactly a cheerful prospect, and the whole *if you're taken do as you're told* thing could take a flying fuck at a rolling donut, as Suze used to cheerfully intone when talking about bitchy customers at the craft depot.

What if she ended up caught by another vampire like Max? Of course, he seemed pretty one of a kind.

The sense of invisible eyes on her returned, now so strong she spun, searching for the source.

Had it always been him?

Max's shoulders had sagged, and he looked... well, almost

tired. Like Dan late at night, staring again at Suze's autopsy photos, dull suffering rage unable to find an outlet. Some of O'Shaughnassey's guys had worn the same expression when they thought nobody was looking; so had Ackerman during the long drive toward this city, his finger tapping the Wrangler's steering wheel as a preacher on AM radio ranted about Judgment Day.

Her heart hurt, another familiar sensation. "Don't worry." Another of her duties, to cheer everyone up before go-time. "I know how to run, been doing it for years now. Where are we meeting up?"

Which was strange—did she really intend to rendezvous, not just head for the hills while he was busy with a whole bunch of other biters?

Except *she* was a biter now, too. How many of them had been forced into it? What was she going to do when she got that terrible word, *thirsty*?

So far she felt all right, but that could be leftover monster blood. Layla was going to have to face facts sooner or later, always an unpleasant chore. Anaphylactic shock and combustion—baby biters couldn't survive daylight, she knew that much.

If all else failed she could head out into the desert and wait for sunrise, right? That way, she wouldn't hurt anyone else.

Not like you've done a helluva lot of good in your life anyway. Might as well.

Max tilted his head, a feline, listening look. "Do you hear? They are firing the wells."

What does that mean? She strained her ears. A thud, a soft faraway hissing, the vibration lingering just at the bottom of audible if she concentrated. "What wells?"

"Petroleum. Hardly *flamme Grecque*, but still deadly to mortals and anything short of an Archon." His eyes half-closed, and a breathless, staticky sense of lightning about to strike pervaded the bedroom. "It will mask your scent unless they draw very close, which may be what Antinous intends. He knows I have hunted in burning cities; this will be no different."

Holy shit. It took a couple tries before she could speak. At least now she knew sort of where this place was located. "You mean we're near the oil fields? And they're on fire?" *That… does not sound good.*

"I could leave you here and the seals would keep this space intact, though the lights would almost certainly be cut." Max spoke quietly, absently, *just the facts, ma'am.* "Yet Antinous will not show himself unless there is a chance to acquire you, and should I avoid this battle he will not cease hunting us in different locations. The world is wide, but if he chooses to let it be known I have a leman? Any sanguinant possessed of a little might will flock to wherever we rest; he will follow, and eventually I may be worn down. Whoever kills me will be gravely wounded, thus easy to dispatch, and then—"

"Hold the fuck on. I thought he was after you, not me." Layla was feeling *distinctly* pale now; her legs, despite the bolstering of monster blood, turned a bit gooshy at the knees. "How… what the *hell*—"

"You will not forgive me," Max said, almost gently. "No sanguinant should ever use their leman as bait."

Layla's jaw indeed dropped; she now knew what it was like to be so surprised she stood literally fishmouthed. A muffled *thwock*, sounding very far away, shivered through the bedroom.

The lights did indeed go out; a deep terrible rushing filled her ears, and a vampire's stone-muscled arms closed around her once more.

The worst thing wasn't the sudden wet-bandage darkness, a complete absence of light which only lasted a moment as she was pressed into his chest. They rose through a dim, quaking, rumbling space which might have been stairs, took a sharp left turn, and exploded through a wall—or window, since the high sweet tinkle of broken glass chimed atop a steady increasing roar.

Sticky, sultry air loaded with concentrated bursts of scent, pictures arriving on each jolt. Dry dirt, yellow grass, metal heated to a dull red glow, and a thick black bubbling smell like tar softening to liquid on county roads during a heatwave. Bright orange blossoms flared in every direction, choking black smoke columns swaying skyward, and the simmering prickle of an approaching thunderstorm covered her back and arms under the T-shirt and sweater.

It was like being on a hellish, rickety carnival ride, changing direction in sharp wrenching reverses which might have turned her stomach inside out if she'd had anything but monster blood for the past couple days. The nausea was sudden, terrible, and unable to complete itself; she couldn't even vomit to feel better.

Layla was almost grateful when a horrific impact slammed in from the right and she was spinning, weightless, flying.

Up and down changed places in sickmaking do-si-do, the world blur-whirring around her, and she had time to think *this is gonna hurt* before she hit.

The biggest shock was that it *didn't*. Stunned and breathless, Layla found herself at full stop, crouching on a deeply bent right leg, her left foot straight out to the side, ankle impossibly bent and bootsole braced flat. Her right hand slapped sandy dirt, her left flung straight out, fingers relaxed as a ballerina's; a small nearby shrub bush rattled warningly.

Did I just do a superhero landing? Far-fucking-out, man. That last bit was all Steve, but she didn't have time to think about her dead… friends? *Crew* was a better word, but…

The roar was massive, titanic, a dinosaur screaming in theater surround-sound. A wall of dry oven-heat rushed past. The orange glares were oil pumps, their heads no longer nodding; a few were twisted like paper and glowing, deformed by billow-ing, liquid orange flame with bright yellow at its heart, the earth's blood turning to smoke in an oddly gorgeous panorama of destruction.

"Holy *shi—*" she began, but a smear of motion tumbled past, thrumming growls briefly slicing the many-throated fire-howl.

Her vision was amped to max, her ears full of crackle-hissing cacophony, her tongue glued to the roof of her mouth. A sudden reflexive movement flung her sideways; Layla ended up crouched next to a giant metal tank, its rounded white-painted sides groaning sharply as another wall of heat swept past.

Not good, not good at all.

Another leap, and she began to get the hang of it. Like rolling down Pratton Hill on a dare in middle school, her one claim to hometown fame. Nobody else was crazy enough to take that steep incline with bike, board, or inlines; she'd done it on Meemaw's ancient rattling four-wheel skates.

Jimmy Nanourek, remember him? Always saying my mama was a groupieslut, and then dared me to go down Pratton.

She'd shut him up but good. The memory was sharp and awful, though curiously darkened, as if seen through tinted glass. Layla gulped a burst of smoke-drenched air and coughed, her eyes streaming.

The flameburst darkness was alive with shadows zipping here and there, a tingle at her nape as she realized what they were.

Vampires.

No. *Sanguinant.*

They streaked between the flames-pillars with eerie floating grace, and the thought that she was seeing more biters in a few square feet than most professional hunters ever did in a lifetime was both hilarious and horrifying.

Especially when several of the streaks swirled like ink on a greased plate, swooping toward her.

A soft, searing breeze eddied—she realized the biters were moving fast to avoid the heat, and also clearly *searching* for something—as a vampire coalesced in front of her. A stocky blond man in a slightly disarranged pale linen suit, full lips pulled back to expose a full set of gleaming fangs, bright blue eyes narrowed and wet, vivid crimson sparks dilating in his pupils.

Oh dear God. Layla darted a gaze to her left, her only avenue of escape, and the biter blurred into motion.

Then he disintegrated, rivulets of rot speeding through his entire frame before a shower of glittering grit exploded in every direction, and Max was there, regal nose slightly wrinkled, shaking his hands briskly as if finishing a disagreeable chore. His claws were out, long and pointed, his hair was a floating mess of curls brushed by heat-currents, and his eyes glowed liquid red from lid to lid. He bent, as if inviting her to dance; her hand reached up of its own accord, and she was yanked away as the tank behind her creaked sharply again.

Then it exploded.

A giant, invisible hand pushed her and Max along, wheeling and tumbling, and the oily biter-streaks collecting in their wake vanished into an expanding edge of shimmering white flame. High, desperate screams burst diamond-bright through the roaring. The world was a madly whirling kaleidoscope, pushing and pulling in random directions as he flew between flame-bolts, through caustic, eye-blurring smoke-veils, breaking through bands of relative coolness. Smoke scraped her lungs, and she coughed rackingly against his shoulder.

Through the smoke-mask she smelled him—a mix of brunet musk, sharp peppery determination, and copper, a deep restful scent with a strange mixed-in floral tang somehow saying *Layla* as well as *Max, biter, male, old.* The mental images made little sense, but the smell reached through the confusion, and the relief flooding her was so intense she could have cried.

Why is that? What the hell?

Sudden stop, nearly jolting all her innards free. Set gently on her feet, Layla had the strange sensation of wanting to stagger, but her body wouldn't let her.

Max cast a quick glance over one brawny shoulder. Tiny spark-dots clung to his clothing—biter dust, she realized, each particle sending up minuscule threads of vapor as it finished cooking. He looked down at her again, the wet crimson light in his eyes snuffed—they were dark, human holes in his face now. "Stay hidden, stay still," he said, quietly but clearly. "Unless you sense a sanguinant approach, then run. If you are caught, *do not resist*. Stay alive. I will find you."

You got it. Another harsh flurry of coughing strangled any reply she could make but he was gone anyway, a puff of smoke-scent and a burst of that comforting, calming cologne.

That ain't aftershave, honey. That's him. She was shivering despite the sticky air, Layla realized, as well as hugging herself. Tiny prickles bloomed where her lengthening nails poked through the sweater's flopping, sloppily folded cuffs. Her hair felt crispy, her skin shiny, the fire's breath a terrible clinging haze.

She was, she realized, plonked smack-dab in the middle of a greenbelt at the edge of a residential district. Dusty, indifferently watered backyards faded into this fringe, before the landscape turned into a long slope leading to the oilfield. Tract houses built on a choice of six-or-so plans—Meemaw had often taken little Layla driving through similar neighborhoods at Christmastime, looking at the lights—all extended their cracked driveway tongues, cars with dusty hoods and windshields reflecting street-lamp glow. Behind her, the rumble took a deep breath and ballooned, sending a hot breeze through rustling branches.

Max had gone back into that inferno.

The sky was a solid dish of cloud swirling with packed-together dots of light; somehow, Layla realized she was seeing stars *through* the heavy overcast. A short sigh of wonder cracked on another cough; she was placed just at the edge of a smoke-smell rivulet. It was probably to shield her from being sniffed out, like a rabbit in a shallow hole.

When her chin tipped back down, a tingle at her nape whispering *danger,* sanguinant shadows streaked through the neighborhood.

Oh, hell. Layla's legs folded instinctively. She crouched behind a thin, rustling screen of leaves and prayed none of the biters would notice little ol' her.

CHAPTER 22

An Archon could bathe in open flame without hurt, it was said. Perhaps they were indeed sanguinant evolved past the summa of daywalking, others averred they were some other demimonde species, though they were said to feed as the children of the Blood did.

He had never met one, and in any case it did not matter.

Half a fractional miscalculation amid the plumes of burning spelled a bright, terrible moment of consumption for a sanguinant elder, no matter how mighty; even the shimmering flows of heated air could tumble a fledgling to the ground and lodge a single spark in eminently flammable skin, hair, clothes. To move in such conditions required care and experience.

To fight while doing so required skill, age, defiance, and a healthy dose of luck.

Twisting, turning, looping, driving a group of elder sanguinant into a wall of flame and veering aside at the last moment, a fledgling's head separating from its neck with a *crack* unheard in the roaring of a burn-beast fed from the veins of earth itself, predicting the likely escape routes of those who decided a leman could not possibly be found in such a hellscape, arriving just in time to send his fellow children of the Blood to whatever underworld awaited their kind—his concentration was a still single point, the rest of him whirling about the memory of grey-blue eyes, wide and soft.

Nobody needs me. There was much to achieve, not least discovering why precisely she would say something so outlandish, but to do so he must needs be alive by dawn.

And every other sanguinant in the city dead, including Antinous. The soldier now knew beyond a doubt that his Maker was aware of the prize, for among the score of elders and as many fledglings roaming the burning wasteland were familiar faces, recognized battle-patterns.

No doubt many were intelligent enough to realize their patriarch was using them against each other. Yet the lure of a leman was overwhelming, a gamble well worth the risk even for fledglings barely past first glut.

For those in Antinous's many territories who thought leman a mere phantasy, the chance to say one had slain Nemesis—whether in a group, after he had been weakened by other combat, or even as a lie—was attractive enough. Now, with the clarity granted by his nymph's shining presence, Maximus could imagine how much he was hated by those the patriarch ruled so stringently.

Some few might even privately think themselves as soldiers capable of killing an Emperor, and witnessing the latter's unequivocal defeat would allow for their own fiefdoms to expand without fear of reprisal.

If, that was, Maximus allowed even a single sanguinant to escape catastrophe.

Quintus, Mure, Eli the Swift, both Roses, Manuel and Pelle, Aries, Silvya Ariste, Dagon and Taika and more, each an elder he had trained and fought beside. They all fell in fiery battle, alongside fledglings they had made.

Others would be roaming the avenues leading from this place. Now that Nemesis had shown himself all would converge, assuming his leman held safely below seal in the outpost. If she by some miracle eluded capture—a nymph given winged feet, indeed—the soldier still knew where Antinous would be resting once dawn threatened.

There was, after all, no need to waste what the former owner of this territory had built.

If she were caught, as was overwhelmingly likely, escalating combat would quickly draw the patriarch's attention. Antinous would be monitoring events closely indeed, listening to the night's subtle whispers, hardly needing spies and runners positioned throughout the city's arteries and organs—dogsbodies and catspaws, mortals aware or unaware of their true master.

None of this mattered at the moment. All he could do was note who he had already slain, anticipate those likely to be creeping elsewhere.

And kill.

Among the flames Nemesis walked, and with him came death for his own kind. The fire naturally escaped its bounds, sending tongues along summerdry scrub. Mortal authorities were no doubt alerted to the danger by now, further adding to general chaos—not that sanguinant cared overmuch, since rebuilding near such a prime resource was a certainty and human calamity most often brought good hunting.

The last to fall, surprisingly, was sneering, skulking Jaye, only recently past fledgling status and much given to tactics of berserker ferocity. Yet even he burned like a candle, resisting the fire-kiss a few moments—a signal achievement, showing he was made of stern stuff indeed.

Nemesis did not wait. He wheeled in the direction he had last seen his leman and put on all the speed he could still muster, riding a searing, invisible wave even as his hair smoked and stinging, smarting eyes nearly collapsed. Burning branches, mortal alarm stirring in a residential area past an overgrown, tinder-dry hedge, distant sirens beginning to howl…

…and a faint thread of rose-scent tinged with musk, fresh

coffee, and the darker note of his blood in her sweet thrumming veins.

His leman was running. The slight trace of her managed to peel a layer of rising ossification from his senses, a sharp jolt of much-needed lucidity filling him for a dizzying moment.

The thrall woke, twisting inside his bones, far hotter than the escaped inferno. Every instinct protective and possessive, predatory or tender, demanded to find her, hide her, make her safe.

Cold unerring logic answered she would never be secure until every sanguinant he could also smell or sense within the city was slain. For their reek overlaid his prize's delicate footsteps, and now it was only a matter of time before Antinous hunted her down.

A soldier's desperate plan now entered its second phase—a running battle instead of siegebreaking. Nemesis was widely held to excel at both.

He hoped the estimation was accurate.

CHAPTER 23

Worst game of hide and seek ever. Layla crouched in a pocket of deep shadow, listening to distant thunder and the frantic call of emergency sirens, her ribs flickering as she gasped. As soon as she evaded one group of biters another appeared, and the only thing saving her was Max's advice.

Listen to your body, it will save you.

She had help. It wasn't so much the way she could streak across open spaces, her braid nearly snapping like a whip as she burst into motion, or the sudden turns and leaps she was now capable of. The real, true friend was a tingle of instinct at her nape, the sense of unfriendly, invisible watchers lurking on an otherwise deserted street, the sudden clear *no don't move* freezing her solid or the *go, go now, go NOW* sending her into places she never would have glanced at as a regular old human.

Time to move, the little voice said. She burst into motion, streaking across four lanes of momentarily deserted highway and catching the top of a chain-link fence. A rattle, a lunging effort, and she was in darkness again—a waste lot choked with weeds, ancient railroad tracks turning to rust, and the backside of a strip mall behind another fence.

O'Shaughnassey and his crew had trained Dan's group in the

art of finding cover, always knowing where the next alley was, never looking at a building without thinking about the exits, all the little paranoid habits which were actually kind of fun if made into a game. Dodging surveillance cameras, working angles, sensing which neighborhoods were likely to be deserted during certain hours and which had nosy eyes at every window day or night—she was no more than an assiduous amateur, really, but it was a lot easier with eyesight turning the darkness to bright noon and hearing jacked up into hearing separate heartbeats inside houses, cars backfiring several blocks away as if they were right next to her, howling sirens and smaller cries of surprise, the bumbling passage of raccoons and other wildlife taking advantage of darkness to scavenge in corners and trash bins.

Layla found she could scramble up downspouts by the simple expedient of throwing her body at a wall, simply letting it find purchase with burning, scrabbling fingertips and boot-toes. Her wrists ached; she was sure she left scratches on brick or paint, and those faint traces might look very much like biter claw-marks to an experienced hunter.

Or to her pursuers, who had to see just as well as she did, hear just as well—the wild pounding of her heart somehow didn't give her away, if she lurked near enough to traffic or occupied buildings active at this hour.

She even had allies, sort of. The animals knew, and their scuttling for cover—cats stray or well-fed, armadillos, rats she shuddered upon hearing the tail-drag scrape of, dogs and slinking coyotes, even a few snakes desperate to avoid contact with anything possessing legs, a whole-ass petting zoo—warned her of the shadow-blurs, sanguinant using their semi-invisibility trick to whistle along at freeway speed. There were strange shimmers she didn't like hanging about streetlamps or lurking in shadowed places; *feeling* a disembodied gaze ooze or slice past was a matter of instinct as well, judging by goosebump and the stiffening of fine hairs.

She was a bundle of exposed nerves, a shrinking animal scuttling between walls, cutting through backyards, scaling fences, slipping along back alleys choked with junked cars or dumpsters half-open amid drifts of reeking refuse, avoiding clusters of human and biter activity alike. No plan to her wandering meant she could not quite be anticipated—or so she hoped as she simply reacted, moving when any kind of notice drew close, often freezing in the smallest, darkest spot she could find when pursuit temporarily drew away.

Culverts were good, for her *and* for nocturnal critters. The furry, scaled, or feathered evinced little desire to bite, rattle, or hiss; she returned the favor.

In fact, she thought she was doing pretty okay, except for the goddamn dry spot at the back of her throat. It grew a little larger anytime she made an extreme physical effort, and though the sensation sharpened her hearing *and* sight it also made her skin sensitive as hell, filled her mouth with a strange numbing almost like monster blood, and worse of all, gave her the shakes when she heard human heartbeats.

Even the tiny skittering pulses of 'dillos or cats woke a dozy trickle of interest from that rough thirst. She could very easily imagine the sensation getting worse, and worse, and over- whelming as the thought of water, coffee, juice, booze, or any other liquid caused faint nausea and an intensifying throb in her throat.

She knew what it wanted.

Would she eventually rip the cloth top off an old, well-main- tained convertible to get at an insistent human pulse? Would another man look at autopsy photos of his dead wife and silently swear vengeance on things that went bump in the night, or would the weird-ass murder be swept under the rug by cops unwilling or unable to investigate, some owned by big-time biters and others knowing all too well not to fuck with strange, inexplicable shit the entire world teemed with under a crust of normalcy?

She was slowing, and that was bad. Stopping to listen at

certain houses where only a few pulses beat, scrambling away from buildings when doors opened and people stepped into the night for a smoke, an errand, an emergency call; parks where teenagers necked in cars, their proud galloping hearts announcing youth and pleasure to the night, streets where crowds gathered or worse, furtive hurried steps meant *easy prey, easy prey…*

One hand clapped over her mouth, where her teeth ached, ached, *ached.* She ran or hid, shrank into pools of darker shadow, heard a mutter of excitement and intensifying clamor as the dozing town noticed a false sunrise on the northwest horizon.

The oil fields were burning, maybe the holding tanks or a refinery as well. A big unholy mess, and she hoped it wouldn't spread.

Layla had no time to worry about other people's problems. Just as she thought she might be able to work down a long sagebrush-starred hill and make it to the freeway heading east— she'd been seeing signs for onramps in the distance for what felt like hours, though unable to even get close to one—she was caught.

A rattle, a crescendo of alarm from her instinctive warning system, and for a single heartstopping moment she thought it was Max, the crashing disappointment of being grabbed meeting a wave of *oh thank God,* that at least the devil she knew had appeared.

But it wasn't him. The hands on her hurt, biting hard; she was thrown over something stonily muscular, and the world spun away underneath her.

Oh, fuck.

Being fireman-carried at high speed might have made her vomit as well, except her body simply refused. Bouncing, jouncing, sharply changing direction at random intervals, she tried to look for landmarks or direction; her braid had come loose and her hair was a wind-whipped cloud, denying even the briefest glimpse and as a bonus, attempting to climb into her nose and mouth as well.

By the time all motion came to an abrupt, screeching halt and she was nearly tossed from her carrier's shoulders, landing on her feet with an effort that seemed to take every last bit of starch from her legs, the thirst was a rage in her throat and her teeth were hot, sensitive razor edges. A faint trace of metallic taste said she'd bitten the inside of her cheek, and the thin thread of coppery taste hit the back of her throat hard.

Jesus, please. Layla fetched up against something vertical, hard, and blessedly motionless—a wall sheathed in heavy dark wooden paneling. She clung to it gratefully, fingernails on her free hand driving in with a small splintering noise.

The cessation of windrush, heartbeats, crowd- and traffic-noise was almost as shocking as the sudden motionlessness. Her pulse was hummingbird wings in her throat, her wrists, even her ankles and behind her knees; a single other drum was beating in this space, slow and terrible. A quick shake to get hair out of her eyes, bumping the back of her skull against the wall, and the sense of being watched was dismally familiar and uncanny at once.

It wasn't Max's gaze, she could just *tell*. She peered through long dark strands, and a flat, quiet voice spoke.

"You reek of my son." A dark, musical tenor, the syllables weighted oddly, bearing the imprint of another language through textbook English as well as a strange, stilted effort to enunciate.

Pretty much as Max had spoken at first, but somehow this guy sounded far more strained. Almost as if he could barely force the words through a janky translating app on a weak, wavering wifi connection.

A shadow snapped into focus—tall and lean, topped with a mess of gleaming dark curls, and though she *knew* it wasn't Max hope sprang up wildly for the second time, filled her aching throat, and was just as quickly snuffed. The figure's shoulders weren't quite so broad, and instead of Max's eerie focused stillness, this guy almost vibrated in place, a flood of jittering force just barely held in check.

Her new instincts spoke again, loud and clear. This creature was *old*, far more ancient than Max. Strangely, though, he lacked the sense of leashed, smooth riptide strength Layla's monster carried. So, old, but somehow not so... not as strong?

Plenty scary though. Oh, Lay, we are in the shit now.

The biter blurred into motion. Layla screamed, the sound trapped against a moist, folded sweater-cuff swallowing her hand—*do vampires sweat, gotta find some research on that,* a darkly hilarious thought—as she tried to back through the paneling. His palm slapped next to her left ear, his breath flooding her nose. The biter's eyes were wide and dark, swelling wet crimson points eating the pupils. He inhaled deeply, and her own new eyesight was pitiless.

He *felt* ancient, but the face inches from hers was barely old enough to buy beer. Skin perfect like Max's, yes, but with a peculiar tender texture implying he'd never shaved; his nose was classically straight, his mouth chiseled though the top lip contorted, both sets of upper fangs fully displayed, gleaming softly.

The biter snuffled so hard his chest heaved, her hair stirred by moving air. His shoulders trembled, waves of shudders down to his rope sandals, and the bizarreness of being huffed by a vampire threatened to give her the screaming-meemie giggles *yet again.*

It didn't help that he was wearing... a bathrobe? No, a sort of knee-length tunic. Dark material gathered at his shoulders, a belt which looked like several different kinds of frayed rope braided together, his muscled arms bare and gleaming, his knees and shins equally naked, and those weird huaraches. Of course, Layla looked like a kid playing dress-up, swimming in Max's sweater and dirty from dodging groups of vampires for what felt like hours, but this guy was just plain *outlandish*.

Then his head darted forward, lizardlike, teeth snapping together with a solid, heavy *chuk* like a clean break on a back-room pool table, and she screamed again as hot breath caressed the side of her throat not shielded by a raised arm. His heavy vibrating growl was a physical weight, pressing her against cold, slick wood, but the vampire didn't bite her.

Instead, he recoiled, almost as if slapped. His teeth champed twice more and the red dots in his pupils dilated, liquid-glowing at the corners as if the light was saltwater tears.

Behind him loomed a cavernous parquet-floored space, and a tinkling overhead was a row of honest-to-gosh chandeliers marching along a ceiling full of plaster gewgaws and furbe-lows. They were only indifferently lit; several tiny electric bulbs loading each glass-and-metal confection fizzed and blinked, on their very last legs. Floor-length drapes clothed the side walls, stiff with dust, and the whole shebang seemed vaguely familiar.

Ballroom? What the hell? Where had she seen this before?

It was almost like trying to remember a red-stripe file while Pete and Dan argued over comms. No time to think, because the biter tilted his head back, his cheeks twitching madly as the fangs receded and normal, blunt human teeth—or the illusion of them—returned.

He had to do that in order to speak, apparently. His chin lowered, loose curls falling softly over his forehead, and this new, exotic terror examined her afresh.

"Not dead yet," he said, that odd accent pushing at the vowels. The words were still clunky, either jammed together or weirdly spaced. "But is no matter. He shall do predicted, I will dispose of what's left. You are indeed *aima-glyza*, that is good."

He likes to talk. But he ain't bit me yet, okay. Layla stared, folded sweater-cuff still clapped to her mouth, and tried to figure out what to do.

Submit if you are caught, Max whispered in memory. *Do as you're told… I will find you.*

Sure, easy for him to say. She was, as usual and as always, on her own. The thought that this creature might try to hold her down and—

No. She couldn't think about that. Bad enough she was almost *missing* Max, in some weird way, but this guy, this *thing* with its red-flashing eyes was somehow completely alien in some essential fashion, as the monster who had killed her team seemed not to be.

It wasn't just the lizard-twitching or the mad flat shine in its eyes when the red light faded, or the jittering, shivering force only barely controlled. It was the singsong voice, the idea that it was wrapped in a world all its own and its intense, casually terrifying power could strike out at any moment, doing something completely unexpected.

Not to mention fatal.

Is this what bit him? Trying to imagine Max being infected by this crazyass thing, living with its moods for hundreds—no, *thousands* of years—was horrifying, but she couldn't waste time on that. Layla twitched, attempting to slide sideways along the wall, maybe buttonhook and bolt for half-open doors at the far end of the ballroom.

Wham. The creature's fist punched through paneling a bare inch from her shoulder, effectively barring escape. Its body heat was a simmering wave, and its rough musky non-cologne wrapped around her as if trying to drown her own scent. It was disorienting to not even *smell* herself, very much like vanishing.

The old biter clicked his tongue a few times, as if admonishing a naughty pet. "Now, now. Let's see. I will name you Pandora, perhaps, or Philomela, though I do not wish you to sing. No, no. You will be Psyche."

What. The hell. Layla lowered her hand from her mouth, slowly; the creature watched, its smile stretching, cheeks bunching up. The effect was at once angelic and deeply, utterly creepifying.

How could Max ever call this being *Father*?

"She wants to speak," it crooned, and did another round of huffing at her hair, snuffling against her cheek with dry fever-breath. "So good, such a sweet little piece. I'll allow it."

This thing is completely fucking batshit. The terror was deep, wine-red, and so overwhelming her legs went rubbery. If this was a father, she was deeply glad she'd never known hers.

"Yes," it continued, and trailed off in some other language, rolling and rhythmic. But the red gleam lit its eyes once more, and she sensed it was working itself up to something. A coiled spring, winding tighter and tighter until something snapped.

Layla had the distinct idea she wouldn't like whatever it had planned.

I thought they weren't supposed to hurt lee-mons, she thought, inconsequentially, and a single spark lit in her midriff, exploding like the oil tank Max had yanked her away from.

Fuck this. I'm going down fighting. She lashed out, blurring-quick with every inch of her newfound strength, and felt her fingernails shear through cloth.

The creature gave a titanic, world-ending yell.

CHAPTER 24

For some while Nemesis followed his leman's scent, twisting and turning—his nymph ran well, and the thread of rose-musk helped sharpen his swiftly blunting edges. Other predators were upon her trail, seeking to take what was his, and the rage was also a weapon to hold the numbness at bay.

He gave himself over to it, a fire fit to dwarf the other blaze now clearly spreading from the oilfields, helped along by a slow hot breeze. Much of the city was now awake, aware of one danger while remaining blind to another battle being fought in alleys and culverts, atop flat roofs offering a vantage of the false dawn, alongside their paved roads and byways.

True sunrise was still some while away. The sanguinant upon watch left their posts, for the firebreath breeze carried both smoke and an enticing tang of roses; those who did not scent the prize felt the excitement of others and streamed after their siblings, eager to join the battle and perhaps be the final victor after all others were weakened.

Now he was not merely hunter but also assiduously followed, and the risk of ambush while he dealt with those chasing lovely, fleeing Leila mounted. Another whetstone to sharpen him against ossification; any tool was acceptable, so long as it worked.

Short sharp engagements or longer running duels, each ending with runnels of quick decay before final explosions or showers of glistening grit. He knew how to kill his own kind, for such was his function as Antinous's eldest son, a prop to Father's power, the once-faithful *strategos* upon whom an Emperor depended.

And every lesson over long centuries of battle was used.

The conflagration spread, sending long bright tongues through two residential areas lain cheek-by-jowl to the oilfields; the sanguinant, in their eagerness to draw him forth, had wrought far better than they could have hoped. Much thick humidity was sucked from the air, though the clouds pressed lower and jeweled glitters leapt between their billows, lightning dancing above columns of rising smoke.

Iuppiter was roused, lazily tossing his bolts from one hand to the other, waiting to see how the creatures below would fight. Were other divinities present as well, briefly called from their long slumber? The question of which had drawn a Persian-named nymph across a soldier's path was unnecessary, unheeded.

If he survived to make a sacrifice of thanksgiving, he would need an oracle's help to aim the smoke correctly. Or perhaps one of Leila's stray utterances would grant him knowledge, though never absolution.

Mortals scurried to contain the catastrophe, shining red beetles of firetrucks accompanied by wailing ambulances, many swarming to predetermined points since flame, like water, followed preferred paths. Invisible messages hummed through a gasping-hot summer night—radio, television, emergency chan-nels, news, and the far more subtle humming of sanguinant awareness.

Thunder rumbled behind the flashes; some mortals prayed for rain, but most of modernity knew better than to count on the divine for aid and so, more resources were mobilized, more personnel shaken from their beds.

As the night wore on, the ranks of the Blood thinned. They turned upon each other in phrenzy, seeking to lessen the competition for a miraculous prize most had now been granted a scenting of.

Among them Nemesis appeared, slaying all he found—until he found another trail, one he recognized.

He stood, head down, breathing harshly. The sandy, shimmering particles of dead sanguinant clung to his flesh and tattered cloth; the killroar vibrating in his chest had dropped to a range inaudible to mortals. The thrum spread for a good distance in either direction, however, maddening his prey just as each other's presence did, and the killglow spread from his eyes in a band of crimson haze.

Yes, he knew this scent. It belonged to the one who had granted him the Gift, the one who had made him a weapon, the one who had named him Nemesis.

The one who had stolen his leman.

A moment later the empty lot was deserted again, air collapsing upon itself with a hard tearing sound as a soldier forgot every other consideration. Thrall and ossification swirled within him, vying for primacy as the oilfields fire leapt a freeway and sent a sheet of hungry flame through the northwest industrial district. Warehouses crumpled, more storage tanks exploded, and the city's second, larger refinery serviced by a railroad spur felt the first touch of a hot breeze laden with cinders.

CHAPTER 25

She'd barely managed to rip its robe, but the biter roared as if suckerpunched. Layla threw herself sideways, or at least tried to—it grabbed her, and Max's assurance that biters wouldn't hurt her seemed terrifyingly like a sadistic joke.

"How dare you!" it howled, its claws locked around her arms, and shook her so hard her head bobbled. "*How dare you strike at me!*"

It gabbled other stuff too, mostly in a collection of foreign gobbledygook, and kept shaking. Layla went limp, and even though the monster was probably going to tear her head off in the next few seconds, she felt curiously… well, deflated.

It was acting, after all, just like a man.

Then it stopped all at once, a flood of terrible, tingling silence. The monster pressed her against the wall bruising-hard, its body a marble statue, its face buried in her hair. A long, endless breath —she wondered blankly if strands were getting up its nose and the thought of vampire-snot hair gel was morbidly, distantly funny—as its ribs swelled like a cobra's hood.

"Ohhhhhh," it groaned. "Look what you made me do, Psyche." Another string of incomprehensible gibberish followed, but its volume was falling.

Just don't let it try to... She couldn't even finish the thought. Every muscle locked in trembling stasis, a deer staring into head-lights as slow dozy hatred swept through its entire body.

She wanted to fight. But if she did, what hideous action would this thing be provoked into?

"—no, no, no." The creature shifted back to English, which was either a good sign or a very bad one. "All will be well, yes, all will be well. We have just the thing."

The world turned over. Layla screamed again, a long desperate wail; Max's father dragged her along the parquet, his ancient bony fist knotted in her tangled hair. It *hurt*, she tried to tear free, kicking and scrambling, the sudden irrational fear that her scalp was going to rip loose swallowing every other consideration.

"*Stop it!*" the old biter roared, bending down to yank her upright again. Another round of shaking, and though she was sunk eyebrow-deep in terror, a hazy realization pierced the shell of panic.

It was nearly as strong as Max, yes, but it was *restraining* itself. Which was almost as terrible as the alternative.

It finished shaking and dragged her along—thankfully just by the arms, not her hair anymore—for a few paces before kicking the ballroom doors open. Hallways unreeled around its floating speed and her staggering attempts to put a foot down every once in a while. Images flashed by, a massive staircase leading to a vast plain of white-and-black squares slippery under her sadly battered boots, and the angle of a doorway set off another firecracker-burst of memory inside her ringing skull.

It's the old Schellburger Mansion. Griskov's place. Their original target—this was his main lair, built by a railroad baron back during the first Texas oil rush, crumbling and renovated by turns, and finally bought by Griskov two decades ago. There were architectural and lifestyle photo spreads of the interior from the previous owner's tenure; Layla had pulled them and put together the initial file herself. Said previous owner had almost certainly been a cocaine cartel lord, and there were whispers of how he'd vanished.

Max's father had clearly moved right in, made himself at home.

Most of the place looked like a war zone now. Furniture was battered to sticks and rags, strange huddled shapes lay flung in corners, spatters of dark fluid reaching in high arcs along certain hallways, and the atrocious, titanic stink she'd hardly noticed—she was, after all, confronted with a batshit-insane biter, and that was overwhelming enough—was recognizable as well.

The clustered shapes were corpses; they reeked of shit, fear, and a thick brassy odor she didn't need newfangled vampire senses to name. It reminded her of autopsy photos, Suzy's poor mangled body, a whole cascade of associations any mortal animal knew when that cold metallic aura drifted on trembling air.

Death.

Grishkov's security? Human, not vampires. These had to be henchmen or employees; now she could see rifles and pistols scattered about as well, shell casings glinting in sprays and piles. They'd clearly tried to defend the place—had Max done all this, coming back to tell her the blood all over his clothes wasn't his, and that Grishkov was *'no longer a concern'*? Or had the creature dragging her along gone for a murderous spree?

Not like it matters, she thought, hazily. The corpses thickened, stacked to either side like cordwood. Another set of doors slammed open; she was hauled through an antechamber and into another dusty, stifling room, thankfully free of dead bodies but holding something even more horrifying—a big white and pink four-poster bed, the kind child-Layla had looked at in catalogs, dreaming about having her own house one day. Not a trailer, not a 'manufactured' or an apartment, an actual *house.*

But not like this. No.

Ohshit.

A big, white-painted antique vanity sat against one wall, a

walk-in closet stood open and empty with a few scattered wooden hangers caught in its throat. The dark cave of what had to be a bathroom exhaled dual scents of rust and damp through an archway, and a vast bank of pink brocaded drapes showed where there was a window, if she could just get to it. Hot, numb-tasting nausea filled her belly, crawled up to swamp the terrible thirst.

And she *still* couldn't vomit. The feeling was completely, utterly horrible, and useless as well.

The biter shoved her against the bed's foot, where a padded bench rocked as she landed, hard. He stood staring down at her, the crimson points in his pupils shrinking, before sucking in another deep bellows-breath and lapsing into motionlessness. A terrible shadow of sanity crossed that strangely young-looking face.

He looked almost forlorn in that moment. Which didn't do her any good, no sir; chills raced down her back.

Layla gripped the edge of the bench, did her best not to look at the window. If she could somehow toss herself out—or at least get hold of some broken glass, there would be a way to saw at her own wrists, her own throat? All it would take was enough pressure, the older biters had tough skin but she wasn't there yet—

"I apologize," the biter said, suddenly. He sounded a lot calmer, but that wasn't helpful at all. "It has been some time since I was... you must understand, I have been alive so very, very long."

So has Max. How much older was this thing? She held herself very still, wondered if it was possible to strangle herself with whatever moldering sheets were on the bed. There were curtain rods in the closet, she was pretty sure—the hangers argued for that luxury, didn't they?

"You must be... frightened, yes. But don't worry." The mad biter's accent had thickened, though the unevenness between words had smoothed out somewhat. He fumbled at his robe, reaching through the slashes down its front—had she done that? Heavy brown velvet flopped, and for a moment the biter looked very much like a human teenager patting himself down for missing car keys. "A treasure made a very long time ago. A pretty, pretty thing, for pretty things like leman."

There was that word again. Did it mean he wasn't going to kill her? But of course, there was something worse. If this thing touched her, if it tore her clothes off and threw her on the bed… she might have thought nothing could be worse, but now she suspected her ever-acctive imagination was failing her, for once.

Why didn't it bite me? Something important about that, lingering just at the tip of her overworked, overheating brain. *Max bit me first thing, why didn't—*

"Aha!" The biter now sounded pleased. Its eerie calm persisted; this sudden attack of almost-reasonableness was far more horrifying than the screeching and throwing her around. "Here we are."

A glitter, a golden gleaming. Thin strands and intricate metal knotwork dripped between long, strong coppery fingers; both he and Max had really good tans even after all the time away from sunlight.

He shook the shining thing out, held it up.

"Do you like, do you find it, ah, acceptable? Gold, of course; silver burns the poor sweet fledglings. But you'll never need worry about that, no." The biter leaned down, arms extending, and the expression he now wore was truly obscene. Eyebrows anxiously raised, a tentative smile with no hint of fangs—except for the robe and those falling-apart sandals, he looked like a boy offering flowers on a first date.

Except for the way he twitched at the end, as if he couldn't stay still. The juxtaposition of human nervousness with powerful, crazy ancient *thing* was nauseating, terrible, *wrong*. Had he been cuckoo-crackers before the vampirism, or had living so long driven him irredeemably 'round the bend? Was he trying to stay sane, *flexible*, like Max said?

She almost pitied him.

Almost.

"It's a collar," he continued. "Very, very old, made in the East with arts now lost. Cost a big shiny penny, a demimonde thing. You're just right for it."

He's offering jewelry? Another desire to bray with heebie-jeebie giggles rose in Layla's throat, dark and terrible. If she started laughing now, she might find out what was even worse than dreading the big pink bed lurking behind her.

The biter darted forward, too swiftly for her to dodge or even flinch. Fabric tore, a terrific yank against her shoulders, sweater-sleeves parting like water. Cool metal touched her throat; the openings in complex metal knots were designed to leave bare spaces to either side of her larynx, while the band to the back of her neck was solid.

Oh, it's so they can bite, she thought. Then the necklace squirmed against her skin, warming rapidly, and the biter's loose dark curls brushed her smoke-tarnished hair as he fiddled with something near her nape—it had to be the catch.

A flash like lightning, an electric white blur filling the world. His cheek rested against hers, cool and hard.

"Yesssss." A long, satisfied hiss. He inhaled again, filling his lungs, then straightened. "You're all right now, little leman, peerless Psyche. Nemesis will be killed by his siblings, then I will destroy whatever remains. Or he will finish them all and come to meet his end upon my claws." A bright, young, careless laugh, all the more chilling for the note of ancient, sadistic glee. "I will let you watch, perhaps. Then we will be alone."

That's what you think, motherfucker. Layla's body would not obey. She sat, staring straight ahead, humid summer air caressing her bare arms below the T-shirt's sleeves.

Her sweater—*Max's* sweater—hung from the ancient vampire's left hand, a dead pelt. Her breath came softly, regularly; her pulse settled. The lassitude wasn't like the warm forgiving syrup of a monster-blood high; it was simple, sheer inability to move. She could feel the padded bench under her thighs, her hands now loosely draped instead of clutching.

"*First the bite*," the young-faced monster chanted, brushing at her hair with his free fingers. He smoothed the strands almost like Max had, sudden gentleness far more nerve-wracking than the roaring, the shaking, the screams. "*Then the claiming.* You'll keep me from true-death, dear Psyche. And I will see that you want for nothing. Isn't that nice? Nod for me, *kardoula mou*."

Her chin dipped without her brain telling it to. Frantic internal signals wouldn't reach her arms, her legs; she *couldn't move.*

Not of her own volition, at least. Her traitorous body performed a slow, dreamy nod.

The creature smiled, rising to his full height, and looked down at her with a nearly avuncular expression. "Now be good, and do not wander. I must attend to some business, but I'll return very soon. It's rather nice to feel again; I will enjoy many years of discovering the limits of... Oh, yes. We shall have *so* many experiences, dear Psyche. So very many."

Warm air puffed, redolent of dust, neglect, and corpses stacked higgledy-piggledy in hallways. The creature's scent faded; she heard creaks and shifting as the house settled, a rumble of what might be distant thunder.

Layla strained to get up, to scream, to lift her arms. Could only manage a tiny rocking motion on the bench. It was the necklace, it was somehow locking her in place.

Oh, God. Oh god oh god oh god…

Her heart, her lungs paid no attention. A breathing statue, she stared at the door to the hallway, her eyelids drifting down at regular intervals to blink, then back up.

And she *could not move.*

CHAPTER 26

THE LAST COMBATANTS WERE A PAIR OF SANGUINANT ELDER SO FAR enraged they tore each other nearly to pieces before he descended to render both into clouds of swirling, pattering dust. Nemesis stood panting, attention briefly focused upon sealing a few rips and gashes in his own hide.

Strips of clothing hung from limbs turned scarecrow-gaunt from fueling the demands of battle. He had lost a measure or two of blood, managing regain some few iotas from unwary fledglings drunk with the faint rose-musk breath clinging in storm-heavy night air. The killing numbness was rising to enclose him, and the flaring, fading trail whispering *Leila, Leila* into the night could no longer hold back the tide of ossification.

He needed his leman.

To think of laying his head in her lap, perhaps while she smoothed his hair and smiled down at him… oh, the vision was sweet yet also a trap, a sucking tar-pit aiding the one who had stolen his nymph.

She was taken, no doubt terrified. Antinous would not injure a leman, but he would certainly *break* her, given the opportunity. Even if the patriarch did not torment her without leaving a physical mark—well within his capabilities, an amusement often indulged in—the thirst itself could be used to shatter any claim to sanity. She would be rendered mad, perhaps permanently.

No less holy, no less tender and fragrant, but utterly lost to reason.

The thought pierced Nemesis's chest as the claws of his enemies had failed to, and that sting was so sweet it pushed back the numbness, the creeping stupidity.

A mortal city, torn and bleeding, was rid of all sanguinant save three—Father, eldest son, and fragile, beautiful sylph. Sirens wailed from every quarter; the fire was breathing hard, gorging itself and making its own weather to some degree. Thickening smoke spiraled skyward, any true thunder hiding behind a lower, closer roar of combustion and air heated to flow thick as oil.

Despite that, a faint green aroma struggled along in tendrils, summer-drained flora anticipating rain. Perhaps the plants prayed as well; would the gods heed their silent cries? Or did whatever dryads and naiads lingering in this age know one of their own was in danger, pleading with silent Olympus?

He realized he was standing uselessly in the open, and her scent was fading. No matter, she was his fledgling, and so long as she was awake he could trace her passage. An internal pull, infinitely faint, could take precedence now that he had cleared away all Father's progeny.

Antinous would not mind the winnowing; no doubt he considered Nemesis had performed a final service in murdering every single sibling, niece, nephew, cousin. The patriarch would create no more children of the Blood to work his will—the risk of another sanguinant, even his own get, discovering sweet Leila was too great.

Far better to use mortals as servants henceforth, and concern himself solely with a ripe, toothsome prize.

Any resistance on her part would be met with crushing, over-whelming response. The patriarch required instant, unstinting obedience as a matter of course; he often made fledglings simply to break and discard them into true-death. Nemesis knew his own cruelty, as only a soldier can; Antinous's was of another species, that of imperial rule. Leila's fragile defiance—so delicious, so attractive—would not save her.

Nemesis could swear he wished to rescue her from a beast even less kind than himself, and perhaps that was so. Yet another, deeper truth overpowered that consideration.

She was *his*, and another sanguinant had laid hands upon the garland.

The soldier had let a mortal male escape at her pleading, wishing to show whatever mercy he could. Nemesis could not allow a mad emperor to retain the prize. If a soldier must die as well, leaving the nymph to wander until another sanguinant found and claimed…

Wake up. Her voice, low but urgent. *You're just standing there, Max. Wake up, for me.*

Of course he would, there was no command he would obey with more alacrity. He lifted his head, finding the night was old, almost fully drained. He knew precisely where his enemy would take her, the battleground Maximus himself had prepared so short a while ago.

I know you're tired. Her fingers, so tentative, along his scarred shoulder. She had deigned to touch a filth-crusted legionnaire, stripped away the dust of centuries, brought him wholly to life for the first time in his cursed existence, mortal or sanguinant. *You can rest, if you want. It's okay.*

No repose until the battle was done. It had been true in his mortal lifetime, true when he fell upon his sword after that awful, crushing defeat he could no longer quite remember the importance of, and remained accurate as he choked and gasped, denied a swift ending by slight miscalculation in angle. Antinous's face, swimming in the bloody darkening haze of true-death's approach.

I can use you, the patriarch said, and indeed he had.

The northwest horizon bore a distinct, sullen red smear; even night-flying mortal vehicles were active now to view and hope-fully contain the blaze—such wonderful, ingenious things. Maximus wished to see what mortals would do next. He wanted Leila to explain this current age to him, longed to use hands and mouth to discover her slim curves, to experiment with different varieties of pleasing her, wanted very badly to ease the thrall's mounting, painful pressure over and over in her hot, unrelent-ingly gorgeous furnace.

Then get moving. Archly amused, as she had never dared taunt him. The voice was another trick of rising ossification, threatening to drown him before he reached Antinous's bolthole.

Maximus blurred into the whispering speed, streaking through clinging, smoke-tainted darkness. The pull of his fledg-ling was oddly weak, as if she were deeply injured; still, it was unquestionably in the direction he had planned for.

The thought of her distress brought another explosion of useful rage, briefly battering aside the numbness. He could not linger.

Especially since the eastern horizon, as if wishing to outdo the northwest glare, held a thin line of grey.

CHAPTER 27

Difficult, like swimming through clear, melted plastic—Layla found she could twitch, concentrating on her own body as if it were foreign territory, a lead-filled puppet with invisible strings.

Reaching to strip away the stupid necklace almost caused her to black out. She decided not to bother and focused instead on standing. Her legs worked, though barely; she swayed drunkenly, new vampire reflexes pulling her back from falling on her ass at the very last moment. Pushing too hard caused the strange colorless lassitude to swamp her, and when she turned toward the window her knees gave way, spilling her to carpet that smelled older than Meemaw Cathy's trailer rugs.

And significantly less clean.

"Do not wander," the ancient, horrible vampire's voice repeated near her ear, and a wave of terror struggled with paralysis. Had he returned?

No, she was just hearing things. What the fuck was this necklace? A magical shock collar? Well, if she could believe in vampires, in Sasquatches, in little green men or invisible curtains keeping her trapped, a magic leman-leash wasn't so outlandish.

Knees. On her knees, pushing upward; she got the trick of

working against the funny unseen resistance. If she moved very, very slowly, concentrating on each muscle and balancing adjustment, it was possible.

The thought of wearing this thing when the young-looking monster came back and wanted to do… whatever else he wanted to do to her, was deeply scary. She couldn't brood on that, though. Moving helped her think, and the only edge she had now was a few ounces of grey matter inside her skull. At least the necklace didn't seem to slow that down—not that she could tell if it had, maybe.

Vampire hunting wasn't for the faint of heart. People didn't want to know about the inexplicable, scary shit in the world; plenty of hunters went full-on paranoid nutbar if they survived the job long enough. Doubting your own senses, your own *mind* was worse than almost anything else in the world.

If she was lucky this Father guy would eventually get bored of playing with her; for once in her life, being abandoned didn't sound so bad. But would he take the necklace off when he did, or leave her forgotten in a corner, a discarded doll?

Do not *think about that, for Chrissake. You're standing, that's great. Now let's try walking.*

Why? Where was she going? She wasn't supposed to wander —the thought was nearly overwhelming, and the most terrifying thing was that some part of her *wanted* to obey, wanted to just sit down and wait for another command, some direction to follow. Nothing else seemed terribly important.

I'm not wandering, I'm just going to look at the house. As soon as she settled on that mental concept the pressure eased—if she concentrated on the fact that she was doing recon instead of roaming around aimlessly, it was fine. Hunky-dory.

At least the necklace made the thirst retreat, blunting the scratchy smoke-laced burning into mild, faraway irritation, a slight but unreachable itch between shoulderblades. Layla reached the bedroom door, stared at the pink-carpeted sitting room—or was it a dressing room?

Doesn't matter. Outside the next doorway was a hall full of corpses, already ripe and gassy from hot weather. If Grishkov had air conditioning in this place, none was working now—had it been switched off? Maybe the ancient, weirdass biter didn't care for modern conveniences, or maybe he didn't know how to turn them on? He seemed a few loops short of a barrel roll, as Suzy would say, tapping her temple with one brightly painted acrylic nail.

Poor Suze. And now, as Layla veered with slow drunken determination across faded pink carpet—the decorating scheme here was something else, dusty discolored furniture hulks mired in what was briefly fashionable a few decades ago—she wondered what in the hell Dan had wanted from vampire hunting unless it was avenging his wife.

If he hadn't loved her…

But that was ridiculous; he'd married Suze, after all. Had he *wanted* Layla to say something before the wedding?

Maybe he did, so he could blame it on you. He always was a lazy piece of shit.

The slow burn of irritation from constantly dealing with men and their bullshit pushed back the lethargy a little more. Always necessary to throttle that anger, keep it low and glowing, coals in her chest. Any flare-up and she'd begin to stagger drunkenly instead of slow-walk, or worse, float away and come back to find herself staring blankly at mildewed wallpaper.

Holy hell and hallelujah, she had a single skill usable against a leman-leash. More than she'd expected; who knew annoyance could be weaponized?

The smell was so goddamn awful. She drifted down the hall, unable even to wrinkle her nose since just putting one foot in front of the other required all her attention, a tricky balancing act between invisible resistance, waves of lassitude, moving her unwieldy limbs, and low-level fury.

Because she had to admit she wasn't irritated, annoyed,

piqued, or even vexed. She was, Layla discovered, absolutely fucking enraged.

I'm just exploring, that's all, she told the necklace silently. *Nothing to see here, nothing to worry about.*

It might have helped to run her hand along the wall, but touching the frequent splatters of drying blood and other horrible fluids was out of the question. Had the crazyass-old vampire done this, or Max?

What was happening to Max right now? The necklace warmed against her skin—really it was more like a choker, stretching from just under her chin to her collarbones, supple but also constricting. She didn't like the word, just one extra letter away from *choke*... but getting caught up in deciding what precise term to apply to a magical piece of jewelry was a waste of time.

Layla came back to herself with a start. Somehow, she'd reached a set of long straight stairs carpeted with faded, threadbare, tacked-down blue runner, her toes arranged precisely at the edge of the top step. The flight stretched downward, a surprisingly narrow pipe lost in a huge house. Why had she checked out this time, goddammit? Had she thought about tipping herself over and tumbling, hoping for a broken neck? Good luck, with her new reflexes—

What the fuck is that?

Rumbling, crashing, a deep vibrating roar. The sounds were distorted, rippling and stretching, but recent events had taught her there was only one thing in the world which sounded like the Tasmanian Devil's snarling run through several staticky amplifiers at once.

A vampire fight.

She stood and thought about this new development. It seemed important, even if figuring anything out took precious concentration away from moving.

Is that Max? It couldn't be. He'd left her behind after having his fun, just like any man—or he'd gone back into a burning oilfield and gotten himself killed, which amounted to the same thing. She was on her own, as usual. The important thing was to keep moving, maximizing her chances of getting away.

Or figuring out what the hell to do about the stupid magical necklace. Her hand floated out, closed around the banister.

First step's a lulu. A faint feeling of amusement surfaced; even now, she couldn't stop seeing the bleakly funny side of things.

Her left boot hung in empty air. Her right knee bent.

Slowly, dreamily, Layla moved down the stairs.

CHAPTER 28

ESMOND'S LAIR WAS A LARGE VILLA, AS SUCH THINGS WENT. Surrounded by thirsty, flagrantly watered ornamental gardens already wilting in the heat, the structure itself lacked any grace or refinement. The outbuildings were similarly either overdone or glaringly utilitarian, drones frozen in the act of servicing a rich, long-dead mortal's overweening pride.

Though aesthetically lacking, the estate was in a strategically commanding position for both the city and the larger, quite valuable territory, and possessed a number of crannies suitable for sealed daylight rest besides. A cloud of mortal death hung upon it now, thick and noxious but incapable of disguising Antinous's scent—broad as a highway, the patriarch taking no measures to conceal his trail.

A breath of roses and fresh-ground coffee intensified on the hot, sluggish breeze as well. It speared the ossification, a sharp poke on fresh bruising, and Nemesis was moving too swiftly to care for things like mortal construction, even if walls and windows had been busily reinforced by the servants of a now-dead sanguinant.

Massive front doors of imported wood exploded, breached as if by ballista or later, far more violent artillery. The great staircase-decked foyer, floored with black and white marble squares —carefully crafted, perhaps the only truly beautiful piece of construction in this entire pile—resounded like a struck bell. The call of his fledgling, a slight internal tugging of shared blood, was still far too muted.

Had his enemy hidden her elsewhere? But her fragrance intensified, vivid and reasonably fresh, a weak but welcome antidote to the encroaching numb lassitude.

He knew where his foe lingered almost immediately. Of course the patriarch would choose the larger of two ballrooms; Nemesis had carefully left that space clear of mortal corpse-dreck, since he knew Antinous's preferences for theatrical display even in battle.

There was no joy in finding that his opponent had taken both baits, leman and location. Why was the pull so faint? Had Antinous injured her, seeking to close his fangs in that luscious relief from slow age-death? Another sanguinant would find it deeply difficult to bite a bonded leman, near-impossible to claim one.

Thus, any challenge must be to death.

More internal walls crumbled before Nemesis. He did not bother with respecting mortal construction. Let this place shatter, brick by board, until he could take her from its hideousness. Was she wounded? Bleeding out? Impossible, no sanguinant would allow such damage to a rare, precious, irreplaceable leman.

And yet. The fear taunted, tormented, sharp spurs used to push at calcification.

More doors, some carved with foliage-shapes, others glimmering with glass insets. All shivered to pieces, flung inward, and the ballroom flowered before him. Parquet floor still gleaming despite a layer of dust, drapes along one wall rippling with several shrapnel impacts, mirrored panels along the other cracking under invisible strain.

And at the far end, a single shape gracefully avoiding flying debris with blurring sanguinant speed, then coming to rest, tall and wild-haired as a statue of Dionysius.

Nemesis finally halted.

The chiton of thick brown velvet, the sandals of an ancient pattern, the belt of braided mortal hair—a similarly old custom, fledglings bringing a lock or two of any prey's fur to their Maker —were just the same. Yet over the long tunic Antinous had draped a torn sweater, black wool with scorched, discolored leather patches shredded at its dangling elbows.

It had been wrapped solicitously about a leman just after dusk. The tatters were still redolent of her.

Antinous's dark eyes held the killing glow, wet crimson spatters waxing and waning, but the slowly accreting dust over their otherwise depthless wells had been scorched away. He would have inhaled as much as possible of a leman's fragrance, shaking away his own ossification; to be so close to the prize and yet unable to sink his teeth until her sanguinant was dealt with must be maddening.

She *had* to be hidden nearby. Had Antinous stripped her bare, attempted to claim what he could not yet bite? It was impossible for Nemesis's rage to intensify, yet it did. The flame was colorless now, a sword in the vitals mounting to his throat, just as dangerous as the rising stone-apathy.

The patriarch's grin was almost winsome. "My boy." Pure old Greek, a tenor singsong. "What a beautiful grey-eyed prize you brought me."

Centuries fell away. The rough, direct bark of an army camp burned Nemesis's throat. "You think yourself Agamemnon? You are not even a second Tarquin."

"You fancy yourself Akhilles, then? Do not forget he died young." Antinous stroked the sweater's rags, palms and fingers sliding with with lascivious slowness. "I will be enjoying her long after Lamia's Children have forgotten *your* name."

Which one, Nemesis or Maximus? Irrelevant, really. None of this mattered since his overarching goal was so nearly accomplished. Now was the most dangerous moment; the cusp of eventual victory could be wasted by exhaustion or arrogance.

Antinous would preen endlessly if allowed, counting upon fatigue and the steadily mounting weakness of a sanguinant denied his leman. Outside the mansion, a city burned and the gates of Dawn quivered upon the verge of opening.

"Too much talking," Maximus snarled, and flung himself into battle once more.

Ripping, rolling, tumbling, tearing, gouging, clawing—the patriarch roared as he fought, concentric waves of sound intended to dizzy, confuse, baffle.

Nemesis remained silent, and he noted almost absently the direction his enemy sought to keep the battle from veering. Leila was indeed nearby, then, tucked in the furthest wing of the main house, but the call of his fledgling was so very weak. It could be a trap, a feint—he tore at his Maker's side, and a spatter of ichor was loosed before Antinous could seal the wound.

Claws blurring, deadly quiet, Nemesis pressed the patriarch through one wall after another, absorbed heavy blows in return, lost a few more drops of his own blood after a flurry of swift deadly strikes, Antinous showing unwonted tactical flexibility for one so old, so rigid.

Even so short a time with a leman bonded to another sanguinant could grant a measure of marvelous, stinging clarity. No wonder the treasures were so rare, so cherished; a single sip of her was enough to shake both soldier and Emperor free of immortal chains, to make Nemesis more than he had ever dreamed of becoming.

He began to force Antinous back to the ballroom, as if he had just realized what the other sanguinant's caution implied. Again and again he battered at the patriarch, demanding retreat. Another sensation intruded, a brazen inner trumpet every child of the Blood knew intimately.

Dawn was nigh.

Now. The roar burst loose of Nemesis's chest, every scrap of strength hoarded through the long night breaking free of constraint. Skating the thin blister-swelling edge of bloodcraze, dangerously close to the glut-rage yet not tipped into the whirlpool, balancing on a single spidersilk strand of her beautiful blue-sheened hair, the memory of his leman's pulse against his fangs, the sweet hot velvet furnace, the throaty, desperate cries as she—

Here. She is here.

A passageway ran parallel to the ballroom's mirrored wall; the combatants had already pierced it twice in wild combat. Now Antinous was aimed squarely at the first hole—yet the aperture framed a slim figure, a familiar, tattered cotton shirt knotted at her waist, her lovely wintry eyes wide and vacant. The wet, smoky breeze carried a murmur of thunder plus a wave of her natural perfume, musk-drenched roses nodding under incipient storm. A glitter at her throat—the cocoon of ossification peeled from Maximus in an instant, shredding to nothingness, and fury unlike even the summit he had already mounted filled him from toes to scalp.

Even the craze of glut was paltry, infantile, *nothing* to this rage.

Collared. No wonder the call of his own fledgling was so muted. The question of just where Antinous had acquired such a demimonde item was unimportant—as was every other consideration, for the sun was just about to breach the horizon.

The killgrowl made words, a single sharp command. "Leila, *down!*"

Distraction was a gift to his enemy. Antinous struck, claws sinking into his eldest son's belly, ripping upward to find the heart.

CHAPTER 29

She floated through nightmare hallways full of corpses, veering as the rumbleroar and sounds of breakage changed, sometimes meeting dead ends, often unable to pick her way past stacked bodies. Each time she got near a window the necklace got worried, swamping her with clear plastic goop, slowing her down and making it hard to think.

I'm not wandering, she kept repeating internally. *I'm doing recon, I'm looking at the house.*

Then the rumbling swallowed her, crashing and creaking all around. She turned down a cramped, dark hall, thankfully free of sprawled, rotting shapes, and saw bars of faint light criss-crossing along its shaft. Not windows, she realized with a burst of muted relief, just holes.

Drywall dust floated in the air, like the glittering poof-grit of dead biters. Splinters and shards of wood, drywall, paneling, glass littered bare linoleum; this had to be a service passageway. A mansion was like a mall or a grocery store, there had to be places for the help to scurry around without visually afflicting their betters, and those passageways were never given more than a slap-kiss of cheap paint.

Pow. Crash-crunch. Boom. The whole structure rocked like a ship in a hurricane, and visions of Looney Tunes chaos made her want to laugh. Her lips twitched as she picked carefully between chunks of wreckage; she reached the first bar of light falling across the hall and stopped, wrestling down the urge to smile since she couldn't afford to spend the extra energy.

The sounds were coming from her left. She turned, staring through floating veils of vaporized plaster and drywall dust at a dim cavernous vista of broken walls, furniture smashed to flinders, bits of ceiling descending with majestic slowness, fierce shining glitters of broken glass.

It was amazing the roof hadn't caved in yet, though a low groan rising under the noise of a vampire fight gave her the syrup-slow realization that it wouldn't be long before that was a major possibility.

Confused motion. Her new eyesight was sharp, but they were moving so *fast* and she couldn't quite tell what the hell. Something else was happening, some new force fighting for control of her tired body.

"Leila!" A familiar voice, cutting through clear, thick lassitude. *"Down!"*

Her knees folded in immediate, unstinting obedience. Something big and dangerous whooshed overhead, the roar swallowing her whole, and crashed along the ballroom's parquet, throwing up more jagged splinterspears. Two combatants, so far as she could tell, both with dark curly hair.

It can't be. There was too much crap in the air, her vision was failing. The necklace was warm against her throat, but it didn't have to work so hard now to keep her trapped; her limbs were leaden, her head filling with the funny floating sensation of drifting off to sleep.

One vampire had his hands buried in the other's midriff; both snarled, their eyes glowing with bars of wet spreading crimson glow. She was still trying to figure out which one was the ancient, crazyass biter when her body shut down.

. . .

Dawn had risen.

CHAPTER 30

THE AGONY WAS IMMENSE, TERRIBLE, ANOTHER SANGUINANT'S CLAWS puncturing viscera, rising for the heart—was this what his own targets had felt, every time Antinous sent his son to kill? It did not matter, for Leila had collapsed almost as he gave the order— the collar would render its wearer quick to obey a bonded protector—and he had managed to wrap his arms around his opponent.

Clinging, clasped cheek to cheek, close as lovers, Nemesis propelled himself for the windows. The last, literally gutwrenching effort, the final piece of his plan, and his mind was very nearly empty as glass shattered, dust-choked drapery shredding with the force of their passage.

Too late Antinous grasped the danger; perhaps he thought his eldest meant to kill them both rather than suffer another's grasp upon the treasure. It did not matter—the sun's chariot was loosed from pink-pearl gates. Swollen and venomously red through a haze of burning, the great enemy of sanguinant both fledgling and elder lifted a rim over the horizon, scattered its light from a lid of heavy cloud closed over the city.

Past the ballroom's window was a flagstone patio meant for outdoor parties, then wide lawn sloping vaguely downward to a thick, spiny-green hedge masking the estate's boundary. No hole to hide in, no stick or stone to break the advance of quickly intensifying daylight—Nemesis's boots had long since evaporated and his bare soles skidded against flagstone, driving hard even as claws nearly reached his throbbing, aching heart.

Is she safe? Was Leila in a shadowed portion of the wreckage?

Eerie bronze glow strengthened. It stung, though weak and filtered through both cloud and smoke; the fire's breath now blanketed the entire city, swirling as the threatened storm lingered over outlying sand-scrub wilderness beyond the borders. Yet even that shadowless glow was more than enough to kindle a fledgling's tender flesh—or induce rapidly mounting anaphylactic shock in an ancient elder.

Only a daywalker or Archon could risk the sun's eye. And Nemesis had discovered just the previous morning, racing to the outpost holding his leman in safety, that he had surpassed elder status.

Age was no guarantee of strength. Perhaps the many deaths he had meted out sharpened and strengthened him in the Blood; perhaps he had been capable of daywalking for some while yet remained unaware, assiduously and habitually avoiding the danger.

Or perhaps the touch of a star-eyed nymph had hallowed him, made him capable of a fresh miracle.

It mattered little. Grateful for the gift, faintly amazed the plan had after all succeeded, he bore down, their furious passage erasing a long strip of yellowing turf to bare dry dirt. He held Antinous in smoke-tinted sunlight as the sun mounted and the dying Emperor screamed, no longer vibrating with a battle-roar but choking on a high whistling cry.

Certainly the light stung Nemesis's hide, scoured sensitive eyesight. It did not raise blisters or swelling, though, and even as his enemy clawed frantically, the balance had been tipped. Steam rose from the roasting of elder flesh, curling grey coils freighted with veils of grit. Muscles shriveled, eyeballs collapsing, the skin of Antinous's face splitting and desiccating with increasing speed. The more damage was wrought, the swifter sun-shock accumulated.

One more violent effort, wrenching the patriarch's arms from his son's flesh. Nemesis held the squirming, struggling, dissolving thing to earth as morn strengthened by increments.

A last gurgle, a final burst of glittering particles, and only yellow steam remained, shredding as thunder once again growled in celestial halls. Along with the smoke-tang, the greenness of petrichor intensified.

Rain was now increasingly likely.

Nemesis remained on hands and knees, shuddering as the gouges in his gut sealed. The sunlight did not quite harm a new daywalker, but he still did not like its inimical prickling, robbing him of strength even as the wonder of survival spilled through nerve and muscle both.

Leila. He was somehow upright, left hand a bar across his slowly healing midriff as he staggered for the house. Shredded curtains waved upon a flirting, strengthening breeze. Bits of debris pattered down, the villa now a slumped ruin. A deep furrow was gouged across flagstone patio, the ballroom's flank torn wide.

Stepping into shadow was a relief.

"Leila," he whispered to the house's shattered depths.

There was no reply.

The storm finally broke midafternoon, lightning piercing skydams, torrents sweeping over long orange-and-yellow tongues stretched from the cauldron of the oilfields. The wrecked pumps still burned, belching smoke—it would take some time for every iron-gantry dragon to be subdued—but the refineries had both been extinguished and all told the mortal authorities were relieved at the rain.

Even if lightning had struck the old Schellburger mansion, provoking a much smaller fire which gutted the historical monument. A certain rich local philanthropist had reportedly been caught in the flames along with several of his staff; that particular item of news would be buried under far more pressing concerns.

Of a ragged, half-naked figure carrying a long bundle swathed with dusty antique window-drapes from the residence, nothing was ever said. The mansion's cavernous garage had largely escaped damage, many of the gleaming vehicles within eventually auctioned off by authorities; if a dark-red SUV with heavily tinted windows had gone missing, nobody cared. It was enough that Grishkov's property was available for new owners; several developers had been eyeing the fraying estate for almost a decade now.

The city would remain free of sanguinant for a short while, but power—and predators—abhor a vacuum. Any territory so prime was meant to be ruled. There was unrelated, much more interesting news buzzing in the subterranean gossip-streams of the demimonde.

It was whispered that Nemesis had turned on his Maker, but none could say for certain. For all of Antinous's get had vanished from the earth.

CHAPTER 31

A BRIGHT, INDISTINCT SMEAR HOVERED BEFORE HER. WATER RAN, the torrent eventually shutting off. The thirst was back, rasping and awful even if the necklace held it at arm's length; she could not scrape up the strength to push against deep swimming lassitude.

Quiet, hoarse instructions. "Lift your arm… there. Good. Tip your head… sit up, yes, like that." A hand at her metal-clad nape, flowing warmth rinsing her hair, sluicing away smoke and terror. The bright smudge was glare on blue and green tile; soap-scented steam rose in slow-motion streams. "Close your eyes."

Her lids drifted down. More rinsing, then she was lifted, a small metallic clink and the slippery sound of draining. The brush of a towel—patting gingerly, not scrubbing hard as she would—drifted along her skin. More movement, cooler drafts passing leisurely over damp skin, and more directions she didn't bother to resist.

Save your strength. The shakes had her, muscles quivering as if after several days of hard workouts and too little food. A small noise, her throat vibrating inside a cage of golden knotwork. Was she trying to scream?

"I know," he soothed. "A moment more, *puella mea*. Then I will feed you."

She strained to open her eyes. Couldn't. The necklace's invisible grip was now far too strong.

Oh, God. Is it the old crazyass? Sharp burst of terror, but she was locked in darkness, in an unresponsive body.

The only comforting thing was a steady, almost familiar *ka-thump*, pause, *ka-thump*. It meant something, she just couldn't remember what.

Fabric draping, heavy and clinging-soft. Pressure moving her one way, then another. She sank into more softness, swayed, was caught and returned upright. Sitting, she was sitting on something—was it the bench? Had the ancient, terribly jittery vampire brought her back to the dusty pink room? It smelled too clean, though—fabric softener, fresh air loaded with the scent of mimosa trees, night air carrying the powder-spice through open windows.

That's nice, but I need to know…

What did she need? The thirst was growing too intense for the necklace to push it away; her throat was an agony of burning.

"Here, my Leila. Feed." Pressure against her lips.

Layla. That's me, that's my name. Oh, good, I'm glad to know that.

A slight shifting sound, her mouth suddenly hot and numb. Teeth clamping, and a burst of something wonderful hit the thirst, surrounded it, drowned the burning in deep comfort. Tangerine-taste, again, and chocolate milk. A hazy drifting memory of Meemaw's stuffing on a particularly good Christmas, the stickiness of cheap watermelon lollipops bought with pocket change after school.

The necklace loosened slightly. Her eyelids drifted up, vague bright blots taking on solidity and definition.

Light. A darkness looming over her, and her heart slammed against its bony cage before another swallow hit the spot where the thirst lived, spreading warmth in every direction. Her hands were locked, held near her face, and between them was a wrist. Sharp teeth buried deep, she was drinking.

Monster blood. She couldn't stop, despite a frantic internal retreat. Her vision sharpened, took on the funny rainbow oscillations and sparkles. Again and again she swallowed, wondering when it was going to stop.

"Enough," he said, finally, and the flow cut off. Her hands fell away, strengthless. But she could blink now, hold herself upright without swaying too badly. The thirst was gone.

Yet the necklace's clear, rippling wall still stood between her and the world.

I passed out. They were fighting. Oh, God, please tell me it's not the crazyass biter in a bathrobe. Funny, sure, real hilarious. But why was she so hopeful it was *another* vampire?

"Be still." The unmistakable note of command, and there was no loophole to exploit. The necklace had a good grip on her, plus the monster-blood high was deep and irresistible, spreading lazily through arms and legs, tingling in her fingers. "I will return in a moment."

Okay, but who the hell are you? Layla was left gazing blankly as the shadow retreated—yes, there was an open bay window, filmy white drapes fluttering on a soft breeze. A table to one side, thick tan carpet reaching from white-painted baseboard all the way to her bare feet. She could move her toes a little, feel the scratch against her soles, and the sensation was utterly luxurious.

Clean skin. Damp hair. Her hands lay demurely in her lap, on a bed of silky wine-red material. So she was dressed? Yes, she felt the straps on her shoulders, the fabric against her breasts and back, the soft folds over her knees.

That's good too. The edge of a mattress under her—she was sitting on a bed, which was faintly concerning for reasons she absolutely did *not* want to think about.

Warm air brushed past her. The shadow had returned.

Layla managed to tip her head slightly. Dark work trousers, a shirt-hem of black knitted material. A sweater, too heavy for a balmy summer night, leather patches at the elbows. Broad shoulders.

"Better?" Max asked.

The world went away on a white-hot rush of relief. Came back full of color and scent, laden with the warmth and swimming sensation of a monster-blood high, and yet she still couldn't move.

She was *still* trapped.

"You need not concern yourself with Antinous. My Maker is dead." He sat on the bed next to her, half-turned, watching her profile as he tucked a strand of damp hair behind her ear. "You were very weak, I carried you from the battle well-wrapped against daylight." A pause, as if he expected her to reply.

There wasn't a single blessed thing she could say, even if the necklace would let her talk. Layla strained against its grip, achieving only a slight twitch.

Max eventually continued. "I did not know he had a collar. It is… a rare thing, and I am amazed you were able to move while wearing it. Any other fledgling would be utterly helpless. But he was not your sanguinant, so I suppose his commands were not wholly inescapable." His hand moved again, smoothing her hair; he brushed her cheek with his knuckles, very gently. "Leila. Look at me."

She didn't want to. Her head turned, calmly, smoothly, and she gazed at his face.

Same curls falling messily over his forehead, same dark eyes —thankfully without those glaring, liquid crimson dots—and same proud beaky nose. His mouth was drawn tight, though, and his cheeks were hollow. Cords stood out on his neck; he wasn't quite gaunt, but he was certainly drawn.

Rolling around fighting with a cuckoo-ass biter will do that to you.

It was a wonderful thought, a *sane* thought, and she clung to it. Her lips wouldn't move; she couldn't talk.

"I am sorry." Almost mumbling, and he looked down—not staring at her chest, but as if he couldn't quite meet her eyes. "It was the only way to make certain he would not pursue us. It was a gamble, and you suffered for it. A sanguinant should not use his leman so, and I never will again."

Between the necklace and tripping on monster blood, she was having a difficult time following. Use her? She'd been decoy, and got caught—but it was sounding like he'd planned for that?

There was a bigger consideration, though.

He hadn't abandoned her. In fact, he'd shown up, beat all to hell—again—and put down a super old, absolutely batshit biter. If that had been part of the plan, it had worked. She couldn't feel anything but relief on that score.

Yet the collar was still on. She still couldn't move, couldn't speak, had a hard time even *thinking*.

He was talking again, still in that low harsh tone, ripping every word free against invisible resistance. As if his own throat hurt, perhaps. "You will hate me, you will struggle, but I will not let you go. I tell you this now, so there is no misunderstanding. You are *mine*."

Which was weird. Nobody had ever… Layla lost the thought, distracted by the light, the wall behind him—this looked like a hotel room, a nice older B&B maybe. Patterned wallpaper, and a mimosa tree outside. How long had it been since she smelled one of those?

"Now I must hunt." Max pushed his shoulders back and rose, stalking for the window. In a trice it swung closed, the sheers fluttering to a standstill, and he drew heavier drapes with quick, almost brutal efficiency, closing any hint of a gap. "You will rest, safely under seals. I shall return in less than an hour."

Uh, aren't you forgetting something? Layla's lips twitched. Her fingers tingled, but the goddamn necklace wouldn't let her move.

He was suddenly at the bedside again. "Lie down." No *please* or *thank you*, and her body moved woodenly even as she fought every inch. He settled her carefully on a comforter of white eyelet lace, and the air grew still. The funny sense of the air turning dead under an invisible force-field was hatefully familiar; almost before she realized what was happening, he had vanished.

CHAPTER 32

THERE WAS MUCH TO DO. DAYLIGHT HOURS FOUND HIM ARRANGING mortal identities for cover, carefully draining no few of Antinous's resources to provide for a leman's comfort, moving steadily through one task after another to build crucial ramparts for defending them both from notice either mortal or sanguinant. He even found a few hours to test his tolerance for the sun's blazing gaze, and found it much greater—though more uncomfortable—than he had imagined.

He could still barely believe she was safe, whole, alive; shock could kill a fledgling and his leman had suffered too much. The collar kept her quiescent enough to heal and possibly ease into a new rhythm of existence. He fed her twice nightly, keeping an iron grip on the steadily mounting thrall.

If restraint was torture, it was also richly deserved. The beast snarled and snapped within his bones, at the floor of whatever soul he possessed; his skin was increasingly, terribly sensitive, an iron bar sunk agonizing roots into depths of his belly, and rinsing her pliant, unresisting limbs nearly drove him to madness.

He wanted nothing more than to take her repeatedly, feel her shudder with pleasure under and around him, fuse himself to her softness. Every time her fangs pierced his pulse, every slow thorough draw against his veins as she fed, made his own true teeth fight for release and the beast struggle for primacy.

She was even more helpless now. Yet her huge, pale eyes were full of pleading. Or did he imagine that? Was the look hatred instead, or the uncomprehending stare of a collared fledgling? He did not dare take a single mouthful of her, though the collar provided more than enough room.

Finally, upon the fourth night since inferno and escape, he could wait no longer.

He rolled his sweater-sleeves up and bathed her as usual, dried her, wrapped her in a soft yellow gown which suited her a great deal, set the seals with care. Settled her on the bed, her pretty hands in her lap, her hair combed—and oh, he would like to spend hours upon that small chore, imagining she was willing, that she enjoyed his touch.

Or at least, tolerated it.

Finally he knelt at the bedside, gazing up at her. Took her hands—warm, almost limp, much softer than the battle-hardened hide of her sanguinant. "Leila."

Those wonderful wintry eyes with lavender threads patterning the iris, a puzzle he could study endlessly as the whorls and ridges on her fingertips. Her mouth, relaxed, lips slightly parted.

"Can you hear me? Nod if you understand."

Her chin dipped, drifted back to level. Her gaze sharpened. Was it fury or grief, begging or disgust? Deceptively fragile-looking gold threads gleaming against pale, lucent skin, a beautiful contrast. He could tell himself it was necessary, required to keep her safe.

"We will leave this place next dusk," he said, past the dry stone lodged in his throat. "Before that, though..."

Under the correct orders, she could even provide a simulacrum of willingness. The temptation was exquisite, especially with the mating-thrall approaching near insanity.

She will hate you. A constant, grinning, grinding reminder.

Each time the answer was the same. *Let her. It is better than this.*

For her dreamy movements, her lack of resistance, her vacant stare reminded him of ossification. He laid her hands back in her lap, took her shoulders, applied gentle pressure.

"Bend down," he ordered, softly. "Just a little… yes, there."

He traced one of the metal knots with a hesitant fingertip, then reached for her nape. The catch was easy, though the collar would dissuade its wearer from attempting to loosen the simple hook, the curved eye. Stretching the warm, near-liquid threads, loosening the restriction, he drew the collar away. It did not wish to leave her—he understood the feeling, down to his very bones —but necessity demanded.

Eventually the threadlike tangles, skin-warm, dripped between his palms. The effect would linger briefly; she sat stock-still, staring not at him but at glimmering metal. Temptation rose again, and he nearly foundered.

No. I cannot do that to her.

Maximus closed his hands. A simple wringing, muscle flickering in his forearms, and an expensive, very rare item of the demimonde gave a thin awful squeal as he tore it to shreds. Again and again he twisted, folded, and crushed, until a fine glittering dust descended to pale carpet.

He did not dare look at her. Brushed his hands together, ridding them of detritus as the fragments split finer and finer, just as sanguinant dust in the final throes of dissolution.

Her pulse, slow and steady while controlled by the collar, now quickened. So did her breathing. Her fingers trembled, the long glossy sheaf of blue-black hair falling to shield her face. Maximus longed to touch her; his hands were fists, denying the urge for as long as possible.

Leila crumpled, sliding from the bed's edge, and screamed.

CHAPTER 33

SHE COULDN'T STOP.

The cries poured out of her, razorfeather birds; when she toppled Max caught her and Layla struck out, wildly, her fist glancing off his stone-hard cheek. Her body jerked, twisted, starfished and kicked as if throwing a toddler-tantrum in Meemaw's trailer. Maybe every motion she hadn't been able to make stored itself up and now broke free, or she'd forgotten how to control her own limbs.

Either way, there was no stopping. Max lifted her, paying no attention to the frantic blows raining against his face and shoulders, her heels or toes drumming his shins. Her back arched, her lungs heaved, and what felt like hours later a long last despairing wail burst from her chest.

She went limp all at once, twitching, but at least she could now blink on her own. Her hands did what she told them to, her legs belonged to her again. Her shoulders tensed, her knees bent, and she kicked, weakly, experimentally.

Oh thank you, thank you God, thank you so much.

She hung in a vampire's iron-strong arms, her forehead against his sweater-clad shoulder. He'd torn the damn collar all to flinders, sure. But she could still *feel* it, warm and terrifying, against her bare throat.

"Ow." Her own voice startled her, faintly husky after the wild yelling. Her cheeks felt damp; a yellow cotton dress she didn't remember ever wearing before was twisted and ripped. Now *she* was the one destroying clothes. "No. No no, don't do it, don't… Oh, please, God, don't…"

Broken pleading, cursing, interspersed with random snippets. Apparently all the things she had wanted to say were pouring out as well. It was such a fucking luxury to *talk* again, to hear and feel her own voice.

Max's heartbeat never wavered. He held her, only moving slightly to avoid a particularly sharp blow; he's absorbed all the pummeling and now listened to her rave, nonsense flooding from her newly liberated throat.

"—I don't *care*, just take the fucking thing off me, I will do anything you want if you just *take it off take it off take it ooooooooffff…*" A final, lung-scouring hiss died away and she slumped once more, boneless against him. "God, oh God… Max? *Max?*"

No answer. Well, he was probably disgusted by the display, but she didn't care. Being able to consciously move again was worth any embarrassment.

She forced herself to breathe deep, her cheek pressed against his solidity. Still shaking, or maybe he was too. He held her at least a foot off the ground, statue-still except for tiny adjustments to keep her steady. His heartbeat continued, a slow even march, and the sound was more comforting than she could have ever imagined.

Even being motionless was good when *she* was the one deciding on it. The shaking intensified; she still couldn't tell who was trembling, her or the vampire who had come to collect her after all.

Who hadn't left her behind.

"Max?" She tested her fingers, swung her lower legs. "Say

something. P-please." A slight stammer, her voice a little rusty from disuse.

His chin shifted, touching her hair. "Are you hurt?" Very softly, as if afraid she was going to go off again.

Of all the things to ask… The wild urge to laugh ballooned inside her ribs, died on a sharp spike of fear, and she wasn't going to get over being magically immobilized anytime soon. At least the still, dead air told her those weird invisible curtains were up, so she probably hadn't disturbed anyone else with the ruckus—which was a weird consideration, since she was being held by an honest-to-gosh biter. "That… that thing, the necklace, the thing—"

"Destroyed. I did not know he possessed that item, Leila." Evenly spaced, the words very careful, now lacking any accent except a faint crispness which could have meant *college boy*. All things considered, he sounded almost modern. "Are you injured?"

I feel about an inch away from losing my entire shit again, if that's what you're asking. "I… no? I don't… I don't think so."

"Good." The trembling increased, and he was definitely the one doing plenty of it.

"Max?" *Are you okay* was probably a stupid question. She'd just punched him repeatedly, not to mention kicked several times. "I'm sorry, I couldn't stop—"

"Do not apologize," he said, harshly. "I used you as bait, Leila. You will not forgive me, but I have you, I will not let you go, and I am finding it rather difficult to stay in control. Be still, or…"

"Or what?" Maybe she didn't mean to say it out loud, but her brain-mouth filter was out of practice as well.

"Or I will take you." Still deceptively calm, though the jitters intensified yet again. They were definitely shared; as a matter of fact, he was shaking more than she was. "I… I need…"

Comprehension hit. Layla's breath caught, and she was very aware of the thin cotton dress, of his body heat through the sweater, of his arms locked around her. A curious feeling, being held so tightly—she was enclosed, but not like the necklace's terrible, smothering pressure.

Protected, almost. When, in God's name, had she begun to feel *safe* with a vampire?

Oh, what the hell. Why not? He was a monster, yes—and there were worse beasts out roaming the night.

Far, far worse.

Layla tested her arms—yep, still working. So were her legs, and a slight experimental movement verified the hypothesis; her thigh brushed against a definite protrusion.

Max froze. His motionlessness was breathless and almost-comforting at once.

Her own quivering wouldn't go away. "Then do it." Her mouth was full of the spice-taste meaning monster blood; how many times had he fed her with the collar on?

But tonight, he hadn't. She was reasonably sober, all things considered. And she hadn't worn panties for a while now, but if she had, they would definitely be a little soaked at the moment. Her own arousal was frightening, body and mind both yanking at straws to prove she was in charge, able to move, no longer trapped.

"Do it," she repeated. Her trembling arms raised, hands finding the muscle-slopes between his neck and shoulders. She couldn't get her legs up to wrap around him, but the urge to simply climb this tall, stock-still vampire like a tree was over-whelming. "Make me forget."

"Leila…" Drawing out her name like he knew the song, almost a groan.

"The bed's right there." Now she could be *sure* she was in charge of her own body again; she could barely believe she'd said that to a monster, but it was unquestionably her own decision. "Although—"

He was already moving, fabric tearing—she felt a momentary, completely laughable pang for the poor dress, first ripped by her own thrashing and now this—and the world whirling like a carnival ride again. This time, however, the ride was controlled, a thrill instead of a careening disaster. The mattress accepted them with a short surprised sound; no matter how everything spun, Layla found, *he* was still right there, solid and real. His mouth on hers, insistent and greedy, the purr of that strange growl spilling through her, his hand curling under her left knee and lifting, and then the *invasion*, a single hard thrust she was more than willing to meet.

Certainly not wasting time, are we. Then there was no more opportunity for thought. His mouth drew away for a bare moment, kissing frantically down her chin, and before she could flinch his fangs struck as he surged forward again, burying his cock completely.

Her back arched; she could scream, but the cry was short and breathless, lightning slamming through every nerve. Fear and dark pleasure swirled, her nails turned to claws scraping frantically against his shoulder and a long furrow down his back, dragging over flickering muscle as he did it again, again, *again*, patient and deadly as the pressure coiled inside her.

Until she shattered, heart pounding, great gripping waves pulsing through every inch, her body entirely hers once more. How the cut opened she didn't know, but hot candysweet blood filled her mouth, and she drank in long starving swallows while he whispered her name, over and over, holding her safely pinned to white eyelet lace.

EPILOGUE

Several months later

"Not ever?" Layla propped herself on her elbow, frankly amazed. The oak tree rustled, night wind caught in branches heavy with damp spring leaves. "Really?"

"Not even as fledglings." Flat on his back, fingers laced behind his head, Max lounged like a big cat. He was impossibly feline sometimes. "Some say the killing sleep holds dreams and that is how it grasps an elder, with memories of mortal life. Or fantasies." One corner of his mouth lifted incrementally. "Much better to rest in a leman's arms."

Layla rolled her eyes. "Except when you sleep in the corner." She picked idly at the plaid blanket he'd spread so carefully atop another weatherproof layer, since the ground was damp from constant rain.

It was a tradeoff. Everything here was so green, all the time.

"That…" A slight, rippling shrug. His every move was so controlled, but he didn't seem to mind her constant need to fidget. "It's different. It's more of a trance."

Sure. Maybe now was a good time to broach the subject. This park had a great view of the city's glimmering, a field of stars mirroring the great vault overhead. The breeze was chilly, but sanguinant didn't feel extreme temperatures so much; still, she decided to slither a bit closer to his comforting heat. "I've been thinking."

As usual, he immediately tilted his head, paying attention. "Yes?"

"About hunting—not to feed," she hastened to add, knowing how he felt about *that* particular subject. No that she ever wanted to grab a human being and take blood, though he said she wouldn't go nuts, swallow too much, and inadvertently murder someone. *Immune to the glut,* was how he put it, and while she was glad about the assertion Layla didn't feel like testing it anytime soon. "But other things. Demimonde stuff."

Max was silent, but not in a dismissive way. His quiet was focused, receptive attention; it was strange to be listened to so closely. She liked the feeling, certainly, but still suffered the same old flutter of anxiety at advancing an idea, risking another hunter's ire.

Especially a man.

"We could do a lot of good," she added, her knee touching his leg. Carefully, because he was apt to take most nudges as an invitation to at least a kiss. "Right? Take care of mad sanguinant, the ones doing bad things."

"Hm." Neither agreeing nor the opposite, a very male noise.

Layla nudged a little harder. "Don't just grunt, *talk* to me."

"Yes, *puella mea.*" A lingering rumble under the words, and his smile was more definite now. He'd even unbent enough to wear flannel button-ups and sometimes even a baseball cap, though the work trousers and boots were a given. *Good for battle,* he said. "As long as you like, always."

More than that, though, he seemed a lot more, well, *human.* Still a little stilted sometimes, but the difference was night and day. Which he said was entirely due to having a leman, but Layla thought regular athletic sex was probably a factor as well. God knew she had loosened up in that department; the things he could do with his mouth, for example… "English, Max."

He wanted to be entirely modern.

"Thank you." Gravely grateful for the reminder, as was every time. "I clear every sanguinant so foolish as to tread in this territory, sweetheart." His eyebrows rose a little, questioning if he'd used the right endearment.

Good job. She risked slipping a little closer, laid her head on his chest. "Yeah, you sneak out near dawn for that, and when you come back you sleep in the corner. Did you think I couldn't tell? Anyway, we could really do some good. Couldn't we? I'm fast, and strong." *Since you keep feeding me, and you're old.*

Finding out he could go out in daylight had been a bit of a shock. A daywalker had erased O'Shaughnassey's entire team; she still wasn't sure how to feel about snuggling with the biter who had wiped out her own.

Sure, they had shot at him first. But still.

"For a fledgling, yes." As usual, he moved slightly to accommodate, then became motionless the moment she finished arranging herself comfortably. "That is not my concern."

It stung, for a moment. "I can train harder. You said yourself it's possible, if you get a blade going fast enough—"

"I risked you once, Leila. Never again." Another touch of purr to the words, vibrating in the cathedral of his chest. When it faded, his heartbeat continued, strong and sure.

"I don't like you going out alone." *There. That's a lot of it, too.*

He was silent for a short while. It smelled like rain, as almost always; the mix of car exhaust, concrete, and the persistent note of fresh-brewed coffee permeating this city was beginning to be familiar. His heart spoke in her ear, and on the other side lingered traffic-noise, a faraway burst of sirens as some accident was discovered, and the drowsy murmur of urban crowding. Between the two was a small, safe cradle.

Sometimes it pinched. Not like a collar, thank God; finding

out how those had been made, what they were intended for, was horrific.

"I do not like it either," he said, finally. "And witnessing my hunting to feed may unnerve you."

"I guess that it might." *I don't ask where you get the blood from.* He was pretty definitive that *he* didn't drink to kill nowadays, and she left it at that. Compromise was necessary in any squad, even with only two members. "But will you at least—"

"I will consider the idea most carefully, Leila-my-rose."

That's a new one. She was going to have to think of some cute little nicknames for him, too. "Good."

"But I *will not risk you.*"

"Fine." *I guess there's time.* If she had to be a biter, she wanted to be the least-objectionable kind. Keeping an eye on the forums and message boards was a lot more thought-provoking now that she had a source right next to her at the keyboard.

And one day, after she'd learned enough, she might strike out on her own. The thought tiptoed around in her head at intervals, a cautious guest.

Layla pushed herself up to sit, almost regretfully. Max followed suit, glancing briefly over the vista. Not because the city was beautiful—though it unquestionably was—but checking the terrain, alert to danger. The constant awareness was sometimes exhausting to witness.

So she poked his ribs, gently, almost like tickling a statue. "Let's do something fun. I'll race you home. And—" She forestalled any incipient objection with another lingering touch, before bouncing to her feet. She liked the local fashion of jersey knit dresses and leggings, especially since she could now afford good boots. Not to mention an actual *house*. Learning how to get funding the vampire way was another item on her list. "If you can catch me before the stop sign at the top of our hill, I'll give you a reward."

It was a short run, after all. For sanguinant.

Max rose, and set about refolding the blankets with swift, exact care. "What reward?"

"How about a shower?" If she could keep him from ripping this particular outfit to shreds, it would be a miracle. "But you'll have to be careful, and not tear all my clothes apart. I'll wash your back."

The tree sighed, combed by a freshening wave full of green scent. He frowned slightly, tucking the wad of blankets under one arm, and regarded her, eyes gleaming almost hopefully. "I prefer baths."

"I know you do, but it's *my* choice of reward." The fidgets had returned, as usual; she had to move, soon.

Of course he liked to chase, and nowadays she didn't precisely mind being caught. They would be lucky to make it to the shower, though he would make sure the seals were set the moment she was inside.

The day she learned how to do that… well, they'd see. Layla shifted her weight, testing her bootsoles' grip.

He had gone still again, unblinking, focused entirely on her. "*Ave, Imperatrix.*"

"English, Max." She was, Layla realized, grinning like an absolute fool.

Which was all right, because so was he. "I am yours, my nymph. You'd best start running."

EXCERPT FROM FLEDGLING & ARCHON, BOOK THREE

The third installment of a scorching new dark vampire romance series by the New York Times bestselling author, Lilith Saintcrow.

Becoming a bloodsucker had fixed her knee problems—which was, so far as Simone could see, the only good point.

Simone Deschants was all ready to begin a new life as a middle-aged divorcée, until a monster's attack turned her into something unspeakable. Now she hunts down vampires while trying to ignore her own terrible, raging thirst. Until one night, an old, powerful specimen finds *her*.

No name, no home, no sanity. An eternity of roaming the night has become madness, true death looming ever closer… until a leman crosses his path. Now the ancient wanderer has found the prize every sanguinant seeks, and his survival is assured—if he can hold what he has claimed. He will stop at nothing, and his hold on her is assured.

Unless, that is, another powerful predator snatches her away. Because someone else has noticed Simone's existence, and has plans of his own…

Chapter One

BECOMING A BLOODSUCKER HAD FIXED HER KNEE PROBLEMS—WHICH was, so far as Simone could see, the only good point.

Well, there was also not needing bifocals, plus her tinnitus had outright vanished. The resultant sensory sharpness was a curse in its own way since there were so many things she would rather not see or hear. Especially when she got through the door of yet another boot-scootin' shithole and found that, as dismally expected, the entire bar stank to high heaven *and* there was another vampire present.

Five bucks to you, Barry. Her finder would be thrilled that his sucker-map algorithm was still tiptop. If it was indeed computer wizardly and not some kind of low-level psychic whatsis, which Simone did not quite rule out.

There was a whole lot she refused to disbelieve these days.

She gave every pair of peepers under cowboy hat or faded baseball cap time to take in her arrival, then stalked across a slightly sticky floor with a little extra strut in her Levi's. Each light bulb hanging in a dust-crusted fixture seemed to have at least two flies perambulating lazily below and the corner jukebox was a knockoff Wurlitzer currently thumpwailing some generic Hank Williams clone. All the boots here were just as run-down as her own deeply vintage Tony Lamas, *except* for the brand-new glossy black numbers with shiny toe-caps worn by the vampire at the end of the bar. No doubt everyone in here just thought he was a weekend-rodeo stranger; his camouflage was as good as her own. The vamp stared over his warm bottle of something domestic like he couldn't believe *another* bloodsucker would have the temerity to walk into this dive.

Sandy-gold hair flopping over his forehead, check. Those narrow, close-spaced hazel eyes, checkity-check. Her sense from the blurry security camera footage was correct, too—he *felt* like a young one, but honestly once she'd hit her late forties everyone looked like a baby. Of more interest were the dark, microscopic flecks on his denim jacket and the quickly snuffed crimson pinprick in each pupil.

Well, I've certainly got his attention. Which was never a problem; vampires seemed a gregarious bunch, despite what the forum posts said. Of course, she probably had a leg up by being a fellow bloodsucking evildoer.

The spot at the back of her throat scratched, lightly. "Whiskey, please." She tried a polite, noncommittal smile on the grizzled, plaid-jacketed bartender, whose bushy eyebrows twitched in what could have been surprise.

Me too, buddy. Here she was, plain old Simone Deschants of Trenton City, looking well over thirty years younger than her actual age and fitting into her college jeans as well. It was a miracle, Lord have mercy—but the price was steep.

"Uh." The bartender's pupils were blessedly human, dilating as his irises shrank. For all that, he seemed nice enough—sad, yes, but that was to be expected in a place like this. "What kind, ma'am?"

Asking for the most expensive firewater would be showy, and too much for her slender budget as well. She had to remember who she was, despite the… the fangs, and the thirst, and what it made her do. "Good old JD's, please. Thank you."

She turned as the bartender busied himself, letting her gaze rove, marking the position of every critter in the room. Mostly male, only two waitresses—both with the type of high, crunchy hairsprayed bangs she hadn't seen since high school, Christ this place was a time capsule—and a couple ladies in what was their going-out best, including large bright plastic earrings. She even caught a breath of drugstore perfume from a blonde in an embroidered chambray shirt, who was staring owlishly at this new babe on the block, and for a moment Simone actually felt pretty.

Except she wasn't really in search of booze or a cowboy to take home for riding. Her business was with the man-shaped thing at the end of the bar, staring fixedly in her direction, and those spatters on his jacket would be all but invisible to human eyes.

Not to her, though. And she could smell the it, stroking that spot at the very back of her throat.

Blood.

Four packs left in the fridge, she chanted inwardly. It wasn't going to be enough, but maybe she could get more once she was out of this pissant burg.

God knew she'd done far more difficult things in the past few years.

So she gave the barkeep a crumpled bit of legal tender, told him to keep the change, and held the other vampire's gaze as she downed her whiskey, exhaling softly afterward as the brief alcohol sting faded. Christ, she couldn't even get drunk nowadays, though lots of the others acted like blood itself was pure-d Everclear.

Once again she was grimly unsurprised that the liquid didn't ease that dry spot. Nothing did but the red stuff, and even the bagged variety only imperfectly.

The vampire at the end of the bar was trembling. Oh, *that* wasn't visible to the normal folks, either; the liquid in his bottle barely moved, a few bubbles shaken free of the sides. But he stared at her like he'd just found new meaning in the universe, and Simone wondered why they all acted so oddly. Was it just because she was perpetually new in town? Did they get bored looking at normal people's faces?

Doesn't matter. Of course vampires were more visibly different to her now, she could see the matte-poreless skin, the wild shine to their eyes, the gloss of their hair. Normal people had imperfections, pimples, scars, bedhead, wrinkles.

It wasn't fair, it wasn't just, it wasn't *right*. But there was nothing she could do except her self-chosen job, so Simone simply gave the bartender another smile and headed for the door.

She knew the other vampire would follow.

It wasn't quite a one-horse town—eight stoplights, the nearest hospital reachable by half-hour highway drive, three churches and four honkeytonks on the main drag. Outside the imaginary village limits, grassy plains stretched westward until purple mountain majesties decided enough was enough and put a stop to that nonsense, thank you very much. The wind sweeping across miles and miles of almost-nothing tasted like grass, cows, wildlife, an occasional tang of balsam or river, and forever. Hard diamond stars glittered endlessly, but she had no time for beauty or philosophy because the bloodsucking fucker was fast and her claws might have a hard time getting through his skin.

Sure, he was 'young'—but now that they were both on the move it was clear he was a bit older than *her*, which seemed to make the bastards far more difficult to deal with. Her only saving grace was that he was weirdly uncoordinated, almost too excited to fight properly. Every bloodsucker she'd interacted with went shaky-psycho when they got close to murder, and Simone didn't have time to think about why *she* seemed to have missed that boat.

It could be a function of accumulated age? Or maybe she just didn't notice her own altered perceptions. Both horrifying prospects, to be sure.

Getting her prey to the city limits was simply a matter of running fast enough, and a carefully chosen gully yawed to her right, precisely on schedule. She plunged into its arms, twisted in midair, bounced from side to near-vertical rocky side, dodged half-seen or merely sensed obstacles, and when he attempted to hit her from behind she was almost, *almost* surprised.

But not entirely, and she had a bit of experience nowadays when it came to ripping up vampires. Plus, visiting this very ravine right after dusk had given her a good idea of its layout—not to mention the tangle of abandoned barb-wire rusting comfortably in its crooked elbow, perhaps deposited by a long-ago flash flood.

She dropped flat just in time; the blond bastard sailed right over her into the mess. A yip like a surprised coyote, followed by a thrashing and a sweetly metallic scent.

Blood. *Vampire* blood.

Okay, he's not so old as I thought. Great. But she couldn't wait around for a motherfucker to die of tetanus.

He stagger-streaked from the iron cobweb-tangle, arms outstretched and claws out. Her own fingernails were extended—tough, razor-sharp, and more than ready.

The hardest part was shoving away a lifetime's worth of training—*you can't do that, girls don't hit people, use your words, be nice!*

Fortunately, her body's hateful new instincts knew what to do. She just had to get out of the way.

Plus, before catching a bad case of vamp-itis she'd been on the downhill side of fifty and the rocks of a bad divorce besides. There wasn't a lot of *nice* left in Simone Deschants, taking her maiden name back in a big way and dodge-weaving close, left hand flickering to open up a big ol' steaming rip in the monster's guts.

During each and every fight she remembered the thing that had infected her, how it had screamed when sunshine poured through the church basement window. She heard those cries once more as she tore at the drunk-staggering bloodsucker, ducking and bobbing, claws ripping over and over until finally, eventually the wet rot racing through its tissues turned to glittering dust.

Another monster went *poof*, caving in as she caused more damage than preternatural flesh could heal until nothing was left but irritating iridescent grit, working itself finer and finer into every crevice. Simone backed toward the gully's wall, rubbing her hands frantically, shaking out her hair, and finally brushing at her clothes with maybe a little more force than necessary.

The grainy stuff itched, but only briefly. Worst of all was the way her conscience dug its spurs in. Maybe this guy had been attacked and turned just like her, and was only trying to survive. Maybe one day Simone herself would go nuts from the thirst's constant scratching and have to be put down like a rabid dog.

She leaned against the ravine's wall, ribs heaving though the fight was indisputably over. "Sorry," she heard herself whisper, over and over. "Sorry, I'm so sorry, I hope it's better now. I hope you're at peace."

A crowd of dry, twinkle-giggling stars watched avidly from overhead, along with the low-hanging, evil-grinning gibbous moon. Neither cared about her silly little emotional pangs. Nature was beautiful, sure, but she was also a stone-cold bitch. Maybe vampires were just an evolutionary niche, biology getting day-drunk and deciding to have a little fun.

Simone let the soft, frantic catechism of regret drain away as she braced herself against the ravine's wall, calculating the hours left until dawn.

Just enough time to get home and check in.

Chapter Two

Taverns, hostelries, inns as a whole smelled far better than they used to, or perhaps his nose was simply dulled with age. Yet the wanderer hesitated before crossing the street, forcing himself to *focus* through the shifting, distracting kaleidoscope of night's wonders.

Neon signs buzz-blinking, showering multicolored light competing with the lamps and blinking traffic-control devices. Arteries and veins of paving turning to dirt as they unraveled from the township-clot, starred at the margins with houses staring blankly at wonderful vistas of grass and weather. A cool breeze redolent of plain and mountain, thick with the everpresent tinge of car exhaust. Mortal heartbeats thundering through the mechanical cascade of pipes, buzzing galvanism, tinny music, chatter, and clatter; the song of wind through tall grass and quiet murmur of high-summer watercourses diving for shelter providing orchestral backdrop.

The wilderness called; for a creature so old and frayed, it was almost a refuge. He almost turned to stride away before remembering his purpose once more—a stranger, an *intruder* tainting his current territory.

The fractures and slippage weren't so bad here. In mortal cities the crowding of prey was a constant quasi-irritation; here, he could visit a few isolated homesteads upon an eve, feeding carefully to avoid glut. Or he could simply linger unseen outside one of four taverns, harvesting the drunken, leaving them weakened yet still breathing. The effort of restraint helped fight the accretion of mental and physical dust upon his joints and brain-folds, hardening slowly to stone, but the wanderer suspected he might be too old to die in the usual manner of his kind.

After all, neither the great fire of the Sun nor open flame itself could kill him. Hazily he remembered how he had discovered the latter fact and shuddered, his fingers driving into the crumbling concrete flank of what had possibly once been a greengrocer's as he lingered in comfortable shadow, again attempting to remember why he was here, now, in this particular place.

Intruder. He clung to the single word, the concept threatening to slip from a mental grasp grown increasingly clumsy and worse, timorous.

The process was accelerating. He would soon be too slow and absent to survive even a fledgling's attack, unless mere reflex was enough to ward off such an ignoble end. An elderly, arthritic dragon, shambling through the dust-heap of centuries—no, a *dinosaur*, that was a good concept, meaty, endlessly interesting. Was he ancient enough to remember such beasts?

It seemed likely. He remembered thinking the steam-carriages of their ilk, snorting and heaving, and fleeing at least one of the things long ago. But no, there was another word for it —*train*, like a noblewoman's dress or retinue, like teaching tricks to a dumb beast. In other languages the connections were differ-ent; he had to focus on the current tongue.

Again the wanderer almost turned away. Later he might brood upon how close he had been to failure, true-death, the treasure whispering past his aching, clumsy fingertips. But at the last moment, recognition of the insult arrived once more—a tres-passer, an interloper in the small realm of one who had survived open flame, by the thunderbolt, by the wounds of God!

So he forded the street's cracked pavement river and pushed at the caupona's door…

No. *Tavern* door, this was a watering-hole, not a sleeping-place. The close almost-pleasant fug of mortal breath and yeasty inebriation puffed outward in a silken cloud. A golden thread buried in the breeze's depth halted him upon the threshold, a long glassy moment between screaming chaos and a precious, crystalline moment of lucidity.

What is that?

Spice and night wind from exotic harbours, a hint of green sap and the faintest stinging touch of mortal alcohol. Sense-impressions flooded the fractured mess his brain had become, layering quick and deft as a master painter's brush—a glance from wide dark velvety eyes, brown curls fragrant as cedar bark, a soft musical murmur he could almost, *almost* hear.

The bartender drew breath to shout at a ragged scarecrow standing spellbound in the doorway; the wanderer's attention fastened upon that stocky mortal, who wisely swallowed whatever he had been about to say.

Marvelous, wonderful clarity. The smell was intriguing, but more than that, it peeled away a thick layer of accreted dust, sharpening every visual edge and burnishing the entire room from its slumped, wheezing music-maker—*jukebox, that's what it's called*—to the flies under hanging lanterns abuzz with galvanism, the spotted mirror behind shelves of liquor to the worn, dust-creased boots of tired mortal males. Quite a few curious glances settled upon the wanderer; he wondered if his cloth were too anachronistic for even simple country folk used to keeping their opinions to themselves.

Layered against that beautiful, phantasmal perfume was the more-familiar intruder's scent. Perhaps *that* was why the trespasser lingered? But if so...

Well, you will simply have to kill him. Not a difficult task. His gaze roved the tavern's interior, marking every living thing, and the mortals would never know how close they brushed against death that night—a feast before battle was always tempting. The golden thread was a frail fence and enticement all at once, drawing him away from such dangerous pleasures.

She—the scent was unmistakably female—had lingered here for a short while, dyeing the air with beauty. A shudder passed through his frame; he turned, allowing the constant whistling wilderness-breath to sweep the door to. Let this clutch of mortals live another night; there was time and enough to drink the entire continent dry if necessary.

Later. Once he had run the most important prey of millennia to ground, and disposed of whoever now held her.

Following a single auriferous thread, the wanderer stepped into the road, loping easily along painted yellow stripes. The buildings blurred to either side, and he plunged past the frail glow modern mortals used to hold back the night.

Remember, remember, he chanted as he ran—almost unnecessary, since the evaporating waft of delicious scent waxed and waned, yet thankfully never quite disappeared. No attempt to mask at all, though the trespasser's spoor was intermittent, showing some recognition of elementary safety measures.

He could not tell if the strangeness was in his own looming unreason or the trail itself. Stars overhead sang to themselves in high tinkling voices, a yellow moon leering, gazing upon the earth's teeming face with interest but no mercy. The trail veered, plunged into the mouth of a gorge, and only the angry reek of recent death stopped the wanderer from leaping straight into a rusty tangle of mortal iron.

Not that it could have harmed him; his hide was ancient, more durable than daylight. But had he been so foolhardy his clothes would have been reduced to shreds.

Now the wanderer could not remember what he wore, or whence the garments had been stolen from. A question literally immaterial; when he met the bearer of that wonderful perfume, he would no doubt seem a bit odd. What mattered was getting close enough to fill his lungs, let the fact of her presence sink in so he could think clearly for a few moments. The constantly fracturing mess inside his skull would coalesce, and he might even be able to remember his own name.

The intruder to this territory had been less than cautious; this, the wanderer could understand. With that lovely, enticing, magical scent filling nose, brain, branching vein-channels, it was a wonder either of them had been able to run without stumble-staggering. No trace of whoever had killed the trespasser, which meant the valuable prey's protector was old and canny—and yet, they had let her slip away?

A sanguinant did not use their greatest treasure as bait. Never, never. It simply was not done; he knew that, as he knew little else about this confusing present time. So, a bauble slipping from a powerful grasp, temporarily adrift until reclaimed? Perhaps, yet her trail led from the gorge as well, *still* with no masking.

How was it possible? The wanderer was missing something crucial, and would most likely die as he challenged another archaic, powerful sanguinant for the guerdon.

If, that was, a creature like himself were capable of true-death. Was it accuracy, hubris, or further insanity to have doubts upon the matter? He had, after all, survived the fire.

For once, remembering that terrible event did not distract him from current surroundings. Slipping between the whispering speed and nearly invisible mistform at places which seemed ideal for ambush, he was more alert than he had been in… oh, two centuries, at least?

How long had it been, precisely, since the quaking riven earth, the walls of flame breathing like living creatures, the agony as their caress swept over him, robbing him of any claim to logic or sense? He knew not what day it was, what year according to which calendar, or even what this mortal country now named itself. The language of its inhabitants eluded him at the moment as well, yet the scent was working upon him in tremendous fashion, for he dimly sensed what he was missing. Great gaps torn in his knowledge, his reason, his very *self*, and he could not entirely blame a city soaked in flames.

Those who lived long became as stone, physically and in all other ways. Unless…

Unless you are strong enough to kill the protector of that scent. Why do they not mask her? Such a simple precaution.

A cold, rational, *sane* thought, one he clung to as he ran

He veered down a gravel side-road, which widened to a small, irregular trampled space abutting the green skein of an aestival-vanished creek. The metallic scent of water was barely a drouth-choked trickle, and a large rectangular shadow loomed. The shape was possessed of wheels as well as two large night-blind eyes watching him, insectile, glossed with starlight.

Ah. Glass, front-facing. Along the thing's flanks were irregular hints of golden glimmer—candlelight? Here?

It was a camping vehicle, he realized slowly, halting at the very edge of what had to be a place for locals to park when the creek was high enough to hold fish, or dabble toes in a cool flow. The scent was very strong; she had been here for some while. That realization peeled another layer of insanity from his encrusted mental processes, and the resultant jolt was almost as pleasant as the great gripping lungfuls of golden-brown spice he took in greedy gulps, waiting for her protector to show.

Nothing. The night wore on. His senses, muffled by age and madness, whetted themselves with each new draught of scent. The murmur of her voice was just as he had imagined, a soft sweet song capable of enticing any sanguinant into the whirlpool, onto razor rocks. A desert wanderer would follow that whisper over the sands until the carnivorous flame-spirits feasted upon his bones; a steppedweller in skins would ride every horse he possessed to foundering in pursuit.

Inside the vehicle, her muffled laughter, edged with some-thing… anger? Disdain? He could not tell. The wanderer, now invisible even to those of his own kind, was patient. Each soft, controlled breath, freighted with her magnificence, was whet-stone to a rusty edge. Perhaps he could gather enough sanity, enough flexibility to fight effectively when her guardian appeared.

Yet why, *why* would any sanguinant announce her presence like this? Did they not grasp the risks? Impossible, even a fledg-ling knew to conceal, protect, jealously shield such a nonpareil.

Unless… was she alone? Which made no sense either, for who had meted out death to the trespasser? One of *her* kind did not engage in combat; it was simply unthinkable. No sanguinant would ever allow such madness.

The vehicle moved slightly, rocking on rubber wheel-feet. A flimsy fortress indeed, and no hint of invisible seals. Either the wanderer was missing a critical element of the scene and her protector was even now stealthily preparing for the kill, or...

Was it possible? It would be a miracle, an insanity in and of itself.

Clicking, sliding metal. A rectangle on the vehicle's side flung itself open, dim golden glow limning a slim shape. A bounce, a hop, and she folded down to sit on a low, handmade wooden stepstool, clearly accustomed to the maneuver.

A cat poised to watch unwary prey would have seemed frenetic next to his utter motionlessness, breath and pulse both in abeyance, his own scent thoroughly masked. In fact, another of his age and experience might have sensed something wrong in a single frozen patch amid the flow of night, camouflaged in long grass and scrub bush greedily seeking the creek's hidden damp.

Between starshine and candleflicker she perched, lithe and graceful, long fingers rubbing at her nape under rippling dark hair just the color he had scented—cedar bark, matching the spice of her scent. Sandalwood, clove, cardamom, cassia, all rich and wonderful savours mixing to fill his mouth with the tingling honey-numbness of change and analgesic agents, his true teeth sliding free without a betraying crackle of shifting bones. His eyes burned, dry and avid; suppressing the pinpricks of killglow required an effort of will he was unused to making.

The wind, capering across miles of empty rolling grassland, wrapped him in her warm, enticing fragrance. Another layer of dust peeled from his perceptions; he marveled at how dull his senses had become.

And oh, was she not superb? Wide dark eyes under winged brows, her cheekbones starkly shadowed, a sweet bow of a mouth drawn with some emotion he could not name, her slimness very obviously tense even as she sighed and gazed at the distant horizon.

He realized the vehicle was deliberately parked to afford her quite the artistic vista, which bespoke some planning. And her thinness was not that of fashion; her scent held a faint edge of burning sugar, caramel turned too dark upon high heat. She was not properly fed, and no smoky screen of another sanguinant's possessiveness hung upon that gorgeous, compelling aroma.

Can't be. His mind trembled upon the edge of fracture once more; the sensation retreated as he allowed another trickle of air past his nostrils. Even the most momentary relief was worth unending devotion; a sanguinant would pay any price, perform any feat to have unfettered access, to be near the source of that surcease.

It simply cannot be.

Yet it was. Sitting before him, in jeans and a soft, clinging long-sleeve shirt, an actual, unmistakable leman pointed her booted toes and sighed. "Fuck," she said, conversationally—an old word, perhaps as old as himself. He almost twitched, looking for her interlocutor. Or did she speak to herself, as the lonely were supposed to?

He had, as the madness waxed over seasons and mortal years, babbled in the depths of night or cave. He had sung, hardly realizing the voice was his own, and howled during storms when the thunder-gods hurled bolts earthward. But *she,* she was too beautiful to ever know such things.

"Might be a good idea," she continued, softly, ruminative. A lovely voice to match the rest of her, low and husky, the sweetest song imaginable. "No harm in trying, I suppose." A long pause, as she leaned against the vehicle and tipped her chin up, examining the sky. The lovely line of her throat—so tender, so exposed, a pleasant torment.

Young. Barely fledgling. The sure instinctive sense of another sanguinant's age spoke, clarion-loud inside his own veins. And it added, *Unclaimed.* That was the important part.

Had she killed the trespasser? Impossible, and yet… so was she. An unclaimed leman, *deva, aima-glyza, imprima,* sitting within his reach, staring at the starstrewn sky. Dawn grew close; she should be behind invisible seals, in a secure, silken nest. His blood surged at the thought, an iron bar with its claws sunk deep in his belly, reaching to the base of his spine. Diamond nail-flickers raced up his back, nerves and strong ancient muscles tensing by imperceptible fractions.

Unblinking, he watched. If her protector existed, they *must* strike now. Yet no trace of another sanguinant lingered upon her, unless it were the fading tang of violent death—the trespasser's. She *must* have been responsible, there was no other explanation. Perhaps their mutual opponent, drunk upon the very glory of her, had been singularly easy to dispatch.

The wanderer was very nearly thus himself, though another invisible layer of madness dropped from him with a stunning silent crash. He longed to flicker across the space, his teeth sinking into that naked, tempting pulse, carry her through the door into the vehicle, and…

She sniffed, heavily, rubbing below her pretty nose with the back of one hand. A strange, almost childlike motion, before she rose and re-entered her egg-thin castle walls. The door slammed, and he was left to wonder if she had indeed been weeping.

Where was the one who had granted her the Dark Gift? Had her protector been challenged and killed? If so, why had the victor not claimed her? A leman was not left to wander.

They were, simply and starkly, too precious. Already the wanderer was more awake and aware than he had been at any time since the fire. And—even more of a gift—the thought of the burning city, the heat, the sounds, the smell of roasting did not drive him to restless motion, seeking escape from an internal enemy.

Dawn comes. A fledgling's unconsciousness was deep and utterly vulnerable, beginning at sunrise. Did she know how to set seals about her place of rest, or was she intending to sleep in this… this tin can? It defied belief and insanity both.

Scraps of that maddening, glorious perfume twist-trailed about him. He longed to fill himself at the font; he *craved* a much closer acquaintance. The fear that somehow she would vanish, that this was a hallucination preceding true-death, did nothing to aid him in discerning the most efficient course of action.

Balanced between caution and the mounting urge to claim this fragile, fabulous, utterly maddening miracle, he waited for dawn.

Order *Fledgling & Archon* at your retailer of choice!

ABOUT THE AUTHOR

Lili Saintcrow currently resides in the rainy Pacific Northwest with her children, dog, cat, a half-feral library, and assorted other strays.

https://www.lilithsaintcrow.com

ALSO BY LILITH SAINTCROW

PARANORMAL ROMANCE

The Watchers

Dark Watcher

Storm Watcher

Fire Watcher

Cloud Watcher

Mindhealer

Finder

The Society

The Society

Hunter, Healer

Sons of Ymre

Erik

Jake

Nigel

Tales of the Sanguinant

Daywalker's Leman

Elder's Prize

Fledgling & Archon

SINGLE TITLE PARANORMAL ROMANCE

The Demon's Librarian

Desires, Known

Taken

Incorruptible

Rose & Thunder

SCIENCE FICTION & FANTASY

Roadtrip Z

Cotton Crossing

In the Ruins

Pocalypse Road

Atlanta Bound

Gallow & Ragged

Trailer Park Fae

Roadside Magic

The Wasteland King

HOOD

Season One

Season Two

Season Three

The Dante Valentine Series

Working For the Devil

Dead Man Rising

The Devil's Right Hand

Saint City Sinners

To Hell & Back

Selene

The Jill Kismet Series

Night Shift

Hunter's Prayer

Redemption Alley

Heaven's Spite

Angel Town

The Dead God's Heart

Spring's Arcana

The Salt-Black Tree

The Black Land's Bane

A Flame in the North

The Fall of Waterstone

Steelflower

Steelflower

Steelflower at Sea

Steelflower in Snow

Romances of Arquitaine

The Hedgewitch Queen

The Bandit King

Single Title Sci-Fi & Fantasy

Moon's Knight

Chained Knight

Rattlesnake Wind

She Wolf & Cub

Coyote Run

Harmony

Blood Call

The Marked

Afterwar

ROMANTIC SUSPENSE

Viral Agents

Agent Zero

Agent Gemini

Ghost Squad

Damage

Duty

Gamble

ALT-HISTORICAL FANTASY

Hell's Acre

Hell's Acre

Rook's Rose

The Bannon and Clare Affairs

The Iron Wyrm Affair

The Red Plague Affair

The Ripper Affair

The Damnation Affair

COLLECTED STORIES

Human Tales

More Human Tales

NONFICTION

The Quill & The Crow Vol. 1

HUMOR

SquirrelTerror

Jozzie & Sugar Belle

WRITING AS S.C. EMMETT

Hostage to Empire

Throne of the Five Winds

The Poison Prince

The Bloody Throne

WRITING AS LILI ST. CROW (young adult)

The Strange Angels Series

Strange Angels

Betrayals

Jealousy

Defiance

Reckoning

Tales of Beauty and Madness

Nameless

Wayfarer

Kin

www.ingramcontent.com/pod-product-compliance
Lightning Source LLC
Chambersburg PA
CBHW021243060726
47590CB00005B/1877